THE LIGHT REMAINS

The Light Remains

by Samantha Keller

CATALYST PRESS
EL PASO, TEXAS

For further information, write info@catalystpress.org

In North America, this book is distributed by
Consortium Book Sales & Distribution, a division of Ingram.
Phone: 612/746-2600
cbsdinfo@ingramcontent.com
www.cbsd.com

Print ISBN: 978-1-960803-47-4

Epub ISBN: 978-1-960803-85-6

Library of Congress Control Number 2025944410

Cover artwork and design: The Stoep Collective
Text design and layout: Liz Gowans
Author photo: Marta Muryn

To all my mothers and their daughters.
Anna, Susan, Evelyn, and Rosemary.
And to Chloe, my gift.

Chapter One

Aloe Afrikana | *March 1975* | Malelane, South Africa

In every letter my mother writes to me, she insists that I am lonely.

The truth is, I choose to live alone. The difference between loneliness and being alone is as stark to me as black is to white, and I'd make the same choice again and again, even if I was reborn into a thousand different lives. She tells me that I am only thirty (I'm thirty-one), which is far too young to be living like an old maid with only cats for company (I have dogs), and how on earth will I ever meet someone "in the back of beyond"? My mother cannot understand that I can live alone and not be lonely because she is far too intimate with loneliness. She believes that one naturally leads to the other, and fears both. Her loneliness was seeded in me before I was separated from her, sown along with the code for blue eyes and light skin in the red throb of her womb. I cannot fear what is part of me.

I fold her letter and the envelope with its Surrey postmark into my pocket and warm my hands against my coffee cup, before knocking a cigarette out my pack. I flick a match to flame and draw the smoke deep into my lungs. It is early. The sun has not yet risen, but emissaries of light tip the hills in gold and soften the sky. This is my favourite time of the day. A holy time through which the world moves quietly, not wanting to disturb the gods. I'm careful to extinguish the match completely, wetting my fingers and pinching off the burned head like my father taught me. This farm, the one I manage and that my mother refers to as "the back of beyond", is a five-hour drive from Lasswade, the dairy farm where I grew up. From where I perch, on the kopjie of red rocks that rise behind the farmhouse, I can see into the Kruger National Park and catch the occasional glimpse of distant giraffes, reduced to necks and heads as they journey through the acacia trees.

I take a slow sip of coffee. Ash drops from my cigarette. I turn my gaze over the neat rows of palms and ferns and the distant nursery where young plants are seeded. The farm grows exotic plants to improve corporate spaces and enhance expensive houses in the city. Plants grown for people who think of them as decor; who wish to cover a stain, or fill an empty space, and never really see the living thing that shares their space.

But what if trees were our first gods? Our first family, rooted in our origins. What if we all began silent and still? Trees are shelter and mantle, lungs and breath, sustenance and medicine. Their unique song hums in our cells and bones – sometimes sorrowful, sometimes joyful, sometimes to offer gentle reassurance. Where people don't always say what they mean, plants are honest and clear: a thousand voices in chorus with each other. Trees counsel patience and show that time is endless and abundant.

If I am very still, I can tune into the slow drip of conversation that travels along branches, down trunks, and into the living lattice of roots. From tree to tree, from my farm to the next, from town to town, across vast acres, carrying me back to the damp smell of willow roots on a river bank, the dry crunch of poplar bark on a small grave, the sharp heat of burning eucalyptus leaves, and the quiet observance of the oak tree that still stands in the driveway at Lasswade and sees everything.

Chapter Two

Stick Insect | *July 1955*

The road from Johannesburg was straight and long and lined to the horizon on both sides with yellow veld. The turn to my father's farm was unmarked. It came up after a small rise, with no warning, where the dirt track met the road in a drift of loose sand and stone. On either side of the track, the ground that had been pushed aside in its making was healed over with wild grasses, which had sharpened in the dry winter. The gate was a heavy metal frame with horizontal struts. A hand-painted sign was attached to the frame with a twist of wire at each corner, which read: *Lasswade*. It was the name of the Hunter family's home in Scotland, reused by my father to give our South African farm a sense of beginning and belonging.

We heard the car before we saw it. Jack whistled and gestured for me to get down. I grabbed a stone from the arsenal he and I had been adding to all morning and pinched it in the rubber of my slingshot, then slid into the fort the way I imagined soldiers slid into their trenches – feet first, kicking up dust. The bare skin on my legs stung, but I didn't flinch.

"Lower." Jack pushed down on my head.

I elbowed his ribs in reply, but edged my body flatter, and we settled side-by-side on our bellies to watch the rise in the road like snipers, our breath clouding the winter air.

Jack and I had spent most of the July school holiday, whenever we could escape our chores, building our fort. We'd scraped a shallow trench into the dirt beneath the barbed-wire fence that marked the top boundary of my father's farm, then covered it with branches, adding a final layer of veld grass for camouflage. A fort needed protecting, and Jack and I had spent the morning refreshing our ammunition – a pile of stones the size of peach pips, chosen for their shape and size. The enemy were mostly imaginary but sometimes took the form of cows, occasionally birds, neither of which we liked to hurt, and our attention was soon drawn to passing traffic. The heavy trucks that ferried men and supplies between the city and the mine, or municipal buses, were both good targets. When one of us landed a hit, the stone pinged and ricocheted off the metal, smashing into a thousand bits or shooting down the road with satisfying violence. We'd duck our heads until the vehicle was out of sight, then dance and whoop in celebration. If any of the drivers heard an unexpected sound, it was likely they'd assume the stone had bounced up from beneath the tyres, not been launched by two friends with muddied faces hiding in the veld. Usually by the time the stone found its target, the vehicle had travelled some distance away from us. It was a good plan. As long as we didn't get caught.

I sniffed and wiped my nose on my sleeve. The hum of an engine grew closer, followed by the sleek shape of a car cresting the rise on the main road. It was a pale green and edged in highly polished chrome, with gleaming silver hubcaps and a clean windscreen. This was not a farm car.

Jack pushed his hair out of his eyes and whistled a low note of appreciation. "Chevrolet Bel Air."

The glamour must have given him pause because he stayed low in the fort while I rose onto my knees, pulled back the elastic on my slingshot to full stretch, took aim, and let fly. I punched the air at the satisfying ring of contact and tugged on Jack's jumper. "Direct hit!"

Jack didn't respond. He crouched unmoving and I followed his gaze to where the car had come to a halt. As we watched, the reverse lights lit up. By the time the gleaming machine started back towards us, we were up and running. Jack was two years older and bigger, but I was fast and panicked. I chased his shirt through the veld and over the stile into the top pasture, disturbing the Friesian herd who lifted their lazy heads to watch us pass. Glancing over my shoulder, I saw the car turn off the main road and judder over the cattle grate onto our farm road.

Jack sprinted towards the fence, and when we reached the barn, we split up. He vaulted on to his father's farm, while I followed the fence towards the chimney smoke coming from our kitchen fire. I skidded through the gap in the weathered bamboo fence my father had built around our kitchen garden and cleared the steps up to the back door in a single leap.

The kitchen was empty. Gasping, I leaned against the wooden table with my bare feet flat on the polished concrete floor, trying to still my body enough so I could hear over the thrum of my breath and my heart. The house was quiet. Rosie's voice drifted from the direction of the bedrooms followed by my sister's reply, then the slip and thud of a sash window closing. The table was set for lunch and an enamel colander of fresh tomatoes sat in the sink, dark orange and still wet from a recent rinsing. I wiped my hands on my shirt, pushed my hair out of my face, and moving quietly, edging out of the kitchen and into the hallway. A hard knock at the front door landed in my chest. A figure shifted behind the mottled glass, stepped back, then came forward and knocked again. Bang, bang, bang! A face peered close to the glass. I ducked back into the kitchen and slid under the table. Rosie's soft house shoes approached along the wooden floor. She passed the kitchen door with a load of laundry in her arms and glanced at me crouched beneath the table – sweating, ashen-faced, so breathless that I would not have been able to form a sentence – and raised an eyebrow but kept on towards the door. She knew the urgent knocking was about me, knew she was heading towards something unpleasant, yet she did not bother to call my mother, who would not have come anyway.

Kate followed behind. She stopped at the kitchen door. "What have you done this time?"

"Nothing!" I kneeled on the kitchen floor and listened to the driver of the glossy American car shout at Rosie. It was the mine manager's wife, Mrs Rodgers. I knew her from church and both her sons from my primary school. Two barrel-shaped boys with close-cropped hair who started every school year with a shiny pair of new shoes. I crawled out from beneath the table and, still on all fours, taking care to keep out of sight, peered past my sister's legs towards the front door. In the gap between Rosie's body and the door frame I caught occasional glimpses of a firm bouffant and two white gloves, flapping like furious birds.

Kate nudged me with her knee and whispered, "You threw a stone at her car?"

"No," I made a face as if my sister could never understand the complexities of my life outside this farmhouse, "I used my slingshot."

"Oh, that's much better, Eve."

"Leave me alone."

Rosie continued to nod and tut sympathetically. She answered all of Mrs Rodger's questions and each of her demands to speak to "The Madam" with, "Yes, Madam," and "my Madam is not here, Madam," followed by a slow shake of her head.

Rosie always took our side. For once I was grateful that my mother seldom came out of her bedroom, and I imagined her like I was right now – hiding and listening from behind the safety of her closed door. This would upset her. Not because I had shot a stone at passing traffic or that there might be damage to Mrs Rodgers' car, but because she'd be embarrassed. Embarrassed that Mrs Rodgers had come to our house, embarrassed about what Mrs Rodgers would think about us, and embarrassed about what she might say to other people in town. My mother wanted people to think well of us, especially people like Mrs Rodgers. Kate and I understood ourselves through our mother's eyes and through the eyes of the people my mother admired. If I came home with dirty knees or a torn dress, she'd ask, "What would the minister's wife think?" If Kate got bad marks at school, she'd say, "What would the headmaster think?" I had no clue what anyone really thought about anything Kate and I did, but, according to my mother, they all thought the worst of us. She left our upbringing to these people. They were our cautionary tales, our models, our aspirations, and our warnings. In all the places our mother could not be.

"Do you understand what I'm telling you?" Mrs Rodgers spoke slowly as if Rosie was dim. "There's damage to the car. She threw a rock!"

"It wasn't a rock!" I said, and Kate kneed me in the side again.

"Yes, Madam." Rosie shifted her body to fill even more of the doorway and close any gaps. She denied having seen me that morning. "Maybe she's with the Master?" she suggested, making a vague gesture in the direction of the dairy.

I looked down at my dirty hands and scrunched my fingers into fists. I was sorry Rosie was the one who had to face Mrs Rodgers, though not sorry enough to go out there and face the angry woman myself. It was better this way. We all knew that there were limits to what Mrs Rodgers could do when she only had the maid to deal with.

"I know who she was with! I saw the Turner boy running away. I'm going over there now. See what his father has to say about this."

"No," I launched myself up past Kate's legs, "Jack had nothing to do with it!"

Kate pushed down on my head and forced me back into the kitchen. "Shhh."

"She mustn't go to the Turners!" I said. Tears and real fear rose in my throat for the first time. I gripped my sister's sleeve. "He didn't do anything. It was me."

"Stay here," Kate said and went down the hall to nudge Rosie aside.

"Morning, Mrs Rodgers," My 13-year-old sister spoke in the voice she reserved for grown ups: all clear vowels and airy concern. "I'll speak to my father when he gets home for lunch. Of course. Yes. I understand. My sister can be wild, I know. Thank you for coming to tell us." She kept up an agreeable patter as she stepped out onto the porch and closed the front door behind her. Through the glass, Kate's distorted shape steered Mrs Rodgers down the path and back towards her fancy green and chrome car, which, thanks to me, now had a brand-new chip in its perfect paint job.

Rosie bent to pick up the laundry she'd dropped behind the front door. She stood slowly keeping her eyes on me.

I wiped my nose with my sleeve. "She mustn't go to the Turners."

"Hau wena, Ntombi." Rosie sighed and shook her head. "Don't worry about Jack. That boy is trouble. You should worry about yourself. Now go and wash, it's time for lunch."

Chapter Three

Light Remains | *July 1955*

It was raining when my father shook me awake before dawn. "It's time," he whispered, and went down the hall carrying his boots.

Careful not to wake my sister, I rushed to follow him, tucking my nightgown into my shorts and not bothering with shoes, grateful to be invited anywhere with him after the stone-throwing incident a few days before. He hadn't shouted at me – although I wouldn't be getting pocket money for a few months – but my father's disappointment was far worse than any punishment. My mother was still giving me the silent treatment, but that didn't really change anything.

Petrus, my father's foreman, was already in the barn when we arrived, standing behind the slick haunches of a labouring cow. High piles of hay bales loomed around us in uneven stacks. The pale dawn light and the heavy rain clouds gave everything the same dull hue. The air and the ground were freezing, and I rubbed one foot with the other. Every time lightning flashed, followed by a low growl of thunder, a motley collection of dogs would dash in through the gap where two new barn doors waited to be hung, falling over one another with fear and excitement. The cow mooed and shifted in the mud.

"Okay, okay, settle down, mama," my father soothed. The cow was a pretty Friesian, mostly white but with bold black markings that ran from her tail and up her neck to cover her head. Her eyes followed my father as he moved around to stroke her forehead.

My father was a big man, broad-shouldered and thick-necked, with a full red beard. "Good Viking blood," he liked to claim. His story was that he was a descendant of a Norse king called Harald Fairhair, who had invaded Scotland where my great-grandparents and all previous generations of Hunters had lived, before my paternal grandparents had moved to South Africa. My mother remarked that he'd have to fish quite deep in his ancestral pool to find a royal connection.

As tall as my father was, Petrus, a bald, dark-skinned Zulu, was even taller. In contrast to my father's Fairhair ancestry, Petrus claimed to be a direct descendant of Shaka, the formidable King of the Zulus. Rosie was Zulu too, but I'd never heard her say the same. She just clicked her tongue behind her teeth and said that all men liked to imagine themselves as kings. "But we all share the same ancestors, ntombi."

Petrus leaned his shoulder against the cow's rump and pushed her around the small pen. Outside, a flock of hadedas, disturbed by the early activity and the dogs, rose from the pasture and flew in noisy formation towards the river and the pale stripe of dawn on the horizon. A crash of bright lightning set the dogs off again. They barked and tumbled and snapped at each other like overexcited children. My father called them to heel with a sharp whistle and a slap on his thigh, and they settled uneasily, looking between their master and the road. The cow pulled back hard against the rope my father held, her eyes rolling white in her head, and jostled Petrus into the wall of the barn.

"Johnny, out the way," my father said.

I pulled myself up onto the wooden fence that divided the pens. My father had called me Johnny since I was a baby. His friends teased that it was because he liked Johnnie Walker Black Label, but Rosie told me that it was because after Kate was born, he'd hoped for a boy.

The cow bellowed and Petrus jumped back as warm liquid ran out from beneath her tail and splashed at his feet. My father tugged his handkerchief out of his khaki shorts, wiped around his neck and winked at me. "Here we go."

The nose of an old Ford truck pushed through the opening in the barn wall. It was the Turners. Mr Turner sat in the passenger seat while Jack's face peered over the steering wheel behind the energetic swipes of the windscreen wipers. Jack was only thirteen, but Mr Turner had taught him to drive as soon as he could reach the pedals. He'd get Jack to drive him to meet his friends at the Army Legion bar in town, where Jack would wait in the car until his father finished drinking.

We hadn't seen each other since the day I'd hit Mrs Rodgers' car with the stone, and I searched my friend's expression for a clue to any trouble he might have got into because of what I'd done. Jack parked inside the barn and slammed the driver-side door. He walked the long way around the truck, giving his father a wide berth. His hair had been cropped short with uneven chunks taken off over his ears and around the back.

"Did you have a fight with a lawn mower, son?" my father teased, coming out of the pen to greet his friend. He reached up as Jack walked past him, as if to ruffle what was left of the boy's hair. Jack dodged his outstretched hand, and both our fathers laughed.

"He needed straightening up," Mr Turner said as he shook my father's hand, then gestured around the new barn. "This looks nice."

"Yes, lucky to get it done before winter." My father surveyed his handiwork with pride. "Just need to hang the doors." He almost had to shout over the clatter of raindrops on the corrugated iron roof.

Mr Turner and my father had been friends since childhood. Long before they'd volunteered and travelled to North Africa with the Transvaal Scottish, where they'd both fought for, and lost, Tobruk. While my father had made it out with the Allies, Mr Turner had been captured by the Italians and had spent the rest of the war in a POW camp in Italy, and then Germany. In stories of Mr Turner as a young man, my mother painted the picture of a real charmer.

"Tommy was one of those boys you couldn't take your eyes off." A young man who drew people to him with his good looks, humour, and an exciting, adventurous streak. Her stories about him always concluded with a sigh and the regret that he was never the same after the war.

When my parents said that Tommy Turner was changed by the war, it was his left arm that I thought about. Damaged by shrapnel, it hung limp at his side, with pale scars like molten flesh puckering the skin from his wrist to his shoulder. In contrast to this inert limb, Mr Turner was in every other respect, a boulder of a man. Tall and broad, the skin on his neck, chest, and powerful right arm was tanned to a permanent dark red from days spent outside. He wore his hair cropped close to his square head as if he were still in the military. My father loved his friend for his big generous laugh and ability to mimic people and tell jokes, but Rosie said that Baas Turner farmed with his sjambok, a tightly-bound leather whip, which he used on both his black staff and his animals.

"If straight was what you were after, you've failed," my father said.

Jack didn't react to the ribbing and pulled himself onto the wooden fence alongside me. When he looked over to nod a short hello I noticed a bruise on the side of his jaw. I touched my face in the same spot and Jack turned away.

The cow mooed.

"She ready?" Mr Turner said.

"Yes, bloody close." My father went back into the pen followed by his friend.

The calf's front hooves, covered with a taut, milky membrane, stuck out of the cow.

My father clapped his hands together. "Right, manne. Let's help this mama out."

Petrus looped and knotted a rope around the calf's ankles. He handed one of two lines back to Mr Turner and took hold of the other himself. My father laid his hands on the cow's flank.

"Johnny." He gestured for me to come over.

"Let Jack do it." Tommy put a hand around his son's upper arm to lift him off the fence. "He needs to learn."

Jack shrugged his father off.

"Eve's got this one," my father said.

His certainty gave me confidence, and aware of the quiet, waiting eyes of the men, I jumped into the pen. Mud squished up through the hay and in between my toes, sharp and soft at the same time. I pushed my shoulders back and rested my palms on the cow's flank alongside my father's. Her flesh rippled.

"There, feel that?" My father's voice was earnest and attentive.

I nodded.

"Whenever you feel that contraction, tell them to pull." My father returned to the cow's head.

We waited, poised and silent. The only sound was the cow's restlessness and the occasional creak of the wooden barn as it warmed with the rising dawn. I pushed the hair off my face and held my breath, keeping my eyes on my father's and my focus on the warm hide beneath my palms. I glanced back at Jack, but only once. It was a thrill to be included in the business of farming alongside my father. I had expected the labour to be a noisy, messy affair, but apart from the cow's agitation, it felt almost reverent. The dimensions of the barn loomed overhead like a cathedral. The rain had stopped, and sun lit the horizon like a blessing. The calm patience of Petrus and my father's kind crooning. Anticipation buzzed like a current through my skin. I leaned my forehead against the cow's bulk. A sea creature rolled in the waves of her flesh.

I stepped back. "Pull!"

"Donsa." My father repeated the instruction in Zulu.

Petrus and Mr Turner leaned back on the ropes.

The cow's muscles released, and I held up my hand.

"Ima." Petrus relaxed his grip and nodded his acknowledgement to stop.

"Pull," I said, a minute later. The men pulled on the ropes until I held up my hand.

We continued in this way for some time. Swaying first towards then away from the mother on the rhythm of her body. Slowly edging the ankles, then the shins, then the knees of the calf out of her, until its black snout and purple tongue lolled into view.

"Pull," I called.

With a final rush of liquid, her calf slipped out and dropped to the floor. My father tightened his grip on the rope around the cow's neck and Petrus and Mr Turner dragged the calf away from her hooves. They worked together to manoeuvre the new mother until she faced her calf, and then encouraged her to lick the baby, cleaning out its nostrils and mouth.

"It's a male," Mr Turner said.

I watched my father's eyes for disappointment – a dairy farm needed cows – but he only nodded briskly, shook Petrus's hand and patted me on the head.

"Good job, everyone."

The calf struggled to his feet. When he began to nose his way beneath his mother's belly, Petrus squeezed the cow's udder, aiming a stream of milk at the newborn's mouth.

Jack and I followed our fathers outside, squinting into the light. A breeze split the clouds apart like candy floss, which drifted away. The sun had risen over the veld and pastures, which had been cropped short for winter feed, and were now stacked in a wall of bales in the barn. A black-shouldered kite hovered in the distance, searching the ground for breakfast. My father turned on the outside tap to wash his hands, and the dogs pushed through our legs to lap at the stream and the puddle it made at my father's feet.

I shivered and rubbed my arms through my sleeves, abruptly aware of my frozen feet and hands.

"You look like you're the one who crawled out the back of a cow," Jack said.

Mud covered my bare feet up to my knees. The long nightgown I'd hurriedly tucked into my shorts was blossoming out the bottom of the legs. I was soaked through, and my hands were smeared with blood and dirt from my wrists to my elbows.

Jack wrinkled his nose. "You smell like it too."

I aimed a half-hearted swing at his shoulder. "I just saw a calf being born," I grinned, pleased with every inch of myself.

He dodged my swing and lifted his hands up in mock defence. Two of his fingers were bandaged together, with the silver tip of a metallic splint sticking out from between them.

"What happened?" I asked.

"Nothing," Jack said. "Well, not nothing. They're broken."

There was a ring of bruising around his right wrist, which matched the bruise on his jaw. I looked with more interest at his buzzed head. Red marks crisscrossed his neck. "How?"

"Ag, you know what I'm like." He shoved the bandaged fingers into his pocket like a full stop at the end of a sentence.

"Jack!" Tommy called to his son from the driver's seat of his truck.

"Want to go to the river?" Jack said.

His question made me aware of the hollow in my belly. "Maybe after breakfast?"

He nodded. "Definitely after you've had a bath," he said, and waved his hand in front of his nose.

That time my punch landed with a satisfying thud on his upper arm.

My father waved his thanks as Jack ran across the yard and jumped into the back of his father's truck. He took both my hands in his and guided them into the tap water to clean the mud and blood off my palms. The sun was falling through the clouds in clear rays of yellow light. There was something majestic and beautiful about them, like a picture from a bible, when God sends a message to his flock.

"Look," I said.

My dad followed my eyes. "Crepuscular rays."

"Crepuscular." The word had a satisfying fullness, and I rolled it around my tongue.

"The light is there but we can't always see it. It takes a bit of unsettlement to show it up. Like dust, or moisture after the rain, like this morning. The clouds make shadows, so we see the light as sunbeams." He lifted my hand and splayed my fingers like the rays he was describing.

My entire 11-year-old hand fit into his palm with room to spare, and he swallowed it up and gave it a squeeze. "You should head back. Your mother is probably wondering where you are. I'm going to finish up here with Petrus."

I headed across the top pasture towards the dairy. I very much doubted my mother was wondering where I was. She never did, as long as Kate and I were back for meals and clean when we were at the table. If she ever wanted us, it was Rosie who would step out into the yard to whistle for us. A single long note followed by three short blasts, sent like a soccer ball to carry the length of the farm and bounce at our feet. Wherever we happened to be, Kate and I knew that sound meant it was time to head home.

Thinking of the coppery smell of the birth, of soft ears, spindly legs, and a wet black nose, I heard those familiar notes and jogged towards the farm track. It would be a faster route home, and smoother underfoot.

Chapter Four

Mopani Worm | *July 1955*

After a meal of fresh bread, bacon, and sliced tomatoes, I wandered out the kitchen door, ducked under the washing line, and plucked a pomegranate from the tree at the centre of the yard. Palming a small flat stone, I beat gently at the woody shell until it split open, then pushed my thumbs into the crack I'd made and tore the pomegranate open to reveal a bed of red seeds. One by one, I lifted them to my mouth and with a careful nip of my front teeth, popped the taut flesh to release the sweetness. My mother's manservant, Moses, sat in the shade of the oak where he provided the service of a local barber to the farm staff, offering haircuts on a three-legged stool in front of a broken mirror nailed to the trunk. He would shave the men and braid the women, and every lunchtime there was chatter and laughter under the tree. Moses was always meticulously groomed. His uniform khaki shorts and shirt were crisply pressed and topped off with a green beret, which he wore at an angle and had embellished with two beaded brooches my mother had given to him for his wife.

I stretched my legs out in a patch of sun on the bare concrete slab that had once formed the base of a chicken coop before it had been torn down. Over the years, what was left of the wooden frame had all but rotted away. With nothing left to secure them, rusted nail heads jutted uselessly out of the slab, and the concrete had cracked with the hardy determination of kikuyu grass pushing from below. Even after a long bath to wash off the remains of that morning's mud, the spaces between my toes still felt gritty. I flexed, then pointed my feet towards the kitchen door, enjoying the sunlight on my bare legs. The watery winter sun was directly above me, meaning Jack would soon be at the river.

My father's dogs lay panting at my feet, occasionally thrusting their snouts forward for a scratch of affection. In a couple of hours my mother would get up, powder her nose, put on fresh lipstick, change from her nightgown into a clean frock, and call from the kitchen door for me to feed the chickens. Her afternoon routine included a short walk to the dairy to log the day's milk yield, and I planned to go with her, keen to show her the newborn calf. She always walked with her back straight and her neck stiff, like the native women who balanced heavy burdens on their heads. On her way to the dairy, she'd smoke a single cigarette. Her guilty pleasure. She drew deeply and left a faded ribbon of smoke in the air behind her, which mingled with her lavender fragrance.

I spat a pomegranate pip into the dust. Next week, Kate and I would be back at boarding school. This was the time of the day we'd leave the dining hall. A hundred feet drumming up the stairs to change for afternoon games. Some of the city girls smoked cigarettes and painted their nails and wore stockings and lipstick on the weekends. It seemed impossibly glamourous. Pale, sun-bleached hairs laid over the dry skin on my legs, which were brown with dust and sun. I popped a pomegranate pip between my thumb and forefinger and stained my lips with the red juice, then pushed myself up and headed into the house. Wiping my hands on my khaki shorts, I moved quietly on bare feet across the concrete floor in the kitchen and onto the cool parquet of the passage, where I was careful to step on the evenly placed, old-fashioned and highly patterned rugs that were collectively referred to by my mother as "The Persians". I slipped past my mother's closed bedroom door and paused at the door of the sun room. Rosie's mellifluous voice sang from the laundry room, accompanied by the click and lift of the iron off the hot plate and the quiet stroke of it across the linens.

My mother's desk stood in front of the sun room window, looking out at a frangipani in full bloom. The exotic plant seemed ostentatious against the modest furnishings of the room. The neat desk, a pale mahogany piece of simple design, had straight unembellished legs and four small drawers. The only decorative features were the delicately faceted glass drawer handles, each inlaid with a small copper ball. I knew what I was looking for and slid out the drawer on the right, alert to any disturbance in the resting household. A silver cigarette box lay inside. Its lid was embossed with an elaborately entwined design of the letters SKB – Susan Kathleen Bigley – my mother's initials before she'd married my father and become a Hunter. I clicked open the case to reveal a row of thin cigarettes on a red satin inlay. They were held in place by a measure of grey elastic with a silver clasp that could be unhooked from the box to remove or replace the cigarettes. Open, the box released the dry smell of mouldy leaves, strong and unpleasant, not unlike my father's muslin tobacco pouch. My stomach rolled and my mouth filled with saliva. I ran my fingertips across the row of tightly rolled columns, each no thicker than a pencil. The taut white paper was so thin around the tobacco that it appeared almost blue, with the words 'Pall Mall' elaborately scripted in silver on each filter. I lifted a single cigarette from its satin bed and slipped it into the pocket of my shorts, then quickly clipped the lid shut and slid the silver case back in the drawer.

"Ntombi?"

I jumped, spun around and in the same movement, pressed the drawer closed with the back of my thighs. Rosie stood at the door to the sunroom with a pile of unfolded laundry draped across her arms. Her dark face was shiny with the heat of the iron and she had pushed the cotton doek she wore around her head off her forehead, exposing a line of tight black curls. The unusual sight of this thin strip of hair seemed almost intimate. I looked away, trying to appear preoccupied.

"I was just looking for a pen." In my pocket, I rolled the small firm prize between my thumb and forefinger.

"Will you help me fold?" Rosie said.

"Not now."

"It's only five minutes." Rosie indicated with a jerk of her head that it was less of a request and more of an instruction. I followed her.

We stood opposite one another at either end of Kate and my bedroom, each holding two corners of a bed sheet, still warm from the iron. Lifting our arms quickly, we ballooned the fabric up and snapped it down, then brought our hands together to form the first lengthwise fold in the sheet. We repeated this over and over, until the double sheet was the size of a pillowcase.

"Why aren't you resting?" Rosie looked at me from under her eyebrows.

"I don't need to lie down during the day," I said. "I'm not a baby."

She handed me a fresh sheet and walked back until it pulled taut between us. "You will always be the baby."

We folded the pillow slips, adding to the growing pile of neat fabric envelopes in the laundry basket.

"Can I go now?"

"Why are you in such a hurry?"

I tried not to think of the cigarette in my pocket. "I'm meeting Jack."

"Don't go looking for trouble," Rosie said. She waved the edges of a sheet in my direction.

Fifteen minutes later, I ducked past the pomegranate tree, through the gate with the buzzing honeysuckle and out of the back yard, occasionally patting my pocket for the thin shape within. Out on the farm track, I turned left towards the river and stepped up onto the grassy mound that ran through the centre of the road. The air smelled of dust and sang with the constant high pitch of insects.

Across the lucerne fields cropped short for the winter, the poplar trees that followed the river stood out crisply against the clear blue sky.

Clear of the house and any watching windows, I felt a release, as if I'd been holding my breath. I took the cigarette from my pocket and held it between two fingers in my right hand. Imitating my mother's elegant walk, I sashayed down the road, twisting my feet in the dust with every step and occasionally touching the unlit cigarette to my lips. In my mind's eye they were still red with pomegranate juice, and I left a drift of smoke behind me. Following the irrigation furrow that carried rust-brown river water to the fields, I hurdled across the juncture where the furrows met and continued to the spot on the river where the bank widened and the water slowed to form a natural pool. Weeping willow fronds overhung the space and made perfect hand-holds to swing on and drop from. As I pushed through the leafed drapes, I disturbed a mother duck and her ducklings who waddled away, tail feathers pert. Jack was not there. Away from the afternoon sun and close to the shadowed water, my skin cooled. I sat on a root that bulged from the base of the tree and inspected the cigarette. I hadn't really considered how I'd light it, or if I even wanted to. I slipped it back into my pocket and settled against the trunk to wait for Jack.

A fiscal shrike darted into the clearing and landed high on the thin stem of a reed. He twitched his arrow head from side to side, keeping his sharp black eyes focused on something at the water's edge. I stood and followed his gaze to the smooth clay low on the bank, where I found the body of a dead chameleon. Black ants covered it like a shifting skin, feeding on the soft skin of the belly and the entrails, to reveal a clutch of translucent, yellow eggs cradled in the reptile's ribcage. Using a stick, I poked at the coiled tail, dragging the body from the mass of ants who rushed around trying to reclaim their meal.

"Johnny."

I spun, startled, on my heels. Jack was balanced on the root of the willow tree. He was shoeless and wore a blue shirt over a worn pair of khaki shorts. With his new haircut, he looked like one of the Afrikaner boys at our old primary school, whose mothers shaved their heads and who couldn't afford school shoes. I turned back to the chameleon and made a show of being unconcerned by his arrival. Jack swung across the clearing on a willow frond, landing hard with both feet in the mud.

"Watch it." I placed a warning hand on his bare ankle.

He crouched and together we inspected the chameleon. Half the creature remained intact; the skin around the front legs and head was still beautifully patterned in bright yellows and green, but the back half had been reduced to bones, naked and vulnerable, her eggs unborn.

"Wow," Jack's head was close to mine, "did the ants do that?"

"Ja. Maybe after the butcher bird ate some of it."

We glanced up at the shrike, which perched in the reeds, its black hood and eye directed at us. Feeling bold in front of Jack, I picked the chameleon up by its tail and flipped it over. The underside had been completely stripped of skin. Jack poked at one of the tightly closed feet with a dry twig.

I tugged at the coiled tail. "Maybe we can wash the skeleton."

"We'd have to boil it," said Jack. "You can't just wash skin off like it's dirt."

I looked at him and grimaced.

"If I brought a dead chameleon home and gave it to Rosie or Moses to boil on the stove…" Before I could finish the sentence, we were both laughing at the idea, which, when taken from our outdoor world here at the river, indoors to the world of adults and washed hands, seemed outrageous.

"Petrus might do it at the fire pit," Jack said.

"Wouldn't the bones just fall apart?"

"One of the boys at my school boiled a cat skeleton for a science project."

"Where did he get the cat?"

"Who knows? But he's the kind of boy that if you asked, you might not like his answer." Jack lifted the chameleon by its tail and carried the small body to the river. With a slow back and forth motion, he washed off the remaining ants, careful to keep his bandaged fingers clear of the water. I was still curious about the injury. I'd never actually seen Mr Turner hurt Jack, and I wasn't sure I wanted my suspicions confirmed.

"Does it hurt?"

He shrugged. "A bit. Where's Kate?"

I ignored the question. I knew my sister thought Jack was handsome, but whenever I called him her boyfriend, Kate would blush and insist he was only a friend. Now that I had him to myself, I didn't want my sister to be the person Jack was thinking about. I turned my attention back to the chameleon, which I had no intention of boiling. At the same time, leaving the corpse to the birds and the ants to further strip it of its flesh and skin, seemed undignified. The bones still cradled the dried, unhatched eggs. I began to scrape out a shallow hole with my cupped hands. Jack came over and helped, using a flat rock to dig. The deeper we dug, the darker and heavier the sand became. We gradually hollowed out a rough rectangular hole. I pulled the chameleon, along with a few of the more determined ants, into the shallow grave, which we filled, patting the sand flat. Jack constructed a rough cross by splitting a green twig, threading another shorter piece through the split, and knotting them together with grass. He positioned the cross at the head of the mound.

I brushed the sand off my hands and pushed them into my short's pockets. My fingertips found the cigarette hidden there and after a moment's thought, I took it out.

Jack's eyes widened and flickered in the direction of his farm. "Where did you get that?"

"My mom's drawer," I shrugged, hoping to portray a casualness I didn't feel. "Anyway, it doesn't matter. I don't have a light." I examined the illicit item and lifted it to my nose. "Smells horrible."

"Not as bad as a cheroot." Jack took the cigarette from me and placed it between his lips. He reminded me of his father. I snatched it back.

"If you want to, we could go get matches from the staff compound," he said.

"We're not allowed there," I said. There were places my sister and I had always been told not to visit on our own. The staff compound and the Abelheiras' store on the other side of the main road were both strictly out of bounds.

Jack was still focused on the cigarette. "I've gone there before, often. Even with Kate once. They don't mind."

"With Kate?" I prickled at the thought of my sister; gentle, sweet, never-any-trouble, why-can't-you-be-more-like-your-sister Kate, sneaking down to the compound to smoke cigarettes with Jack.

"Why didn't you tell me?"

Jack shrugged. "You weren't there."

A breeze lifted the willow leaves, and I pretended to be preoccupied with a butterfly that was making its haphazard, indirect way past us. What had been a private game, taking the cigarette and playing at being grown up, was edging into territory I hadn't really intended to explore. If I said no, Jack might think I was a baby. If I said yes, I could return to boarding school with the badge of having smoked my first cigarette. Like Kate, apparently. I thought of my mother and Rosie in the farm house and the heavy drums of chicken feed standing along the garage wall.

"I have to get back to feed the chickens."

"We can go this way," Jack indicated towards the cattle path, formed by the farm boys bringing the herd down to the river to drink, but otherwise used mostly by Jack travelling to and from the Turners' farm to the swimming hole. "It's shorter."

"Alright, but we must be quick."

Jack jumped over the willow root and ran. I chased him. The

path left the shadowed copse surrounding the swimming hole and opened into the veld, following the gentle turn of the river's course in the direction of the poplars. We ran for about five minutes before we veered away from the river on a faint footpath through the veld. When we reached the poplars, we slowed and wove in single-file through the thin line of trees with their tall, pale trunks. It was dead quiet. The buzz of insects was absent and the usual bird calls were muted, as if coming from a distance. Even the trees were silent. Dry twigs and sharp leaves snapped beneath our feet as the path led us past the old graveyard. A low, wrought-iron fence enclosed the space where previous generations of white farmers and their families were buried beneath standing gravestones engraved with their names. On the other side of the path, a more modest, unfenced plot of cleared land held the graves of the local black workers, marked mostly with flat shapeless stones or wooden crosses. I strained to hear the familiar liquid hum of the river and fought the prickling sense that I was being watched. I felt as if I was breaking the rules, although I couldn't say why exactly. Unlike the compound, nobody had ever told me *not* to come here.

Jack crouched over a simple headstone outside the limits of the graveyard fence. Although it lay low in the ground like the black people's graves, the stone was polished, and decorated with bevelled edges. The grass around it had been trimmed, and a fistful of roses, their stems clipped of thorns, had been left there, which had since dried. Jack cleared away the flowers and fallen poplar leaves to reveal four letters engraved in the stone.

"John," I read out loud.

"Like you, Johnny."

I pushed him. Hard enough to knock him off his haunches and onto the grass. Jack laughed as he scrambled back to his feet. I patted my pocket saying, "I'm going to be late," and started to run, reassured by Jack's footsteps behind me.

Beyond a rise, hidden from the main farmhouse, was a small family of rondavel homes the colour of dust and stone and veld. Each was thatched with grass that had been blackened with creosote. The walls were plastered with mud, and apart from a single square opening alongside the raw-wood front door, windowless. The houses had been arranged so that all the front doors opened more or less evenly onto a patch of cleared earth. At the centre of this clearing, circled by rocks, stood an open fire pit. It had been recently swept and a fresh pile of firewood was balanced there in a neat triangular stack. Kindling and tufts of brittle veld grass poked out between the gaps in the wood. There was nobody around, but a fine trail of smoke drifted from the chimney opening of one of the rondavels and as we approached, two thin dogs raised their heads from the dirt to watch us.

I glanced over my shoulder. Our farmhouse was just over the hill. A quick ten-minute run. Maybe not even that. My mother was there, and Rosie. As we got closer to the compound, one of the dogs jumped to its feet and began to bark a harsh alarm. I grabbed Jack's sleeve. My blood thudded an echo to the dog's bark and the air got hot. My underarms pricked sharply. Jack looked at me with a small smile and I snatched my hand off his arm.

"There's no one here. Let's go back."

"It's fine, I come here often. They won't bite." Jack ignored the dogs and crossed the swept yard to call through the open door of the house with the smoking chimney. "Johannes?"

A man emerged, having to duck his head under the low door frame. He wore a white vest, which was threadbare and frayed at the arms and neck. A pair of trousers, belted in loops at his waist, hung a few inches too short revealing bony ankles and bare feet. His dark skin was greyed with dust and age and stretched taut across his bones. His face was expressionless, and his milky, unseeing eyes drifted untethered and unblinking in our direction.

"Ubani?" he asked, and lifted his face as if to sniff the air. "Ubani?"

"Molo, Johannes," Jack said, and reached for the old man's outstretched hand.

"Master Jack." Hearing Jack's voice, the old man smiled to reveal a sparse collection of long, yellow teeth angled chaotically in his gums. As he took Jack's hand, a frown disturbed his face. His fingertips investigated the bandage and the metal splint they found there.

"Hau, Master Jack." He clicked his tongue against the roof of his mouth and shook his head, "not again."

"It's nothing," Jack said. His eyes flicked to me as he pulled his hand away.

The old man turned his face in my direction.

"And who is with you?" he asked.

How did he know I was there? I traced the pathway home in my mind as Jack waved me forward. I widened my eyes and mouthed at him, "matches," while making a striking action with my hands.

"It's Eve. Baas Hunter's daughter," Jack answered, then to me, "Johannes used to be our foreman."

"Ahh," said the old man. He had a deep, gravelly voice, which seemed to catch on something in his throat. "The last born. Your father is a good man." He extended a thin hand in my direction. His palms were unexpectedly pink and his fingers were topped with long yellow nails. A slight smell of decay hung from him, like the time one of my father's dogs had had an infected ear. I shook the tips of his fingers, then pushed my hands deep in my pockets and stepped back.

"Kunjani?" asked Jack.

Johannes shook his head and placed his thumb and forefinger loosely around his wrist, which floated in the skeletal bangle he created. He clicked his tongue against the roof of his mouth. "You see how thin I am. I am too tired, Master Jack. In the morning, I wake up and think about living, but in the evening, I think about dying."

"No, Johannes," Jack took the old man's hand again. "You are like the hills. You'll still be here when all of us are gone."

Johannes's rasping laugh turned into a shaky cough and he leaned on the door frame for support. Finally his cough settled into a rough wheeze and he retched once, then spat. A fat blob of yellow phlegm landed in the dirt at my feet, like a fallen mopani worm, squashed under the hooves of passing livestock. Black and white rubbery skin split open, slimy green innards oozing over the ground.

Swallowing hard I looked up towards the blue hills unsettling the horizon. All of the farm's residents would come and go – Johannes, Jack, me, any future children, and those children's children, many times over – before the hills changed. The idea carried a sense of endlessness. An untethered drift in space. Silence in the dark. I pulled my focus back to Jack and the cigarette. My mother would be looking for me to feed the chickens, who bustled around me like dowager aunts, occasionally giving the top of my feet a sharp peck to speed up the feeding process. "You're just food," I would remind them.

I tapped Jack on the shoulder and indicated towards the trees, half whispering, "I have to feed the chickens."

"Johannes," Jack said. "Have you got any matches?"

Johannes reached into the pocket of his trousers and brought out a small rectangular box with the illustrated profile of a red lion decorating the yellow cardboard. He gave it a single sharp shake. The contents rattled lightly.

"Ee, just a few." He handed the box to Jack.

"Ngiyabonga, Johannes." Jack held out his open palm. "Pass me the cig."

I shook my head. "Not here."

"No one will look for us here." Jack kept his hand out and flicked his fingers twice.

I snorted with frustration. My skin prickled. I wanted to be closer to the farm house. Away from this watchful place with its thin dogs and thinner air. I glanced towards the distant line of trees that twisted along the river, picturing the slow-moving water in the shaded sanctuary beneath the willows. "This was a stupid idea."

"Eve." Jack looked at me. The old man stood silent. The dogs rested in the shade.

I took the cigarette out of my pocket. It had been bent, and a strip of brown tobacco showed through a slight tear in the fine paper. Expertly, Jack placed his finger over the tear as he held the cigarette to his lips and handed me the box of matches with his broken fingers.

"You'll have to light it."

I slid the small cardboard drawer out. Three wooden matchsticks lay at the bottom of the box. One was blackened from a previous light. The other two were clean, their little heads tipped with brown. I lifted a match and closed the box, licked my dry lips and avoided Jack's eyes. Pressing the match head against the flint, I flicked my wrist, and the powder sparked and flared, releasing the sharp smell of sulphur. I blinked and held the yellow flame up to Jack, who brought the tip of the cigarette into its centre and sucked. The smell, immediate and pungent, stung my nose. Jack dragged in and lifted his face to exhale the smoke up in the air. He grimaced and swallowed hard.

Johannes chuckled. "Hau, you young people."

Jack offered me the cigarette. "Your turn."

I took a deep breath. Where was my mother now? Still asleep? Or standing barefoot in front of her mirror, pulling a clean dress down over her bra and slip, maybe putting on lipstick and brushing her hair. Or perhaps she was already in the yard, calling my name. The air was completely still. The dogs had retreated to the shade and lay on their bellies, heads down, eyes fixed on me. A fly landed on my cheek and I brushed it away. The tobacco smoke floated up undisturbed, anchored to the end of the cigarette. A grey ribbon that twisted and vanished. Johannes tilted his head slightly, as if listening for my decision. I looked at Jack, and he raised his eyebrows a fraction.

"You don't have to, you know."

I took the cigarette from him and held it between my thumb and forefinger. Jack guided my finger over the small break in the paper where a pale wisp of smoke had begun to curl.

"Block the hole, otherwise it won't draw properly."

I nodded and lifted the filter to my mouth, and took a shallow pull on the end. I was anticipating heat, but instead, what I got was a dry, powerful taste that filled my nose and my mouth and caught hard at the back of my throat. The urge to cough was immediate and I held my lips together, suppressing it. My stomach jerked with the effort. My eyes watered and I held my breath until I felt some control, then released a flow of smoke into Jack's face. He ducked and laughed, holding his hand out for the cigarette.

Jack took another drag. He blew out the smoke and offered it back to me. I tried again. This time, I took a shallow pull, managing to suck the smoke back and hold it for a beat, then blow it out through neatly pursed lips.

"You're a natural," Jack said when I handed the cigarette back to him.

Instead of taking his turn, he passed the cigarette over to Johannes. I watched the old man lift it to his brown lips, specks of saliva gathering in the corners of his mouth. I glanced down at the green phlegm drying in the dust. Johannes drew deeply, creating a finger of silver ash that drooped slowly, before dropping onto his vest. It hung there and I wondered if it was hot enough to burn through the fabric until, with some sixth sense, Johannes brushed it away. He took another long drag before handing the cigarette back to Jack, who held it out to me.

"Do you want some more?"

I definitely did not. I shook my head and tapped my wrist as if I wore a watch.

Jack took one more quick pull before guiding the cigarette into the old man's hand. "You have it, Johannes. We have to go."

The old man dipped his head. He clapped his hands together once then presented his palms to Jack to accept the remains of the cigarette.

"Come back soon, Master Jack, or I might not be here anymore," Johannes said. He began his rasping laugh, which soon became the choking cough. He turned his white eyes in my direction and bowed his head respectfully. "Hamba kahle, Miss Eve." He dipped his tall frame back into his house.

"Let's go." Jack brushed past me and grabbed at my hand. His fingers were rough and hot, and as I closed my palm around them, his momentum pulled him out of my grasp.

At the sudden movement, the dogs rushed from the shadows, barking. My blood thudded in my head and adrenaline sparked through my body. I released my limbs into the freedom of running, letting my feet fly and land, gripping the soil with my toes and pushing myself into longer and longer strides. I ran my tongue through the taste of smoke in my mouth and set my eyes on the distant poplars. Jack's blue shirt flashed ahead of me. I caught up to him a little farther along the path. By the time we reached the trees, I was ahead.

Chapter Five

Aloe Afrikana | *March 1975* | Malelane, South Africa

I rub my cigarette into the dirt, stand and stretch, and take a final deep breath before I turn from the view and follow the path back to the farmhouse. As the morning brightens, the chitter and chirp of a dozen different birds build on one another. A small flock of hadedas pass overhead calling in their loud braying way. A shrike darts across the path in pursuit of an insect, and geese call from the river. I toss the remainder of my coffee in a wet splash on the side of the path, and follow a masked weaver with his bright yellow feathers through the bush and over the low stone wall that borders my lawn. Overnight rain has pushed a feast of earthworms to the surface, and the hadedas land clumsily and hop to the business of breakfast. They strut and grumble like old men, their only vanity a flash of iridescence in their feathers, worn like bright pocket handkerchiefs in their otherwise dull suits.

A concrete bird bath stands in the centre of the lawn, and the weaver heads there, sips, fluffs his feathers, and shakes himself awake. Weavers are social birds. They build their nests among their neighbours, forming entire communities that dangle like new fruit in springtime. To him, family is essential. There is safety in numbers. His cousin, the sociable weaver, does one better and builds a single communal nest that hangs in an enormous disarray of sticks and dried grass. Like a dam in the trees, it holds back the weight of seven hundred or more family members, growing so heavy that branches sometimes snap beneath them.

The weaver's nest in my garden hangs dry and empty and after his bath, the male busies himself with its destruction, tearing and plucking at each carefully woven element and letting it drift away on the breeze. There is a crisp note of autumn in the air as the days grow shorter. It will soon be Easter. In the northern hemisphere, where my mother has lived for over a decade, April is the season for fertile beginnings. Here in Africa, it is harvest time. A quietening. Time to drape the plants in hessian, store feed, and refresh the wood pile.

Although she will never say, I know my mother is concerned that my choice to live alone has something to do with her, with how she was when we were growing up. Perhaps it does, but not for the reasons she imagines.

Chapter Six

Weaver Bird | *March 1960*

Through the window of the dorm room I shared with my best friend, Elizabeth "call me Libby" Peele, I watched a group of boys play a pick-up game of touch rugby. One side was shirts and the other skins. The negative space of their t-shirts was still present in their tan lines, their pale backs and shoulders contrasting with darker arms and necks. They tumbled over one another like lion cubs with oversized paws, and I rubbed my feet together under the desk, imagining the itch and scratch of the close-cropped grass on the players' bare skin.

"If I was an animal, I'd be an antelope," I said. Quick and light and as pale as the veld.

"What?" Libby did not look up from her book.

Our dormitory was on the second floor of a Victorian mansion that had originally been built as the home of a wealthy mine magnate, but had lost some of its ambitious elegance in its conversion to a boarding school for young women. Painted an institutional beige, the room's best feature was a large picture window, which occupied almost the entire top half of the end wall. It looked across the fields of the boys' high school next door and beyond, to the concrete skyline that marked the southern edge of Johannesburg. Libby lay on her bed while I sat at the desk beneath the fixed centre pane, which was flanked by narrower windows that opened outwards with a hard twist and push on the iron handles. The morning light cast a yellow rectangle that flowed across the desk and pooled on the floor between our beds. It was in this light that I was failing to concentrate on the glossary in the Transvaal Education Department Std. 9 Biology textbook for an end of term test later that week.

Absorption zone, adventitious roots, anatomy.

The textbook was full of dried veld grass, flattened leaves, and a selection of wild flowers that my father collected as he made his rounds on the farm. He mailed them to me once a month with his letters and I would press them between the pages of my textbook. They smelled of sunshine and soil, and even in this one-dimensional, desiccated state, the plants still resembled their living selves. I could picture exactly where each had been picked; down by the river, behind the barn, or beside the track that ran past the dairy.

I reached over to grip the handle of the window and jiggled until it turned the required forty-five degrees to release it from its frame. Shouts for the ball and a thud of contact carried in on the warm breath of the March morning. A church bell tolled in the distance. I breathed in, and was transported by a note of damp earthiness within the metallic smell of the city to early mornings on the farm.

"We should be outside."

Libby lay on her stomach with a book propped up on the pillow. This time, she stopped reading when I spoke and followed my gaze out of the window. "We *should* be at church," she said, and returned to her book.

My sister had come by on her way to church to ask if I wanted to walk with her. I usually didn't like saying no to Kate, but I had studying to do. Now I wondered if sitting for an hour on a hard pew next to my sister would have been a better choice.

"Come on, Libby. I need some fresh air."

"I have to finish this book. It's my mom's only copy and she wants it back before her book club." Marking her place with a finger, Libby folded back the brown paper cover to reveal the title: *A World of Strangers*, by Nadine Gordimer. The banned novel was like contraband, a single copy passed from one reader to another. My mother kept a similarly wrapped volume of *Lady Chatterley's Lover*, in the back of her drawer in the sun room.

"Is it terribly racy?"

"It's not racy, it's *subversive.*" Libby rolled her eyes to dismiss the claim. "My mother is making me read it."

I knew the real reason Libby didn't want to go outdoors was because she didn't want to miss a call from Jonty inviting her to the Freshers Ball at WITS University where he was a first year. The buzz throughout the boarding house was all about the dance: who was lucky enough to be invited, who was going with whom, who was wearing what, hairstyles, makeup, handbags.

I sagged back into my chair, swivelled around and put my bare feet up on Libby's bed. The eiderdown was more expensive than anything I owned. A richly woven cotton, embroidered with white roses that stood proud of the fabric and rubbed with a pleasing pressure against my soles. Libby's toenails were painted with *pink-pearl* while mine were bare and uninteresting. She was only six months older than me, yet seemed so much more grown up. Born in Johannesburg, Libby had lived in the city all her life, had been to the theatre (more than once), had travelled overseas, knew how to ski, and was going steady with Jonty. I'd been thrilled when we were paired up on our first day at boarding school. The idea that this sophisticated girl who styled herself on Jackie Kennedy wanted to be my friend was still hard for me to get used to.

We frequently spent weekends together at Libby's home in Houghton where I was given my own bedroom, just one of many unoccupied guest bedrooms Mrs Peele had available for visitors. Unlike the farmhouse, where Kate and I had shared a room all our lives and where, on the few occasions we did have overnight guests, the two of us slept top-to-tail on the sofa in the lounge. Libby's mom was liberal in her politics and had a whispered association with the Black Sash. She'd once told us off for being dismissive about voting when we turned eighteen. "There are people in South Africa who have lived and died for the right to vote, girls."

Mr Peele, on the other hand, was an intimidating and distracted businessman who only half listened to the conversation between his wife, his daughter, and her little friend, and seemed to tolerate his wife's politics as if they were a feminine hobby she'd taken up, like book club or sewing, and that could be just as easily set down if it became inconvenient, or interfered with their social or travel plans.

The first time I'd sat down to dinner with the family, served by a maid, Mr Peele had responded to my explanation of where our farm was by observing with a smile: "...the other side of the tracks." Mrs Peele had leaned over and aimed an ineffectual slap at her husband's shoulder. "*Shush, Frank.*" I knew that we literally lived across the main railway track that ran through Johannesburg (and probably a few other railway lines, too), but I saw my friend's gracious embarrassment and understood the true meaning of the phrase, and it stung. The Peeles were rich. Rich in a way I could not really comprehend. Mr Peele's family owned a copper mine in Northern Rhodesia. They had a holiday home on the South Coast and a game farm near the Bechuanaland border. Although I'd never thought of my family as poor, there were things we simply did not have, things I'd accepted we'd never have. Things I'd never realised I wanted. I reacted defensively, exaggerating my family's role as milk producers. The size of the herd and the acreage they managed were given dimensions that I then had to maintain, and after that dinner, whenever I met Libby's friends and was asked about my family and where I came from, to my shame, I referred to our home as The Farm. "My parents are on *The Farm* this weekend." As if it were a second home we used for leisure, visiting only on the weekends or during holidays.

"Why don't we walk down to the church and see if Jonty is there?" I suggested, knowingly trying to manipulate my friend. I wanted to feel the lawn beneath my feet, the pebbled path, the cool water in the fountain at the centre of the quad.

"He's not. He's camping in the Magaliesberg with his family this weekend." Libby rolled onto her back and carried on with her book.

Bracing my legs against her bed, I rocked back on my chair and closed my eyes. The sun dissolved into molten light behind my eyelids as I relaxed my muscles, lengthened my legs, softened my shoulders, and focused on balancing on the chair's back legs.

A movement, like a shadow passing quickly across a lit doorway, followed by a flapping and a short scream from Libby, knocked me out of my reverie. All four chair legs and my own two feet dropped to the floor. A flash of bright yellow in the corner of the room revealed a male weaver, flapping hard in the gap between the ceiling and the top of the regulation wardrobe.

"It came through the window," Libby said from behind her book.

The bird landed briefly on the slight curve of wood that passed for decoration on the top of the wardrobe, then flew up again, working its small wings against the ceiling in quick, surprisingly loud taps, like a flag in a strong wind.

"Keep still, I'll try to herd it out," I said.

Before I could get to it, the bird, drawn by the illusion of freedom beyond the unseen barrier, launched itself from the top of the wardrobe and flew directly at the centre pane. It struck the glass hard and dropped onto the open biology textbook I'd been revising moments before. The small feathered body curled into itself with its black and golden wings folded behind its body, and the pale orange legs and feet, tucked into its belly. The weaver's eye was open, as round and as red as a Lucky Bean, its black centre was dull and unfocused.

Libby's brown eyes peered over the top of her book. "Is it alright?"

"Just stunned, I hope."

There was a knock on the door and a voice called, "Hunter? Are you in?"

Without taking my eyes off the bird, I replied that I was.

"Telephone call," the voice said.

Libby and I glanced at each other, then back to the bird. A foot twitched. Libby hid her face again and shrunk back against the wall. I called that I was coming, then rushed to grab a shoebox from the top shelf of the wardrobe, discarded the lid and turned the patent leather heels I saved for special occasions out onto my bed. I grabbed a pen and stabbed a few rough holes into the base, then up-ended the box and placed it carefully over the bird. "Leave it under there until I get back. It'll feel safer in the dark."

The messenger, a girl from my field hockey team, was waiting at the top of the stairs. At my appearance, she called back in a sing-song voice: "It's a boy!" This news was met with a chorus of *oohs* and *ahhs* from within the row of rooms that flanked the corridor.

Jack.

My face flushed pink. First with the unwanted attention, then because I was blushing at all, and finally with irritation that I hoped it might be him. Jack had recently turned eighteen and planned to join the Air Force. It had been a long time since we'd spent any time together, and he would never think of me as anything more than the slightly scruffy little girl from next door he used to build forts with. It was stupid to even imagine anything different.

The telephone hung inside a wooden booth in an alcove beneath the grand staircase. I looked for Kate in a group of her friends who had gathered in the common room. They were dressed in their Sunday best, either waiting to be picked up for lunch or having recently returned from church. Each girl was wearing a dress in a different pastel colour, and clustered together, they reminded me of a bowl of ice cream: a scoop of strawberry, a scoop of mint, a scoop of lemon. The only man I ever spoke to on the phone was my father, who called every Sunday. He'd ask a couple of questions about classes, field hockey, and then sign off with an awkward, business-like phrase: "Keep well," or "Let's keep in touch," as if we ever wouldn't.

"Hello?"

"Johnny?" It was Jack. His voice sent a rush of heat through me. It sparked down my arms and fizzed in my fingertips. I became aware of the weight of the telephone in my hand. I pressed a flat palm over my sternum, certain that the thud-thud-thud of my heart would be picked up by the receiver, conveyed through the wires via the central telephone exchange, and into the entrance hall at the Turners' farmhouse where the phone sat on a small mahogany bench and where Jack would be standing. To punish my old friend for having this effect on me, I did not reply.

"Hello?" he repeated.

I kept my voice even, "Who is this?"

"It's me," he paused, then irritated, "Jack!"

"Yes." I lengthened and softened the vowel to affect a more urban sophistication. I rolled my eyes at myself.

"Is Kate with you?"

Annoyed that he was looking for my sister, I decided not to tell him Kate was at church, "Why?"

"You need to find her."

The antelope inside me lifted its head with an instinct for danger and froze. When I spoke, it was in my own voice. "What's the matter?"

"Hold on a minute," Jack's voice muted as he covered the mouthpiece with his hand and spoke to someone else in the room. "Tannie, Eve's on." He spoke in fits and starts, as if he was listening and talking at the same time.

"Jack?"

He didn't reply.

"Is something wrong?"

"Hang on, Eve. I'm waiting for your ma…," he paused, and in the background I heard a woman's voice. He continued, "…I'm sorry."

Jack's voice was followed by the sound of the telephone being passed, as if someone was threading the instrument through one end of a woollen sleeve and pulling it out the other side. The slam of a door, distant voices, a woman's high keening cry. Heels advanced across the floor. I felt a wave of something elemental rush towards me, an impulse to run. I held the handset away from my ear and covered the black bloom of the earpiece with my hand. The wave pooled inside my bare feet and crept up my ankles, filled my thighs, circled my hips and leaked into my stomach. When I lifted the phone back to my ear, my mother's voice was explaining about a fault with the electric drill up at the barn. That they tried to revive him, but it was too late, that the shock was too severe and sustained. A short in the wiring. I pictured the stunned bird's clawed foot. My father's clawed hand. Electricity buzzing blue beneath his skin.

The girl in lemon was leaving. She grew small as she walked towards the front door where a young man in a dark suit waited. Her kitten heels clipped across the wooden floor, were quiet on the carpet, and clipped again on the other side. As she reached the man, he opened the door and a sudden burst of light burned them both into silhouettes, smoking their edges. They went through together and the door swung closed, leaving the lobby darker than it had been before.

"Eve?" My mother's voice was thick and unfamiliar.

I felt a disconnection from my own name. Eve. A numbness like when I fell asleep on my arm settled through my body. Heavy and unresponsive. I sat down hard on the small bench built into the side of the phone booth.

"Why are you telling me this?"

"What do you mean?"

"Over the phone."

My mother inhaled and exhaled inside the ear piece. "Evie, find Kate. Jack is leaving now to pick you up."

"Is he alright?" Something in my voice must have drawn the attention of the strawberry and mint girls at reception. They turned in my direction. I spun my back to them. "Where is he?" I said.

"He just left. He'll be in Johannesburg in about an hour."

"Not Jack. Where's Dad?"

There was silence, broken by my mother drawing a breath. When she spoke again it was through tears. "Evie, you need to pack a bag."

The strawberry girl pushed the phone booth's concertina door open. Sounds from the boarding house – calling voices, music, quick footsteps across the floor – came to me as if through a shell held to my ear, with the hiss of wind across sea. The girl looked concerned and offered me her hand. Uncertain about what she intended, I placed the telephone handset into her open palm and, shoulder first, nudged past her out of the wooden booth.

"My dad died."

I had never considered what life might look like after my father's death. I knew, of course, in the same way I knew that birds flew, that he would die one day, as everybody did. It was my mother's death I'd often imagined, accompanied by the uncomfortable thrill of excitement at the temporary celebrity that my mother's loss would bring. For as long as I could remember, there had been periods when my mother was absent, drifting in and out of our lives like a season. The times she was present – when she laughed and joined in with games or met us in the morning, already dressed, hair neat, preparing breakfast – was like essential sunshine, and I harvested what I could, quickly and regularly, constantly alert to the possibility that the axis might tilt and she would fade away again. But my father was different. Solid, present, and reliable. My future lay before me as a straight road highlighted by important events that lit up like street lamps and my father appeared in all of those events. Standing on the steps of the school at my matriculation, helping me move into my first flat, teaching my children how to swim in the river, how to drive, holding their small bodies securely on his lap behind the wide, thin steering wheel of the old blue truck. In all these projections, my father existed forever on the farm, where my future family would visit every Sunday for lunch.

I waded across the lobby. At the staircase, I gripped the banister with both hands and lifted each foot, higher than was necessary, as if I were stepping over an invisible barrier.

Wood was hard. Stairs went up. Light cast shadows.

My pale feet stepped heel-to-toe, heel-to-toe, heel-to-toe along the wooden floor. I opened the door to the dorm room. From Libby's reaction, her wide eyes and o-shaped mouth, and the sudden way she was on her feet, I understood that my new reality was etched on my face.

"My dad died."

Died, not *is dead*, as if it was an impermanent state. A passing event that could still be rectified. I paused for a moment in the truth of this statement, *my dad died*, and felt into myself for the appropriate emotion. There was shock. There was disbelief. But mostly, there was a hollowness, not unlike hunger. An empty, yet steadying practicality, asking: what now? "Stiff upper lip, Johnny." The words arrived in my father's voice. I crossed the room and dropped into the chair in front of the desk, where I had begun a very different Sunday morning only a short while ago. Through my dampened senses, the rugby players thudded against one another on the field outside, a car engine fired into life, was revved then faded, and the opening notes of Perry Como's "Some Enchanted Evening" floated in from the corridor. As I stared, the light coming through the picture window split into tiny molecules of colour that distorted the room.

"How's your mother?" Libby said, and I was embarrassed to realise that I hadn't thought to ask. I shook my head.

"What happened?" Libby said.

"An electric shock."

"Oh my God. I'm so sorry, Eve."

Libby knelt before me and took both my hands in her own, her eyes filling with tears. I could tell that she was holding herself back from asking too many questions, and I was grateful for the consideration. Not because I didn't have any answers, but because I didn't want to dwell on how someone dies of an electric shock. Does it hurt? Is it quick? I recalled a black and white photograph I'd once seen in a magazine of a wooden chair screwed to the ground, leather straps hanging from the arm rests and from the front legs, a domed metal cap positioned above it. I didn't want to imagine my father's clenched teeth, his frantic limbs, his hands clawed and reaching. How would I tell my sister? The wave swept through my chest and choked me. Stiff upper lip. Don't let the side down. Family business is family business. I withdrew my hands.

"I need to find Kate and pack a bag. Jack is on his way."

"Let me do it," Libby said and immediately busied herself with the task. She told a girl in the corridor to find Kathleen Hunter, then pulled an overnight bag, smarter than anything I owned, off the top of her own wardrobe and filled it with items from my shelves. Underwear, stockings, a nightdress, two school blouses and a pinafore, a navy skirt. Like a sick child whose mother does all the caring, I allowed her to make all the decisions, even about what toiletries I might need (a toothbrush, toothpaste, a tub of face cream,) as well as to respond to the concerned line of faces that appeared one after another at our door, until Libby closed it.

"Bad news travels fast," she said, sifting through my school uniforms and the few dresses hanging in my wardrobe. I only had a couple and they were both in the lighter shades of blue that I favoured.

"Nothing black or even navy here, Evie."

"Kate will have something for me to wear." My sister was taller than me, and more shapely, but she was sure to have an appropriate dress in her wardrobe.

The upturned shoebox on the desk shifted with a light nudge from within. Securing the box with one hand, I slipped my other hand under the textbook and carried both to the windowsill in front of the open window. Slowly, carefully, I lifted the side of the box that faced the window while keeping the side closest to me closed against the book, like my father had taught me to lift rocks in the veld in case a snake rested underneath. There was a quiet hop. Then a scratch like a sharp pencil moving across paper. The bird came into the light, blinked its hot red eye, then pushed and flapped in one movement and it was free.

A print had been left on the glass by the weaver bird's impact. Ghostly flight feathers tipped splayed wings, individual tufts of down on the soft crop, the small head and even the tiny nostril were etched on the glass in oil, like a memory.

From the back seat of the Turners' car, I kept my eyes on the smooth skin of Jack's neck as he explained how a faulty wire had caused a short that killed our father as he hung the door on the new barn.

Kate, sitting in the passenger seat next to him, began to cry, and he took his hand off the steering wheel and reached across the bench seat to comfort her.

"It'll be alright, Katie. Things like this don't happen to us," I said.

I very badly wanted to believe my words, but my voice faltered. I was younger but I had always been braver. I was the one who would determine which part of a stream was narrow enough to be cleared in a single jump, which branches could be trusted to climb a tree, which berries were safe to pick and eat. Kate would cuddle the new chicks, while I would kill the rats and snakes that threatened them with my slingshot. But now, as Jack pulled Kate into his shoulder, my certainty unfurled like the soft whorl of a new fern. Jack's eyes met mine in the rear view mirror. His were vivid with pain and something deeper that I suddenly understood. The time for false confidence had passed. The safe world my sister and I occupied, and had never thought to question, had been shocked open. Reality had elbowed its way in with the painful realisation that things like this did, indeed, happen to us.

Out of the rear window, the city folded away like the pages of a magazine, and the road ahead opened to wide horizons of field after field of grazing cattle, yellow veld, and the familiar landscape of home. I became aware of the biology textbook in my lap and tried to remember when I'd picked it up or why I'd brought it with me. To study for a test that had seemed so important only a few hours ago? I allowed the heavy book to drop open and found a dried oak leaf, which I spun by the stem, investigating the pale delta of veins that spread across its surface. Using my thumbnail, I picked off a clutch of moth eggs that had hatched there, blackened and dried. They dropped to the pages of the textbook. As I swept the eggs away with the side of my hand, the truth of the day flooded in, along with my father holding my small hands beneath a flow of cold water, describing how the crepuscular rays that fall like blessings are made visible when dust or moisture move through light, but that light remains, even when it cannot be seen.

Chapter Seven

The Black-Shouldered Kite | *March 1960*

After the funeral, the mourners gathered on our lawn to eat cake and tea served by Rosie and Moses. My mother and Kate received them, while I stood apart, watching and wondering why all these people were here. For my father's sake? My mother's? Or because it was the right thing to do? Kate and my mother smiled politely, offering gratitude and occasionally comfort to people who could return home to their everyday lives, where nothing had changed. Kate's dress was too big across my chest, and my body shifted inside it as I moved. I picked at a spot on the bodice and swiped at the dust on the skirt. I didn't know how to respond to words of condolence, and worried that I'd say something wrong, like when I was very small and people would wish me happy birthday, and I'd reply, "Happy Birthday!"

It was a Monday afternoon, a week after my father's death, and many of the mourners had come from work. The crowd bulged out of the house and onto the lawn, and as the formalities were dispensed with, conversation started to lift and drift into everyday topics between people who had not seen one another for a while. "The Carpenters want us for tennis on Sunday afternoon," a woman's voice announced. Mr Abelheira, who owned the local farm store, promised the minister's wife in his soft syllables that he would bake pastéis de nata for the coming Easter Fair. A man I didn't recognise complained that he was hungry.

Jack's mother was alone when she reached the front of the line. Mrs Turner was a soft, pale woman, who reminded me of the vanilla sponges she was so fond of baking – buttery and sweet. She wore a black skirt, and a blouse in the same creamy tones as her skin and hair, which gave the overall impression of whipped cream on top of meringue. She offered my mother and Kate her condolences before joining a couple from the local tennis club. The woman asked Mrs Turner if she'd heard about the trouble in Sharpeville that morning, while her husband complained about the price of labour and how lazy the South African blacks were. Mrs Turner advised him to get boys from Nyasaland: "Tommy says they're cheap, they work harder than the Rhodesian blacks, and they don't bring their hungry families with them."

I plucked a white rose from the trellis that ran along the low wall around the stoep, and pianoed my fingers along the stem until I found a thorn, then pushed the soft pad of my fingertip against the sharp tip until my skin popped. I tasted the coppery pain before I felt the sting, which arrived in a wash of relief, as if I'd lanced a boil. I did it again and again, until blood bloomed on every fingertip.

Mrs Turner caught my eye. "Evie, what are you doing here all on your own?"

"Where's Mr Turner?"

"Oh, he was at the church," she jumped to an explanation, "but this is all too hard for him." She gestured with a sweep of her arm at the gathering on the lawn. "And they say we are the weaker sex." She nudged me conspiratorially, almost continuing into a laugh, but gathering herself. "You know your father was Tommy's closest friend. More like a brother." She took a deep juddering breath and offered me a syrupy smile, soft eyes blinking with emotion. She cleared her throat and adjusted her hat, pulling it more firmly onto her head, as if to contain whatever it was that had almost come out, then clutched me to her bosom. I gripped her shoulder, leaving four bloody spots on the pale fabric of her blouse, and thought: it should have been him. She released me. I dropped the rose in a splash of petals on the path.

"Cigarette?" The pack of cigarettes Jack offered caught the sun and briefly dazzled me.

I pushed it away and shook my head, checking that my mother was still preoccupied. She was. "Not here."

The corners of his eyes softened in the folds of a smile. He'd grown taller since I'd left for school at the beginning of the year. I was aware of how his throat moved when he swallowed, how his eyebrows terminated in a fine, sun-bleached spray of hair that thinned to a soft down at his temples, and how the crease between his eyes was paler than the rest of his skin, shaped by his way of squinting in the sun.

I'd never not known Jack. The Turners' farmhouse was a quick ten-minute run from ours, and our fathers' close friendship meant we'd been raised more like cousins than friends. Jack had taught me how to load and shoot a pellet gun, and then comforted me when I'd unexpectedly hit my mark and killed a hoopoe, its mate calling his gentle *poo-poo-poo* from a tree above us. I usually regarded my old friend with a thoughtless familiarity, as I might my own hands and feet: ever-present, reliable, and not requiring any deliberate attention. Recently, however, it was like a switch had been flicked that lit him up.

I looked at my feet. "Dad would have hated this," I said.

"It's good they all came."

He pulled a cigarette from the pack with his lips and struck a match. The smell was my father's, and for a cruel moment I looked for him in the crowd – a head taller than anyone else, red beard, blue eyes – before the realisation arrived. I folded into my grief.

"Come," Jack said.

He steered me beyond the mourners and around the corner of the house where I cried into his chest. He waited until I was composed and offered me his handkerchief.

I blew my nose and dried my face. "It's not fair."

"I know."

"Jack?" Mrs Turner stood at the corner of the house. "Have you offered your condolences to Mrs Hunter?" She waved her son over.

Jack looked down at me. "You alright?"

"Yes."

He shook his head when I tried to return the handkerchief to him. "Keep it."

Jack's mother ushered him across the garden, through the crowd, to the line where my mother and Kate were still accepting guests. I went up the steps onto the stoep, through the French doors into the living room. I took my father's pipe and tobacco pouch from their place next to his ashtray, and headed out of the kitchen door into the yard, through the gate and onto the path. Instead of turning to the river, I followed the track to the dairy, sticking to the fields until I came to the top pasture. Wildflowers tipped the veld, turning it into a summer meadow. Proud pretty ladies, lilac baboon's tails, cosmos in white and purple and pale pink, and Matabele violets sang to honeybees that travelled back and forth to the yellow pollen displayed there. I ran through my father's herd of Holstein Friesians. They lifted their slow black and white heads, and moved their mouths over the cud, unaware of the significance of the day. My plan was to take my father's pipe to the barn, the place where he had died. I wanted to make some sort of offering to him, a private ceremony that was more fitting to the man I knew.

My father had always made it clear that when his time came, he did not want a church funeral. "No coffin for me," he'd say, "just put me into the ground so I can return the favour for everything I've taken out." Throughout the service that morning, I'd felt his discomfort itch under my skin. The minister's sermon had included too many empty, clichéd platitudes about my father's value to our family, the community, and to God. I didn't like listening to other people talk about my father. Mr Turner, red-eyed and slightly unsteady on his feet, stood up and described versions of my father I'd never met: as a boy, as a young man, as a soldier, a friend, a husband. The more he spoke, the more indistinct the man I knew became.

Above me, a black-shouldered kite soared and circled against the blue sky. It dived into the grass and emerged with a lizard in its beak, which it carried to a low branch in a blue-gum tree.

Hammer blows knocked open the quiet air. I slowed and tuned in to the direction and regularity of the sound. Everyone was at the farmhouse. No one, on either the Turners' farm or ours, would be working during my father's funeral and wake. The distant blows sounded again, coming from the barn. The image of blue lightning, a burst of electricity, flashed in me. I lifted my face, gripped my father's pipe, and continued with renewed purpose.

The structure emerged from behind a low rise like the hull of a ship, with its beams rising like masts, and the weathered corrugated roof rising like a sail above the wooden frame. The barn smelled of wet wood and dry grass. A handpicked bouquet of flowers, tied with twine, had been nailed to a corner post. A hammer had been discarded in the grass. The faint notes of a song floated up on the breeze – a man's voice. I stopped on the path and held my body still so I could hear over the swish and snap of the grass under my feet. The voice sang a low, slow song that I'd heard my mother play on the piano. It was one of my father's favourites.

I skirted the outside, and as I rounded the corner, came across Mr Turner's truck. The driver-side door stood open, and music played on the radio. His Rhodesian ridgeback, Bantu, sat on the truck bed with his hunter's eyes trained on something beyond the barn. The animal was Mr Turner's shadow. He flicked a black ear in my direction and glanced my way before turning back to whatever held his attention. A new tension rose through my muscles and I ran my tongue along my teeth.

Done with its meal, the black-shouldered kite called its high call from the blue gum. I took a few careful steps around the corner of the barn.

Mr Turner stood with his back to me. He was still wearing his dress shirt and smart trousers, but he'd become untucked. His tie and jacket hung over the open door of his truck. By the deep inhalation and expansion of his back, and the sweet smell of tobacco, I could tell that he was smoking a cheroot. He faced away from the barn, looking across the weft and warp of his fields, which were stitched together by barbed-wire fences. Like ours, the Turners' land flowed all the way down to the line of poplars that followed the curve of the river. Mr Turner kept his eyes fixed on the horizon, although nothing moved there, and when the kite pushed off the gum tree to glide overhead, he lifted his face and watched the bird's slow, focused spirals through the sky. His shirt sleeve was rolled up to the elbow of his left arm, which hung scarred and thin at his side. He spun a coin absently up and down the staircase of his fingers. Between each draw on his cheroot, Mr Turner sang along to the song playing from his car. "*Many dreams have been brought to your doorstep. They just lie there, and they die there.*" His voice was so sweet and so unexpectedly beautiful, that I took a step forward.

He flicked the cheroot down and ground it into the earth beneath his boot. Then he reached decisively under his shirt tail and in a single, effortless motion – as if he were returning a tennis ball over a low net on a summer afternoon – he swung a pistol to his temple. Tension took root through his body and was mirrored in mine. His jaw clenched, his neck became rigid, and his shoulders tightened. His back, his thighs and his knees all stiffened as if he'd been called to attention. He pushed his heels deeper into the sand and sucked in a breath. I did the same. He pushed the gun barrel against his skull, and the taste of cold metal filled my mouth. The sky buzzed bright white over the soundtrack of rock and roll music, and the world stilled, as if all available attention was concentrated on this man, in this place, on this day. On the muscles and blood pumping in his right forearm and his fist gripping the hard hilt of the gun. I dug my nails into my palm.

Into that taut air came the sudden, pitched call of the kite seeking its mate. Mr Turner answered with a rush of noise from so deep within him I felt it vibrate in my chest. He flicked the gun from his temple, pointed the barrel at the sky, and fired.

Somewhere, a dwarf dormouse froze in its grass nest. At the river, a dragonfly pulsed on the velvet head of a reed. A dozen guests gathered on the front lawn lifted their heads, shrugged, and turned back to their companions. And into the pocket of silence that followed, the black-shouldered kite folded like a paper plane. It landed with a puff of impact in the dust at Mr Turner's feet. The man dropped the pistol to his side.

"Bantu, fetch," he said, his voice rough. The sleek dog jumped down to claim the bird as his master moved to his truck and got in behind the steering wheel. With his right side driving all the movement in his body, Mr Turner leaned across his own lap to shift into gear and release the handbrake with his good arm. He slammed the door, turned the volume up, and backed onto the track, where he straightened the steering wheel and kicked up dust as he drove away. Bantu chased behind the vehicle with the soft prize in his jaws.

The earth appeared, hot and hard beneath my feet. I stepped back, tripped over an anthill and fell, spilling my father's tobacco and dropping his pipe before vomiting onto the grass. I scrambled to my feet and ran.

Chapter Eight

The Silk Moth | *March 1960*

My mother, still wearing her hat, sat alone at the dining room table with her back to the door. Even in grief, she carried herself as elegantly as a dancer. Although, if my father ever asked her to dance, she would dismiss him with a wave of her hand, saying, "I don't dance," as though it were an undeniable part of her, like her auburn hair or her fair skin, rather than a choice.

I leaned against the door frame and balled my toes into the carpet, rolled my shoulders, and moved my head from side to side, feeling the click and slip of the bones in my neck. I didn't feel I would ever be able to shake off the tension in my body after what I'd witnessed at the barn earlier, and a day of holding every part of myself tight for fear of falling to pieces. The dirty dishes, platters, cutlery, and glasses from the wake had been cleared to the kitchen where Rosie and Moses took special care not to make too much noise washing up. The French doors stood open. In the perfect light that immediately followed the sunset, the plants glowed gold.

Are you here?

I imagined my father's ghostly presence beside me. If he was here, it should be me that he contacted. An image of him waving his hands in front of my face floated in my mind's eye. Did you know you were dead, when you died? Were you blessed with an immediate understanding of the mysteries of life? Or did the dead experience the same phase of numb confusion and disbelief as those left behind? A time when they did not know they were dead and couldn't understand why the people they loved were ignoring them.

Send me a sign.

God set a bush on fire to talk to Moses. That would be useful now.

Kate came down the passage, lifting her heels as she walked to keep them from clipping on the wooden floor. She carried an armful of linen tablecloths and serviettes and spoke to me in a low voice. "Jack and the boys are finished packing the chairs and tables we borrowed from the Turners into the truck."

"Is everything else in?"

Kate nodded. "Rosie and Moses are washing the last of it." She gestured towards our mother. "She alright?"

"She hasn't moved."

"How are you?"

Heartbroken. Incomplete. "Tired," I said, and leaned against my sister. "I hated today."

"It's almost over," she replied.

The fading day and the rising moon worked in concert to lengthen the shadows until the dining room was dim throughout. The electricity had not yet been reconnected, and Rosie came in to light the fire, the gas lamps, and all the candles that had been arranged on every surface. She and the rest of the farm staff had not been allowed into the church, but they'd come to the funeral anyway, to show their respects from beneath a jacaranda tree in the church yard; Rosie in a dress that had once belonged to my mother, Moses in neatly pressed khakis with his beret at an angle, Petrus in a frayed collar and thin tie, his bald head covered by a worn trilby.

Careful not to disturb my mother, Rosie moved quickly from one gas lamp to the next. She lifted each glass shade with a brief clink and scrape against its brass base, using a single match to light them all. My mother's influence was evident in Rosie's careful frugality. When she'd completed her circuit through the room, she took the linens from Kate's arms and gestured with a quick tilt of her head towards our mother. I nodded, took a deep breath and stepped over the threshold.

"Ma?"

My mother's shadow flickered in the candle light.

"We finished clearing up," Kate said. She pulled out the chair next to our mother and sat.

"Thank you." My mother's voice was dull with fatigue. "How about a nightcap, girls?"

The liquor cabinet stood in the corner of the room. The door was patterned with diamond-shaped glass panes trimmed with lead, and when I opened it, the sweet smell of liquor and cedarwood transported me to a scene of my father, kneeling in the very spot where I crouched, selecting a bottle. I sucked in a breath and exhaled, consciously releasing the fist of emotion that threatened to choke me.

"A sherry please, half a glass." My mother held her thumb and forefinger an inch apart to indicate the small measure.

From the neatly arranged rows of cut-glass tumblers and wine glasses, I selected a stemmed sherry glass and carried it, along with a bottle, back to the table where I sat across from my mother and Kate. My mother retrieved a coaster from the pile set at the centre of the table. I pushed the glass across to her before pouring out the liquor.

"Aren't you joining me?" she asked.

"Are we allowed?" Kate was only seventeen. I had never drunk alcohol before.

"Of course. The day demands it."

I got two more glasses and poured a second and a third drink.

My mother lifted her glass. "'To live in hearts we leave behind is not to die.'" She quoted the poet, Thomas Campbell, and her voice broke as we clinked.

The drink was musty and aged, and I coughed once on the unexpected rasp in my throat. Warmth flowed to my belly. My mother tipped her sherry back in one shot, and held her glass up for a refill. Kate raised her eyebrows at me over the lip of her glass as I topped up my mother's. She sipped the second drink, then set it on the table. Her wedding ring tapped against the glass stem.

"What am I going to do?" she said.

Kate and my mother were so similar it was like sitting opposite the same person at different stages of their life. Both beautiful, with thick, dark hair, my mother had only a few fine threads of grey in hers, as if she'd tipped her fingers in silver paint and run them through her temples. But tonight, she seemed old. Her wrists looked thin in the cuffs of the dress she'd filled so elegantly this morning. She slipped a cotton handkerchief out of her sleeve, and wiped her eyes. It was one of my father's, with his initials neatly embroidered in blue onto a corner of the white cloth. I was abruptly aware that although Kate and I had lost our father, our mother had lost her husband, her partner, her love. My parents had spoken about selling the farm one day and moving to Johannesburg, finding a small home with a manageable garden in the suburbs, where my mother could grow her flowers and my father could keep his dogs. All of that had been taken from her. All those plans. She'd have to create a new version of the future for herself, alone. Sadness softened my bones.

"It seems backwards to me, that the family of the…" I faltered over the description of my father as the dead person and rearranged my thoughts, "that the bereaved have to be good hosts when it's the last thing any of us feels like doing."

"We do it for them," my mother said.

"For the guests?"

"For everyone who loved him."

"*We* loved him."

"Yes, and he deserves an appropriate send off from us."

"But it's too hard." I wiped my wet cheeks with the back of my hand.

"It's because it's hard that the people who loved him most are the ones who must do it."

Kate topped up all our glasses. "Tell us the story about how you and Dad met, Ma."

My mother blew her nose into my father's handkerchief. "I don't feel like that now, Katie."

I'd heard my parents' origin tale so often that I'd stopped attending to the details. Told so regularly, it included repeated phrases and pauses for anticipated responses. A typical Joburg thunderstorm on a summer afternoon. My mother was on her way home from secretarial school when my father jumped onto her bus carrying a bright armful of lilac, pink, and white cosmos. The bouquet was sopping wet. It "fidgeted" with bugs – my mother always used this word, followed by a pause for a laugh – and the roots were still attached, muddy and frayed. My father hadn't been traveling anywhere that day. He'd spotted her through the wet bus window and chased the bus through the rain, plucking the flowers from the roadside as he ran, until he caught it at the next stop. She always ended the story the same way: "That was the moment I fell in love with him." I pictured my father, young and brave and soaking wet, offering flowers to a stranger on the bus. Compelled to reach her, after a single, fleeting glimpse of her face. I sipped the sherry, enjoying the warm, blunting affect it was having on my senses. Was he with her now? Offering up a ghostly bouquet that she'd never see, making her wonder where the sweet, familiar fragrance was coming from?

"The ceremony was nice," Kate said.

Our mother scoffed. "He would have hated it."

I agreed. "We should have buried him on the farm."

"Oh no. No." My mother shook her head, vehement with refusal. "I wouldn't make that mistake again."

"Mistake?" I said, wondering about the *again*. Kate met my eyes and frowned.

My mother polished the edged table with the handkerchief, as if to rub out her own words. "When you bury someone you love in a place, it becomes impossible to leave." She took Kate's hand, then reached across the table, and gripping my fingers hard, she looked from me to my sister with an urgent expression. "Don't bury me here, girls. Don't tie yourself to this place." The candle flames flashed in her eyes.

I withdrew my hand and tipped the sherry into my mouth. I refilled my glass, Kate's, and my mother's, then set the bottle on the table, careful not to make a sound, or a mark.

The wall clock ticked quietly, and from the kitchen came the final sounds of the day's end: cabinet doors were opened and closed, dishes were stacked and put away, the kettle was filled in preparation for the morning.

"We should hold a small service at the river for Dad, just the family. Maybe sprinkle his ashes there?" Kate said.

My father had once told me he believed God lived in Africa. Every night he'd stand at the edge of the lawn, where a slight dip in the land offered perspective across his fields, past the line of trees that marked the passage of the river, to the blue rise of hills in the distance. He knew the weather the sky foretold, what the call of a certain bird or the appearance of a certain insect meant for the coming crop, and the coming season.

My mother shook her head. "I'm so sorry that you girls have to go through this." She waved her hand around the room as if all the loss and grief of the last few days could be encapsulated in this space. Neither of us was able to reply.

The warmth of the alcohol covered me like a shawl. The night darkened, and the candles brightened as they found their element. The three of us sat together in the gentle background noise of night, that seemed like silence but was alive with nocturnal conversation. Frogs, a scops owl, crickets, the buzzing impact of insects colliding with the glass sconces. The candlelight carved my mother's and Kate's faces into planes of black and yellow that constantly shifted against one another. I'd hugged my father for the last time on the station platform three months ago when Kate and I had left for school. Now he was gone, utterly and completely, even while the sense of him was still so real. Pushing off his dusty work boots toe-to-heel at the kitchen door, flicking out the blade of his knife to slice into a bag of feed, whistling his high, sharp summons for his dogs, and dropping into his chair for a meal. As real as if he was sitting in his usual seat at our dining table right now. The familiar soapy dustiness of his smell arrived in my throat and pressed against the back of my jaw.

My mother cleared her throat. "Tommy Turner has offered to buy the farm."

A silk moth flew into the candlestick and dropped to the table. The mouthless insect gathered all the energy it would ever need during its time as a caterpillar, transforming to its winged form with the sole purpose of finding a mate to breed. I rested my fingers at its head, pushing into the pain of the pinpricks I'd made on each tip that afternoon. Blood pounded into my temples, and the retort of the gunshot rang in my head. The moth investigated my fingertips with a few feathery touches of its feelers before walking onto my hand. I wanted to tell my mother about what I'd seen that afternoon, but I didn't know how to describe the scene, which was overlaid with a feeling of shame, as if it was me who had done something wrong.

"I hope you said no," I said.

My mother looked down at her empty glass.

My insides hardened. "He can't. It's too much." Too much loss, too soon.

"Do we have to decide right now?" Kate said.

"Do you want to be a farmer, Eve?" My mother asked the question earnestly, but her eyes held the answer.

"Maybe." I could imagine myself on the land at dawn, the dew-powdered fields, the seeded heads of the veld grass stretching awake in the sunrise.

"It's not all river-swimming and wading romantically through the long grass," my mother said, as if she could read my mind. "It's vaccinating bulls, and docking horns, helping to birth calves, and then killing the ones who are weak and sick. Sowing and harvesting. Praying for rain, then praying for sunshine. Dealing with the blacks. Hard, messy work. Men's work. Tommy will take over the day-to-day responsibility of the dairy and the staff, and Jack will help him."

"Jack doesn't want to be a farmer either." The pitch of my voice betrayed my emotions. Jack spoke about joining the Air Force, learning to fly planes. "Does he know about this plan?"

"He's the Turners' only child, Eve. What else have they got to offer him?" My mother helped herself to the last measure of sherry. "I certainly don't want to be here anymore."

"But it's our home," I said, feeling a different kind of tears from the sort I'd cried all day. Hot, angry tears. I understood that my mother couldn't manage the farm alone, but I couldn't bear the thought of Mr Turner – broken, damaged, mean Mr Turner – taking over what had been my father's, and the only home we'd ever known.

"He won't kick us out, Eve." She paused and reached for Kate's hand. "The hope is that Jack and Kate will get married one day. We can stay in the house as long as we like. The intention was always to unite both farms. Tommy will caretake until Jack and Kate can take over. It's what your father wanted."

"Kate!" I appealed to my sister.

"I don't want to talk about any of this now," Kate said.

"I know Tommy is not the man your father is… was. None of this is ideal, but I can't cope with things on my own."

"You don't even like him."

"That doesn't matter, Eve. Your father loved Tommy. I don't think Anne-Liese has much time for me either. She thinks I'm a soutie."

Kate gasped at our mother's uncharacteristic indiscretion. "Ma!"

My mother was bold after a few glasses of sherry. I'd never heard her speak that way. A soutie, or sout-piel, was an offensive Afrikaans term for an Englishman who lived with one foot in South Africa and the other foot in England, straddling the ocean with their piel, or penis, dangling in the salty water.

"It's true. She thinks she's special because…" She stalled, as if remembering something. Her eyes flicked to Kate's and she shook her head. "Never mind."

"What?" I said.

"It's nothing, just stagnant water under a very old, well-trodden bridge."

"What were you going to say?"

She sighed deeply, drank the remains of her sherry, and pushed the glass away. "She thinks she's special because she has a son."

"How does that matter?"

"To have someone to pass on the family name."

"I'll keep my name," I said. My body felt warm and liquid, as if my insides were floating.

"Jack is nice," Kate said. "And I'd like to have a family."

"Yes." My mother leaned forward and rubbed her hands over her face. "Luckily for him, he does seem to have inherited the best of his parents." The taut look around her mouth was gone, but her eyes still carried the strain of the day. "Think of him as the one who'll benefit most from this, Eve. Think of him as the one taking over from your father."

"You don't know what Mr Turner's like, Ma. He's mean. I saw him today, up at the barn…"

"That's enough!" My mother sat up straight and lifted her hand up to stop me. "Please don't fight me on this, Eve." Her cheeks were flushed and there were beads of moisture sprinkled along her top lip. Sharp and star-like, her eyes darted to mine, then to Kate, then back to her glass, as if she was searching for a thread. "When I was a girl, living in London, we kept chickens. They lived in a fenced hock at the back of the house. We didn't have a big backyard, but it was common for people to keep chickens in the city. For the eggs mostly. We seldom ate the birds. I wanted a dog, but my parents wouldn't allow it, so the chickens were like pets to me. I even gave them silly names, like Dolores and Mable. Somehow chickens seem like old ladies, don't you think?"

I nodded and thought affectionately of the dowager aunts I fed every afternoon.

"One evening, when my parents were out, a fox got into our back garden and dug under the fence of the hock, determined to get at those chickens. We heard the noise, of course, dozens of panicked birds screaming and thrashing around that contained space, unable to escape." Her hands flapped along the table. "It was terrifying, but strangely beautiful. I mean, the fox was beautiful. I remember her burned orange coat with flashes of white and black-tipped ears. She leaped and spun around the hock like a dancer, completely overwhelmed with the buffet at her disposal. She'd catch a chicken and rip out its throat and in the same movement, thrust herself forward and catch another. One after the other, in this bloody ballet, until every last one of them was dead. When she was done, the fox stood absolutely still. It was as if she comprehended the carnage. A dead chick hung out of her mouth, bodies littered the floor – one lay in the water trough, another hung over the roost, dead where it had perched. She was still hungry. The slaughter did her no good, but it was in her nature to kill. She could not stop herself." My mother stared at a point in space, her eyes liquid. Her chest moved over shallow breaths.

"Why didn't you stop her?"

My voice seemed to tether her and she blinked, focused, and brought both palms flat onto the table with enough force that Kate flinched.

"Because, my dear, a fox is a fox. People are who they are. Sometimes you have to take the bad with the good. Accept what you can't change. You cannot interfere with nature."

"It's not nature if the birds are trapped." I pushed my chair back and carried the moth out the French doors, across the stoep, and down the steps into the garden. Frustration blossomed into anger, and I kicked at the trimmed edge where the lawn met the loose, dug soil of the flower bed. The moth clung to my wrist like living jewellery while I held back my tears and struggled against thoughts of the vast loneliness of eternity. The fact that my father's body was no longer part of the substance of life, but was grit and dust and ash, as fine and intangible as a wish. The moth crossed my palm on its gentle feet. I shook it onto a firm strelitzia leaf, and went back up the steps. The dining room was empty. My mother's heels clicked down the passage.

Moments later, the candlelight was extinguished in the kitchen, followed by the quiet catch of the back door as Rosie went out into the night, across the yard to her room.

Chapter Nine

Aloe Afrikana | *March 1975* | Malelane, South Africa

I sit on the back step of the farmhouse and light another cigarette. My mother would be reassured to know that this morning I'm not entirely alone. Catherine, my mother's only grandchild, is visiting. I smoke and tune into the sounds of the girl fumbling her way from sleep to wakefulness. The click of the bathroom door, the flush, bath water running, her quiet singing. She has spent the last week with me as she has every year since she was born. It's a family tradition that allows Catherine and me time together, and gives my sister time to herself. Our week is over and I am driving her home today. I promised my sister we'd be back in time for lunch.

The sun casts an abrupt brightness across the garden, and the birds open their necks to celebrate. It is March, the month my father died. A breeze unsettles the trees and twists at the loose leaves. It's been fifteen years, and still the thought of him brings the cold wash of loss.

My father showed me that loving Africa was more than an appreciation of nature; it was a connection with something huge and unknowable. It was walking barefoot through a conversation with the earth. My mother is a Christian. Her people were banished from the garden. Her relationship with nature is as its master. A tourist who visits to prune and organise, shaping and reshaping things to fit her ideal of beauty. Yet, one season of neglect and the most manicured garden will be undone. Mother Nature does that. Cultivated fields are soon re-wilded by the rough tangle of time. Sunlight bleaches paint, rain rusts metal, and plants split stone. Fire turns flesh to ash. Bodies are absorbed into the soil. That is my idea of loneliness: working to mold nature to your image, only to find it does not reflect you.

Thoughts of my father conjure his presence, and I smell his pipe and turn on the sound of his boots being wiped on the kitchen mat. Catherine stands in the doorway. She is dressed. Her blonde hair is pulled into two neat braids, tied off in bows that reach her shoulders. She has fair skin and a smattering of pale freckles cover the bridge of her nose, as if, in her creation, God absently flicked his celestial paintbrush at her. She's taller than I was at twelve, but reminds me a lot of myself at that age. Fine-boned, almost skinny, her knees touching just beneath the hem of her skirt. She looks at me with her father's eyes, the same air of expectation in her expression.

I want to take her in my arms and shield her from all possible hurt.

"I can't find George," she says.

Chapter Ten

Blue Vervet | *April 1960*

The local farm store was about half a mile from our gate, following a right turn onto a rough track, which travelled perpendicular to the main road. It was run by the Abelheiras whose daughter Zita had been in my class at primary school. I'd never walked to the store on my own, and the closer I got, the more restless I became. I whistled, like my father always had. A perpetual tuneless sound that preceded him to and from whatever job he had going around the farm.

On a dusty patch worn in the veld, trucks and buses pulled over to disgorge and absorb bodies, while a bicycle wove in and out of the line of people waiting at the informal bus stop. Black farmworkers and mineworkers came to the store to buy their weekly mielie meal, bread, boy's meat, and beer, as well as matches, batteries, thread, cool drinks, sugar, and other necessities. The single-story building may once have been freshly whitewashed, but over time it had blended with the landscape in tones of dust and veld. Worn lettering announced *Algemene Handelaar/General Store*, and an oval red and white Coca-Cola sign jutted from the side of the building. Behind the store, two teams of black men played soccer with a deflated ball, which they kicked barefoot up and down a sand field towards rusted, netless goals. A man stood where the dust met the grass, urinating into the veld.

That morning I'd gone into my father's garage, where the air smelled of oil and warm metal, and where my father's presence was remade in light and shadow. I'd sorted through the tools and torn boxes and old feed sacks, opening and closing drawers, and pushing myself up onto my tiptoes to reach the highest shelves. I hadn't been looking for anything in particular. I had only wanted to be among his things – to touch objects that he had been the last person to touch, and find evidence of him among the rusty nails and paintbrushes, measuring tape, balls of string, and forgotten tobacco pouches.

I unwrapped a small parcel of butcher's paper tied with string, and found a small wooden horse. It was hand carved, and stood on a rectangular platform with tiny wooden wheels on each corner. A child's toy. I left it on the shelf and twisted the rim band on an old mason jar to pop open the lid. The dust of empty silk moth eggs and dried mulberry leaves had swirled together with copper coins and a roll of one-pound notes. It was my old silkworm jar, which my father must have repurposed at some stage as a receptacle for loose change. I fished the money out, lifted my father's wide-brimmed leather hat off its hook, pulled it low on my head, and went out into the sunlight.

I searched the crowd at the algemene handelaar for a familiar face. A group of women at the bus stop were restless, speaking loudly. One of them was openly crying. Black men stood or squatted in clusters beneath thin trees that offered little relief from the warm day. I recognised Simeon, who worked at my father's dairy. He squatted with an open envelope of tobacco in the dust at his feet, hand-rolling a cigarette. He spat a loose piece of tobacco off his tongue, put the roll-up to his lips and lit the cigarette with a box of matches, which, now empty, he dropped to the ground. I caught his eye and he looked away. I was used to a more formal greeting. On the farm, all the boys knew my name, or called me Miss Eve, but this was his territory and it was clear the same rules did not apply. I fingered the crumpled notes in my pocket.

There were two doors into the store. The first – beneath a stencilled sign that read *Whites Only, Slegs Blankes* – was empty, while the second doorway – *Non-Whites, Nie Blankes* – was filled with a queue of black men and women that ran out into the yard as they waited for their turn to be served. A small naked child held his mother's skirt while she spoke to a woman carrying an infant strapped to her back. Rosie used to carry me that way when I was little; secured with a blanket that was pulled tight, with the corners knotted across Rosie's breast and waist to hold my little sausage legs snugly around her hips. Rosie smelled of Vaseline and Sunlight soap, and would offer me wedges of lemon to suck on while she got on with her chores. The little black boy was carrying a doll. Its pink plastic body was also naked, with one leg extended at an unnatural angle. Missing chunks of blonde hair revealed a line of dark holes across the dome of the doll's plastic head, and what remained was dry and matted. A bus pulled up, its brakes screeching, and a group of school children got off, girls in regulation black pinafores and white shirts, and the boys in black shorts. Most were shoeless and carried plastic bags filled with their belongings. With their arrival, the general note of restlessness rose among the small group of women. The crying woman pulled a child into her arms and began to wail. I slipped in through the *Whites Only* entrance.

Mr Abelheira ran his store with a benign impatience. He was a big-bellied, dark-haired man who spoke broken English with the rounded sibilant sounds of his native Portuguese. He stood behind the counter in front of a faded poster of Madeira, shouting, "Yes?" to whoever was next in line, and repeating each word of the order to his wife in the back of the shop. Mrs Abelheira turned from shelf to shelf gathering the goods, which she passed to him. He'd put everything into a paper bag, add the total in his head, and scrawl the price in pencil on the bag. He held the bag with one hand and presented his not insubstantial palm until the money owed was pressed into it, at which point he relinquished the parcel and shouted, "Yes?" to the next person in line.

I shouldered my way through the press of bodies towards the

counter. Some people resisted slightly, some ignored my efforts, some even braced themselves against me. A young man, his eyes yellow and glazed, turned abruptly and complained in Zulu, "Wena, stop pushing." But when he saw me, he dropped his head and stepped back to let me pass. I was ushered to the front of the line where Mrs Abelheira waved me forward.

"Evie, what are you doing here?" She lifted a section of the counter and gestured for me to duck under into the back of the shop. "Why aren't you at school?"

My mother had decided that Kate and I would not return to boarding school until after Easter and the April school break, which we'd readily agreed to. We worried that if we returned to Johannesburg, our mother would shut herself away completely. But despite our presence, she'd spent the weeks since the funeral in bed anyway, her closed door a silent instruction to the rest of the household. Kate and I tiptoed and whispered around. The daily newspaper was delivered and remained unread. The wireless in the kitchen was silent. Moses had taken his annual leave and travelled home to Nyasaland. Rosie pottered around the house, swept, tidied, made chicken soup and our beds, and did the laundry for our diminished family. My father's dogs, who'd vanished into the hills after he died, returned to the house every few days to find an easy meal or to rest, their snouts often stained with blood from a night's hunt.

"What's going on outside?" The wailing from the bus stop could be heard inside the shop and a few shoppers craned their necks to peer out the door.

"That's the bus from Sharpeville." She handed her husband a bag of sugar.

"Did something happen?"

Mrs Abelheira turned the pile of Daily Mail newspapers on the counter so I could read the headline. *54 DEAD, 191 HURT IN RIOTS. Anti-pass demonstration leads to Vereeniging bloodshed. A total of 51 non-Whites were killed in their location near Vereeniging and 191 were injured in violent clashes with Police.* I wondered if the crying woman's tears were of relief as she met her children off the bus, or mourning because one of them had not come home. Thoughts that took me straight to my father. I had to blink hard and hold my breath. Mrs Abelheira had stopped spinning around the store and regarded me, taking in my father's oversized hat, my bare feet, khaki shorts, and my shirt, which I knew was dirty and missing a button. Or maybe two. I wiped my palms on my shorts and scrunched up my toes, aware that I was dressed more like an eleven-year-old boy than a sixteen-year-old girl.

"Did you come here on your own?" Mrs Abelheira looked for my mother's face over the heads of the shoppers, while still collecting items from around the store in response to her husband's direction, and handing them forward.

I nodded.

"You walked?"

"It's not far."

"How's your mom, Evie?"

Mrs Abelheira was really asking, how is your mother now that your father is dead and she's all alone with two teenage girls to raise and a farm to run? There was too much to say in answer to this. *Well, Mrs Abelheira*, I knew I'd never say, *Ma seldom comes out of her bedroom. She doesn't cry anymore, but she sleeps all the time. The food Rosie carries into the bedroom on a tray is usually returned, uneaten. Sometimes I worry that she'll die too.*

I took the fistful of notes out of my pocket. "I'd like to buy some of your egg tarts." They were my mother's favourites.

Mrs Abelheira grabbed a small brown paper bag. Using tongs, she placed four tarts inside. "Pastéis de nata," she said, as she handed them to me, waving my money away. She reached behind her waist and began to undo her apron. "Come, I'll take you home."

Mr Abelheira interrupted her with rapid Portuguese, and she pulled a few loaves of bread from a pile on the shelf and put them on the counter next to him. A man shouted from the back, and there was a general wave of impatience through the small crowd.

Mrs Abelheira looked from me, to her husband, and back to me. She ushered me towards the door. "Go straight home, Evie. Tell your mom I'll come visit."

"I will," I said, knowing I wouldn't tell my mother anything and that she would never receive guests anyway. "Thank you, Tannie."

"Straight home, see? Straight home!"

Rolling the paper bag into my fist, I pushed through the boiling hive of waiting people and set off down the path towards the main road, warming to the thought of my mother's happy surprise when I returned home with the pastries.

One of the mine boys had positioned himself at the side of the path close to the road. He looked about my age, and was holding a small bundle in his arms. As soon as he saw me, he stepped into the path and lifted a hand, as if he had been waiting for me.

I paused, feeling the distance between myself and the farmhouse, and the acute sting of my father's absence.

"Come see," he indicated to the package in his arms. A pale blanket, that might once have been lemon yellow but had dirtied to a colourless beige, was wrapped and tucked into the size and shape of a rugby ball. I straightened my back, posturing a confidence I did not feel, and approached him.

"Look, miss," he said, "just a baby." Two dark eyes peered up at me from within a pale pink face. The monkey's tiny mouth was toothless, and a fine fuzz of dark hair started at its brow and grew back across its domed head. The mine boy put the tip of a yellow nail against the monkey's lips and it suckled, not taking its eyes off my face.

"So hungry," he said and laughed. His open mouth revealed a few missing teeth.

"Where did you find it?"

He shrugged. "There by the mine. The mother, she's dead."

"How did she die?"

"The dogs chased her onto the fence." He jerked his body and slacked his mouth. The mines were surrounded by electric fences, and I didn't think it would take much voltage to kill a blue vervet, with their bird-like bones. Not as much as to kill a man. I looked down the path to the road. A car approached and passed. The white family inside turned their heads to look at me as they drove by.

"Those boys want to sell it," he indicated to a cluster of young mine workers in their blankets and muddied hair who watched our exchange from a few feet away. Simeon was standing next to them with the roughly rolled cigarette in the corner of his mouth. Avoiding eye contact with me, he took a last drag on his roll-up and tossed the remaining nub onto the dirt.

"What do I want with a monkey?" I said, loud enough for the others to hear.

"How much you got?" he rubbed his thumb and forefinger together, then leaned closer and offered the monkey to me. His breath smelled of stale tobacco. "How much?"

"I don't want it," I said, sensing in the tone of the exchange that my options were limited.

He pushed the bundle into my chest and held out his palm. "I know where you come from."

The group of mine boys sniggered and shuffled their feet in the dust, pretending not to watch.

"I haven't got any money left." I held up the recently purchased bag of pastries.

"Then give me your hat." Without waiting for an answer, he lifted my father's hat off my head.

"That's my dad's." I swiped for the hat but he held it out of my reach.

The other boys laughed. I bit back tears and glared at Simeon. "I'm telling Petrus," I shouted, but he shrugged. I wanted the hat much more than I wanted some half-dead monkey. I also understood the fate the creature was likely to suffer if I didn't take it home with me. My mother was not going to like this, but I was quite certain my father would put an animal's life above something he wore on his head.

I tucked the monkey against my chest and turned towards the main road. Rosie would know what to do. I began to run. Away from the dirt and the dust and the smell of wee, the wailing women, and the small black child clutching the naked pink doll. The sweet smell of the pastries caught in my throat. A wave of nausea filled my mouth with saliva, and I swallowed hard. Slowing just enough to ensure there was no traffic, I raced across the hard, hot, tarmac, reaching my fingertips into the folds of the blanket to feel for a heartbeat.

Chapter Eleven

Monkey's Wedding | *April 1960*

"For God's sake, Eve. It's a wild animal." My mother had come to the kitchen. She had pulled a cardigan over her nightgown and her hair was unbrushed. She refused to touch or hold the monkey. She couldn't bear the pressure of its tiny fingers on her skin, clinging and needy, and stood an inch inside the kitchen door that led to the passage, like she might dive through it at any moment.

"I didn't have a choice, Ma."

"What were you doing by the store on your own anyway?"

I avoided her question. "The mother was electrocuted."

Silence hung between us as Kate took the monkey from me and tucked the blanket around its tiny face. Even Rosie's hands stopped moving through the dishes in the sink for a moment. Kate cradled the monkey like a mother would her newborn child, resting his back in the crook of her arm. "He's only a baby."

My mother made a noise in her throat, which she turned into a cough. "It's not a child, and it might still die, Eve. What about the dogs?"

"They'll get used to him. He can live indoors until he's stronger."

"I don't want it in the house. Wild animals are not pets." The energy seemed to drain out of her, and she slumped into a chair at the kitchen table. When she spoke again, her voice was tired. "You don't understand how much work it is to look after a baby. You can't leave it alone for one minute. It's a full-time responsibility."

The small creature squirmed in Kate's arms. Four tiny pink fingers clutched the yellow blanket. With its round eyes and human features, it looked like a faerie child, stolen by elves. I hadn't wanted him, but now we were home, it seemed essential that I persuade my mother to let me keep him.

"I'll look after him," Kate said.

"Don't be ridiculous. It's probably not even weaned," my mother continued.

"I'll feed it," Kate said.

Rosie muttered in Zulu and purposefully clattered the dishes in the sink, making sure we all understood that she expected – but did not want – the task of caring for the monkey to fall to her.

"With what exactly? We have no idea what it needs," my mother buttoned and unbuttoned her cardigan.

I crossed the room to get the milk jug out of the paraffin fridge and lifted off the crocheted doily – weighed around the edges with pea-sized, glass beads – which Rosie draped over the mouth of the jug to keep the flies out. The beads clinked against the china as I set the jug on the table. I moved with certainty, projecting a confidence I didn't feel. Just as I had with the mine boy at the store.

My mother watched me and shook her head. "You can't feed an infant monkey cow's milk and hope for the best, Eve."

I hadn't had time to think about any of the things my mother was worrying about, but her concerns burrowed into me. At the time, I truly believed I didn't have a choice, but maybe I should have been firmer and insisted on keeping the hat and abandoning the animal. Now I was safely back home, it was easy to dismiss any fear I'd had that the mine boy or Simeon were dangerous to me, or that I had to give them what they wanted. The truth here on the farm, and in our lives generally, was that there were limits to their power. I'd brought the monkey home because I couldn't bear the thought of anything unpleasant happening to it. It was helpless, and I could do something to protect it. The mason jar, the mulberry leaves, the silk worm eggs, the money that smelled like my father's garage, the mine boy's bitter breath, and the distressed wail of the mother at the bus stop all jumbled together with my need to keep this small animal alive. I had no doubt that my father would agree, but confronted by my mother's emotion and the reality of the situation at the house, I second-guessed my decision. I had expected my mother to be upset about the monkey, but not quite as upset as she seemed to be. She was close to tears, almost afraid, and her fear was infectious. I looked at Kate.

My sister handed the monkey back to me and crossed the room. She unhooked my mother's fingers from the cardigan button she was twisting and worrying, and spoke gently, "Ma, the monkey is not going to die."

"I can't take on any more responsibility."

"You won't have to, I promise. Eve and I will look after it." Kate kissed our mother's cheek and glared at me over the top of her head, reinforcing my commitment to this promise. She fetched the milk jug from the table, and poured milk into a pan to heat on the stove.

Rosie left the dishes to light the gas and shifted the pan over the flame.

I stroked the monkey's chin and he gripped my finger firmly in both his hands, so small that they could barely reach all the way around. His ears, pink and paper thin, were huge compared to the size of his head, and he had a musty smell that reminded me of the time we'd found a mouse nest in the linen cupboard. "What should we call him?"

"For God's sake, don't give him a name, you'll just get attached." My mother scraped the chair legs across the concrete floor as she stood, and abruptly left the room. Her feet sounded down the wooden passageway, followed by the click of her bedroom door.

Kate and Rosie looked at me.

"I couldn't just leave him with them. He's just a baby." My voice sounded whiny even to my own ears. The even keel I'd maintained for my mother's sake pitched over now that she had left the room. "I don't want him to die."

Rosie clicked her tongue and shook her head. "Hau wena. We don't need more trouble." But she stirred a measure of porridge into the warming milk, sprinkled it lightly with sugar, and carried it to the table. I unfolded the tiny animal from its swaddling. Together we spooned the cereal into the monkey's mouth, but although he seemed hungry, nothing would go in. He sucked what he could off our fingers, but most of the milky porridge ended up stuck in his fur or running down his chin. Kate took over.

The greasy brown paper bag from the Abelheira's, battered and bruised after my run home, lay abandoned on the kitchen table. I emptied the pastries onto a plate, choosing one that was in reasonable shape, and left Kate and Rosie to the monkey. I waited in the cool passageway outside my mother's closed bedroom door listening to the silence within before I knocked. "Ma? I brought you something." Across the hall, in the bedroom I shared with my sister, the curtains lifted on a light breeze. Fresh roses from my mother's garden, the same kind I'd seen nailed to the beam at the barn, were displayed in a vase on our nightstand. Bright dust motes floated in the slant of afternoon sun that lay long shadows across our bed. I waited, tracing the wood grain on the closed door with my fingertip, until my bare feet began to ache on the cool floor. Maybe she hadn't heard me. The familiar uncertainty of not knowing whether to knock again or to give my mother her quiet time kept my knuckles silent against the wood. I left the plate with the single sweet pastry on the floor and returned to the kitchen.

Rosie made us each a jam sandwich and ushered Kate and I out of the house to "get some fresh air", which we both knew actually meant "get out from under my feet". Leaving the monkey asleep in a shoe box, we crossed the yard to join the dirt track that took us to the bend in the river, where the water slowed and pooled into our swimming hole.

We ducked through the willow's sweeping fronds and into the shade where I dropped my towel. I tugged my dress over my head and ran down the bank until I splashed into the water, letting it wash over my head, my face, and my body. In only a few quick strokes, I had pulled myself into the middle of the river, where I somersaulted and rolled, enjoying the sensation of the water, concentrating on my body and how easy it was to change direction with just a flick of a hand or to propel myself forward with a short kick.

Kate cleared the small patch of dirt beneath the willow, sweeping away discarded leaves with a hand-held brush of twigs bound together with grass like the black girls used in the compound. She up-ended a stump of wood and laid her towel over it like a tablecloth before unwrapping the sandwiches. When she was done, she came down the bank and stood ankle-deep in the water.

I aimed a splash at her. "Take your dress off and get in."

"Stop it, Johnny." Kate kicked spray back at me and I dived deep to where the water was cold and I could feel the pull of the current. With my eyes closed, I relaxed my body and allowed myself to drift upwards. As I broke the surface, I starred my limbs and floated on my back, enjoying the sun's warmth and the muted calm of the water. A pied kingfisher perched on an exposed willow root that jutted horizontally from the mudbank. The bird tilted its head, watched for a movement below the water's surface, then dived with precision, emerging with the silver flash of a meal in its beak. Drifting with the current, I allowed my body to lift and sink on every breath, and closed my eyes. The branches and their leaves shifted like shadows across my eyelids.

The river exploded and my body jack-knifed as my mouth and nose filled with water. I flailed to the surface to find Jack emerging at the same time. He'd dive-bombed me, and he and Kate were laughing.

"I could have drowned!" I swam at him, put one hand on his head and the other on his shoulder and pushed him under. His skin was warm and smooth, and I felt his shoulder bunch and flex under my hand. He spluttered as he went under, still laughing, then kicked downward out of my grasp and into the deep. Paddling at the surface, the thrill of his presence and the anticipation of another underwater attack was mixed up with my irritation that Jack and Kate had conspired together to play a joke on me. I spun around and around again, watching for his reappearance.

"Where'd he go?" I aimed myself at the bank, but before I could reach it, I felt a hand tighten around my ankle and I was dragged under. I struggled and kicked and my foot connected with his body. He let go of me and I took a few hard strokes, found a foothold on the soft river bed and half-swam, half-ran out of the water.

"Stop laughing!" I splashed Kate as I ran past her in the shallows. "It's not funny."

"It was Jack's idea."

I stomped up the bank and wrapped my towel around me like a shawl.

"You're a stupid, bloody idiot, Jack Turner."

Jack, still paddling out in the middle of the river, feigned shock. "Did you just use a bad word, Johnny?"

"Serves you right for almost drowning me."

"I hardly drowned you." Jack flipped onto his back and dragged himself with a few lazy pulls through the water. He was bare-chested and swam in a pair of khaki shorts.

"It was just a joke, Johnny," Kate said, smiling at Jack.

"It's only a joke if everyone finds it funny, Kathleen. How would you like it?" I used her full name like my mother did when she wanted to show her disapproval with something we'd done. How could my sister take his side? I perched on the willow root with my towel tucked around me.

"You look like an angry crow," Jack said.

"Come on, Evie," Kate said.

"Leave me alone."

"Suit yourself," Kate pulled her dress up over her head.

She was wearing a bathing suit I had never seen before. It was pink with black polka dots, gathered at the waist and tied in a halter at Kate's neck. Unlike my unflattering shorts-style swimsuit, that my mother had crocheted for Kate and had been passed down to me, Kate's suit finished in a flared skirt that edged the top of her thighs. From behind, her shapely body reminded me of our mother. I shifted in the itchy yarn which was wet and heavy against my thighs, and in contrast to Kate's suit, seemed hopelessly shapeless and childish.

"Where did you get that?" I asked.

"Margaret," Kate said. Margaret Webb was Kate's best friend from school. She lived in Johannesburg and her parents would drive all the way to the farm to pick Kate up and take her back to their house for weekend visits. My sister moved deeper into the water. "She's too tall for it now, so she gave it to me." She ran her hands over the shiny fabric. "It's pretty, hey?"

"Yes," I answered before realising that Kate was talking to Jack. He was still up to his neck in the water and he sank lower until only his eyes peered over the surface like a crocodile. He nodded.

Kate rippled her feet through the shallows as if she was posing for a photograph.

I jumped from the branch, ran towards my sister and pushed her hard from behind, knocking her face-first into the water. She emerged, breathless from the shock of the temperature and her unexpected dunking. Her dark fringe stuck flat across her forehead.

"Evelyn Roberta Hunter! You're such a baby!" Kate said.

"I told you you wouldn't like it," I said.

Jack laughed.

The afternoon passed and my anger lifted on the soft wind that brought rain clouds over the horizon. I sheltered under the willow tree between Jack and Kate, as a light sunshower sprinkled through the foliage and dotted the dust at our feet, falling even though the sun still shone strong enough to dry our skin.

"Monkey's Wedding," Jack said.

Kate passed around pieces of sandwich to me and Jack. Yellow and black weaver birds balanced in the openings of their new nests in the reeds, coming and going in the fine rain.

"We've got a monkey," I said.

Jack looked at me, his eyes wide. "A real one?"

"Of course a real one, silly," Kate said. "We're a little old for toys." She was talking in her grown-up voice, acting as if the monkey was all her idea.

"Kate treats him like he's her baby."

"Well I like taking care of him," Kate said. "Is that so terrible?"

"No, except he might still die," I said. I didn't like to imagine how losing the monkey might affect my sister. My mother warned us about getting too attached and I was beginning to understand why.

"He's not going to die." Kate dug her elbow into my side.

"He's not weaned and we don't know what to feed him."

"One of our bitches just had a litter." Jack spoke through a mouthful of sandwich. "She might let him suckle."

Kate and I looked at him with expressions of horror.

"We had a cow who suckled a goat once," Jack insisted. "Better than him dying."

"He's not going to die," Kate said with emphasis on every word. "I'm going to make sure of that."

When we'd finished the sandwiches, I lay in the sun on the riverbank, flopped my arm over my face and peered through my lashes at the shapes of Jack and Kate sitting together in the willow's shade. They spoke quietly, their bodies angled towards each other, their feet and knees almost touching. They were a good match – him fair, her dark, his broad height and her elegance. Kate and Jack both had the gift that I'd seen in other good-looking people, the gift of being at home in their skin. I was the goose-berry, the third wheel. I squeezed my eyes shut and wished that the idea of Jack and me was as inevitable as the idea of Jack and Kate.

It had been two days, and George, named for the last King of England, did not look well. Kate had taken over most of George's care, mothering him and seeing to his needs. She had been awake most of the night, trying to persuade him to eat, and now lay curled in a deep sleep at the bottom of our bed, with a blanket of unbrushed hair covering her face. The monkey, panting shallowly, lay in a nest we'd made of an old towel lining a shoe box, which I'd set in a patch of morning sun on the windowsill. His head was turned to the side. I dipped my finger into a glass of water and held it to his lips. Too weak to suck, his tongue took a half-hearted jab at the moisture before he closed his eyes. I nudged his chest with my knuckle, but he did not respond.

The box was so light it might as well have been empty. In the kitchen, Rosie had set the table for breakfast and whisked eggs in a glass bowl.

"I think he's dead."

Rosie peered into the box. The monkey's hands were too weak to clutch the blanket and had fallen open on either side of his head, exposing the soft pads of his palms.

"Let me see, ntombi." She put the bowl of eggs down and licked a fingertip, which she held in front of George's nostrils. She placed the thumb and forefinger of her other hand on either side of his tiny furry chest.

"He's still breathing," Rosie showed me her finger, as if evidence of the monkey's breath would be there to see. "Take him to Madam."

"She doesn't want anything to do with him."

Rosie steered me towards the door. "It'll be good for her."

My mother was standing at her bedroom window. It overlooked the front lawn and her rose garden, with a view across the fields all the way to the poplars down at the river. She stood with her back to the door. The window was open, and a breeze lifted the few hairs that had escaped her loose chignon. I called twice before she turned into the room. She arranged a smile on her lips, but her eyes were distant.

"You're up?" It was hard not to feel like I was intruding.

"It's a beautiful day." Her smile travelled from her lips to her eyes as she took me in. "What have you got there?"

"I think the monkey's dying."

She motioned me into the room and bent over the box. She smelled of roses and sleep, and unexpectedly, I felt as if I might cry. I sniffed. "He won't eat and now he's not waking up."

"Where's your sister?"

"Asleep. I think she was up with him all night."

My mother looked at the small creature lying limp and unmoving in the shoebox. She laid a tentative fingertip first on its chest, then on its cheek. A muscle in the monkey's eye twitched, and by instinct or with hunger, it puckered its lips and made a weak sucking motion.

"Alright, enough of this," my mother said, and moved to take the box out of my hands. Her response was so decisive, so unexpected, that I fastened my grip. For a long moment we looked at one another. Her pupils sharpened and focused. "I won't hurt him, Eve."

I relinquished the box. She reached in and lifted the monkey out. His arms and legs fell open, and his head, no bigger than an egg, flopped back, too heavy for his neck. She unbuttoned her blouse and slipped the monkey under her satin slip, against her skin. I could imagine exactly how it felt. His light, fur-covered bones. Her smooth, warm comfort. I couldn't remember the last time my mother had held me so close.

"Do you want a cloth?" I offered the towel the monkey had rested on.

"No, he needs body warmth. Go and ask Rosie to boil some water."

I put my arms around my mother's waist and pressed my face into her neck.

"Don't be silly, Eve. He'll be alright." She unwrapped my arms and swiped her thumbs under my eyes. "Quickly now, I'll be there in a bit."

My cheeks tingled where her thumbs had touched me.

"What's his name?" she asked as I reached the door.

"George, like the King."

"Hello, Georgie boy." Her gentle tone followed me through the house.

Chapter Twelve

Rough Skin Lemons | *April 1960*

My mother wore George close to her body like a secret. She was entirely preoccupied with his recovery, as if her own wellbeing depended on it. She'd fashioned a small feeding bottle by trimming a flexible latex bladder usually used to hold ink in a fountain pen. She'd boiled it clean and stretched it over the mouth of a glass medicine bottle to create a teat that was the ideal size and shape for George's mouth. Every couple of hours, she'd open her blouse to the furred face that nestled there and offer him a drink. She wouldn't let anyone else hold him, even allowing him into her bed. Although her confidence that George would recover was reassuring, I found her close attention to him unnerving. On the upside, she left her bedroom and ventured out into the garden sometimes, telling us it was beneficial for George to be exposed to "healing sunlight."

I found her in the morning sun with George on his back in the join of her thighs. The monkey was feeding. His translucent blue eyelids were closed, but his cheeks pulsed as he drank. He clung to the bottle with both his hands and both his feet and his belly was as round and tight as a drum. My mother was excited. "This is his second bottle." She lifted the teat out of the monkey's mouth and he immediately opened his eyes and strained his lips towards it. She laughed and indulged him, allowing him to continue suckling. "He's getting stronger."

"Can I have a go?"

"Next time. He's comfortable now." She tucked the monkey closer into her lap.

Death had brought a new routine to our days. I was embarrassed to notice how quickly people had stopped calling, had stopped coming around, had stopped treating us – my mother especially – as if we had any authority. Just as my father's presence in the world had expanded infinitely, so ours had shrunk back and back and become small. Earlier that morning, a cow had gone into labour, and the first we'd heard of it was when Petrus had reported to the back door after breakfast that the calf had been born. The local bush telegraph meant news travelled quickly across both farms, and instead of coming to my mother, Petrus had sent word to Tommy Turner for his help. This made me defensive of my mother's incompetence and protective of my father's memory. All we needed was a few weeks to catch up, a short holiday from it all, but life continued – milk was produced, cows gave birth, crops waited ready for harvest.

When Mrs Turner appeared unexpectedly at the house in the middle of the afternoon, I guessed that Mr Turner had gone home and told his wife that my mother was not coping.

My mother was resting under the jacaranda with George tucked away, fast asleep beneath the warm folds of her blouse and cardigan. Kate and I lay barelegged on the grass. We planned to go swimming after lunch and wore our bathing suits under our dresses, but dozed beneath the high buzz of insects, the warm sun and full bellies.

I had just closed my eyes when Mrs Turner yoo-hoo'ed from the driveway. She crossed the lawn to my mother, bearing a homemade melktert and calling for Rosie to bring us some tea. She'd been dropped off by Tommy, who was taking Jack to the bank in Johannesburg to do the wages, she announced, and expected her son to pick her up later. Her sudden appearance did not give my mother the opportunity to duck away behind her closed bedroom door, and she blinked like a kitten into the flurry of Anne-Liese

Turner's arrival. Compared to our visitor's robust homeliness, my mother seemed especially thin. Her face was so pale that the skin beneath her eyes looked bruised. She was not a vain woman, but she was proud and deeply private, and I knew that appearing this way in company would be agony for her. When Rosie carried the tea tray out, she also brought my mother a blanket to tuck around her lap.

"We'll need plates too, and some cake forks," Mrs Turner said, "and a knife." She made a slicing motion over the tart with the side of her open hand.

Rosie paused and waited for my mother to nod before returning to the house.

Along with sweet dessert Mrs Turner had brought gossip. "Nellie Erasmus's husband was discovered – by Nellie! – in the back bedroom of the maid. In the bed of the maid. With the maid!" Mrs Turner made her eyes big and her pale eyebrows flew up to her pale hairline. "Nellie noticed that the girl, who's been cleaning for them for a few years now, was getting fatter." She nodded knowingly. "Not fat, as it turns out," Mrs Turner whispered, demonstrating with her lowered tones the size and scope of the scandal, as if even the trees and shrubs and round agapanthus blooms might lean in towards the skinner. "Not fat at all," her eyebrows raised even higher, "but *pregnant*." The final word was not whispered, but mouthed.

A look passed between Kate and me.

"Erasmus insists he's in love with the girl." She scoffed at the impossibility of the relationship. "And then he left with her, headed for the Bechuanaland border in the Ford. Poor Nellie." Mrs Turner began to pour the tea, adding milk and a heaped spoon of sugar to each cup without asking how any of us liked it. "It's the child I feel sorry for in these situations. It's unnatural." This last word was also mouthed.

Unaware of the disturbance she'd caused in our lives, and basking in her Good Samaritan glow, Mrs Turner handed out the teacups, and maintained a constant, chipper monologue with news of mutual friends and happenings at church and in town.

"You must get out, Susan. Isolating yourself like this will not do you any good." She gestured around our small garden with the teapot. "Betsy Vos is hosting a pistol-packer's party next week. Everyone brings a plate of sandwiches or biscuits and after tea we get in some shooting practice. Have you got a gun? Never mind, I've got a .22 you can borrow. You're on your own now. You can't be too careful, you know." She flicked her eyebrows with weighted meaning at Rosie who'd returned with the side plates and forks, which she left on the table at Mrs Turner's elbow. Mrs Turner sliced the melktert into generous wedges. She placed each one on a plate with a fork and handed it to Rosie to serve to my mother, Kate, and me. When we each had a slice, Rosie turned to go back to the house but Mrs Turner shifted to the front of her chair and grabbed Rosie's wrist.

"Did you tell your Madam that your daughter is back?"

Both my mother and Rosie stiffened, as if a fishing line laced down each of their spines had hooked a catch and pulled taut. Neither responded. We were all suspended in the silence that swelled between them. Mrs Turner leaned back in her chair and folded her arms across her chest. Kate and I watched our mother. She sat absolutely still, only the tension in her jaw and a slight flare in her nostrils betraying any emotion.

I'd always known in the unquestioning way children know things about the adult world that Rosie had a daughter, but I'd never thought to ask where she was or why she didn't visit her mother here on the farm. Details of a distant day, a day I had not recalled until that moment, flared in my head. A black teenage girl in an old dress and a thin cardigan beneath a face with round, youthful cheeks; brown eyes; hair that sprung from her head in tight curls. But just as soon as it appeared the memory faded, like warm breath on a cold window.

"Rosie?" My mother's voice was rigid. "Is it true?"

Rosie clasped her hands in front of her apron and leaned towards my mother from the waist. Her posture and the speed at which she spoke added urgency to the situation. "She's only just come back. Just a few days now. She couldn't stay in Sharpeville, after everything that happened."

"Why was I not told?"

"Because, with the Master's funeral… I didn't find a good time."

"Ma, what's wrong?" I understood how Rosie's daughter's absence from our lives made her return significant, but it was unclear why it was so upsetting to my mother.

"It's Ruth, isn't it? I remember her." Kate said.

Rosie nodded at Kate's question but kept her eyes on my mother's face. She bunched her apron in her fist. "She's here, Madam. In the kitchen. I said she should come and see you…"

Before she could finish, my mother was shaking her head. "Absolutely not. We told you then, Rosie. We all agreed that you could stay on one condition," she held a finger up to emphasise the number, "that Ruth *never* came back."

"But she was there when the policemen were shooting those children. She had to run away. She didn't have anywhere to go. She's grown now, Madam. She's a woman. A teacher." It was unusual for Rosie to talk back to our mother and we all waited in silence for her to respond.

My mother's face was fixed. The skin around her mouth was white while her cheeks and neck flushed red. She pushed the blanket off her knees and let it drop to the ground. "It's as if she's just been waiting for Robert to die."

"No, Madam, it was because of the trouble in Sharpeville. Not because of the Master."

"What happened in Sharpeville?" Kate said.

Mrs Turner still clutched the cake knife. She spoke as if her mouth was watering, but her eyes were not on the cake, they were on my mother. "There was a riot in Sharpeville on the Monday that we buried your father. A mob of troublemakers went to the police station and threatened the police, and some of them were shot."

"School children," Rosie said.

"What?" The shortness of Mrs Turner's response suggested Rosie's reply was unwelcome.

"Not troublemakers," Rosie said and stood up straight, "they were children."

"Doesn't matter, there were hundreds and hundreds of them and only a few police. Throwing sticks and rocks and destroying property. If they don't want trouble, they shouldn't go looking for it."

"Why don't you girls run along?" My mother interrupted. She lifted the slice of melktert off her plate and folded it into her serviette, then held it out to Kate. "Go and have a picnic at the river, and a swim. It's such a lovely day." Her voice was calm, but her eyes flared, brittle as glass.

"But, Ma…" I started to speak.

"Off you go." She stood and ushered us out of our chairs, wrapping a second slice of cake as she waved us away. "Here, Evie." I took the offered parcel.

"Don't upset yourself with all this, Susan. I'll take care of her." Mrs Turner pushed herself out of her chair as if to follow Kate and me to the house. "You say Ruth is in the kitchen, Rosie?"

Rosie's face darkened and she shifted herself between the house and Mrs Turner, but my mother spoke up. "I think you've done enough, Anne-Liese. I can see to my own household."

"Whatever you think is best. I'm only here to help." Still standing, Mrs Turner cut a fresh slice of tart for my mother. "Let's at least try to enjoy our tea." She walked around the table to place the slice onto the empty plate in front of my mother, and as she did so, George's little face appeared in the V of my mother's blouse. Mrs Turner faltered, dropped the cake, screamed, and batted her hands towards my mother's chest.

My mother placed a protective palm over George's head, and slapped Mrs Turner hard across the face.

"Calm down, Anne-Liese. It's only a monkey."

Chapter Thirteen

Aloe Afrikana | *March 1975* | Malelane, South Africa

I drop my cigarette into my mug, and follow Catherine around the back of the house and down the path towards the tree nursery to look for George. The old vervet is spoiled and grumpy, but Catherine loves him, and he goes everywhere with her. The past week, George has shown a preference for the nursery, where the palm trees that are fully grown wait with their massive root balls contained in hessian wraps to be transported to the city. They require a front-end loader to lift them onto the back of the truck. George exercises in their canopy and fancies the bugs that live on the hardy stems.

We find George in a *Musa*, a banana tree. His pink, human-shaped hands are clasped at his chest and his tail is curled between his legs. His small body is hard and still, and he does not respond to Catherine's touch. Her eyes shimmer and her chin shakes, but she does not let the tears fall. It is the first time something she loves has died.

"It's okay to cry." I do not want for her the stiff upper lip that was expected from me and Kate.

She nods and sniffs, but holds her composure. "Why did he go off on his own?"

"Animals know when they're going to die. They like to be somewhere safe." I place an arm around her narrow shoulders.

She looks up into the canopy of wide green leaves above us.

"Maybe the trees reminded him of the jungle."

I follow her gaze and nod, even though I've known George his whole life and am aware that he's never been in the jungle. But that's the way with trees. Stitched into our genetics, they are ancient and familiar.

"Should we bury him before we go?"

Catherine shakes her head. "I want to take him home."

I agree, imagining for this furred family member a spot beneath the poplars in Lasswade's graveyard, where we scattered my father's ashes, where Jack and I would pass through on our way to the labourers' compound, and where my mother buried her secrets.

Catherine makes a hammock of her skirt and carries George back to the house where we wrap him in an old dish towel. I don't have an appropriately sized box, so we rest his curled shape in a Dutch oven. Catherine lays a sprig of rosemary over George before she covers him with the lid. "For remembrance," she says.

When we leave to drive Catherine home, she settles in the passenger seat with the closed pot on her lap.

Chapter Fourteen

Weeping Willow | *April 1960*

Leaving the failed tea party, Kate and I ran across the lawn, through the backyard, and burst out the gate at a full sprint, giggling and falling into one another with glee and horror, only slowing once we reached the dirt track. Neither of us had ever seen two adult women argue, never mind be physical with one another. In our experience, disagreements between grown ups were private. Kate and I were punished if we purposefully hit or hurt one another, and it had been years since my mother had spanked either of us, a punishment reserved for the times that we'd been especially naughty – cheeky to a grown up, telling a fib, or behaving badly in public. The humiliation was far more painful than the smack. To see my mother raise her hand to another person was shocking and thrilling. The fact that it was Mrs Turner was more than a little satisfying.

"If anyone ever deserved it…" Kate glanced back at me over her shoulder with a smile, as if she'd read my thoughts.

"Your future mother-in-law."

"Stop it, Eve. That's just adults talking. Ma's in a panic. I haven't even finished school."

"Yet."

"And Jack hasn't asked me."

"What if he does?" I wanted Kate to say she would never marry Jack in a million years, that she had no interest in being his wife and living on the farm, but she just shrugged.

"He might not want to marry me after Ma klapped his mother."

The same nervous thrill coursed through both of us in laughter. I hurried to catch up and walk alongside my sister. "Do you remember Ruth?"

"Yes. I think so. Maybe. I don't know." Kate shook her head, not in denial but confusion. "I mean, I know the name and that she's Rosie's daughter, but now I'm not sure I ever actually met her, or if I made her up around stories I'd heard."

"I think I met her once."

"Was I there?"

"Maybe, I must have been very little. I can't really remember that much about her or what she was doing here, but I do remember an older girl visiting when we were little." I seldom saw Rosie's hair unbraided, and the full uncovered afro of the girl I recalled had made a big impression on me. "I think that she pushed me off the swing or something. I have this image in my mind of her looming over me while I lay in the dust."

Kate widened her eyes and managed to frown at the same time. "Maybe she's dangerous? Maybe that's why Ma didn't want her around."

I dropped behind but followed Kate closely, putting my feet into her footprints and thinking of all the times I'd listened from other rooms to Rosie's sweet voice singing the lullaby, *thula thul, thula baba, tula sana,* and wondered what she'd been thinking about as she sang. "Why would she lie about having a daughter?"

"I don't think she lied. I mean, Ma knows about Ruth. It's more like Rosie kept her a secret."

"Or maybe she didn't have a choice. Mrs Turner knew that Ruth being here would upset Ma. She brought it up on purpose."

Kate slowed until I walked beside her again. "But why?"

"I don't know, but there's always been something about Ma, something... ?" I didn't really have the words to describe what I wanted to say about our mother. Or maybe I did have the words but didn't want to say them out loud, which would somehow make my worries real. In many ways, it was obvious, like the times when Ma didn't leave the house, which had become more and more frequent over the years. But in other ways, I could only feel how my mother was too quiet, too deeply inside her own head. Being with her was like playing tennis on my own – I would serve the ball, but it was never returned. "She can be… you know?"

Kate completed the sentence, "… Different?"

"Yes," I said. Different. My mother was different to Mrs Peele, Mrs Webb, and even Mrs Turner. Different to Rosie, and different to how our father had been. Even different to herself at different times of the day. She reminded me of the set of Russian dolls my music teacher kept on her piano at school, each identical, but distinct and separate, stacked one inside the other, like reflections.

"I know what you mean," Kate said.

"Do you think that's got something to do with Ruth?"

"How could it? No, I think Ma has always been really, really sad. And now with Dad… it's just made it worse."

I squinted into the afternoon brightness. Kate made sure to step on the grassy patches along the path to avoid the hot sand, and I did the same. I didn't want to ask Kate if she thought we were the ones who'd made our mother sad, because I didn't want to hear the answer. I matched my sister's leaps and hops from one tuft of grass to another all the way to the river, landing on each clump of wildflowers that had been crushed soft beneath Kate's foot.

Kate lay on a towel in the sun and I used a willow frond to swing on and splash into the water. I was familiar enough with the eddies and rises to know exactly where to aim my drop to avoid hidden roots and shifting sand banks. The cold water took my breath and I gasped to the surface.

Jack waded in the shallows with his fishing line angled into the water. "You're disturbing the fish, man."

I ran past him and flicked my wet fingers at his bare chest. He flinched, but kept his eyes on his float.

"Your ma said you'd gone to Joburg with your dad."

"He only takes me so he has someone to drive him home after lunch with his army buddies. I'm not his bloody driver," Jack said, casting into the water.

Kate and I had not mentioned what had happened between our mothers. It seemed embarrassing now, for both parties. For my own part, I wasn't sure I could keep my delight out of the story.

I dropped onto the towel next to Kate and with my hair dripping into my lap, used my father's pocket knife to cut the slice of melktert into three pieces. Jack propped his rod on a forked stick to keep the line in the water and sat on the sand next to us. I offered him a piece of tart on the end of the blade and he popped it into his mouth in one bite. His fingers were still wrapped, but the bandage was dirty and had begun to fray.

He saw me looking and lay back, concealing his fingers behind his head.

When the dessert was finished, I carried my father's knife to the water's edge to wash it, aware of Jack's eyes on me and resenting my clumsy crocheted swimsuit. I hiked the pants up on my hips and crouched to rinse the blade.

Kate stood and stretched her arms over her head. "We should head back, Johnny."

"In a bit," I said.

"We need to check on Ma." She used her eyes to express the things she couldn't say with words.

"Later." I clipped the blade into the hilt, tossed the knife onto my dress, which lay in a discarded heap under the tree, and returned to my spot on the towel.

"Suit yourself." Kate pulled her dress over her bathing suit and nudged Jack with her foot. "See you Monday?"

He nodded but did not sit up.

"What's happening on Monday?" I asked Jack as Kate left through the willow fronds.

"My Ma invited Kate for dinner."

"Only Kate?" I kept my voice even, not wanting to betray the dark jealousy that coiled through me.

"It's stupid," Jack said. His body was constructed of a series of flat planes and angles that unfolded into long limbs, where muscles moved directly beneath his skin. His stomach tensed into six even facets as he shifted onto the towel into the space Kate had vacated. He bumped up against me and our hips touched. I pulled my knees into my chest. Jack straightened his legs and crossed his ankles, still resting his head on his hands, and let out a long, satisfied sigh. "No school for three whole weeks."

All the Transvaal schools were closed for Easter break. It was almost the end of April, and the weather hadn't yet turned. I lifted my face to the sun. It was still warm enough to swim and lie in the sun, but by the end of the Easter weekend it would feel like autumn. Kate and I would return to boarding school at the end of April wearing our winter uniforms.

"You've already had a whole week of no school, lucky." Jack said.

"Ja," I said, "I'd rather not have though."

Jack touched my arm. "Sorry, man. That was stupid."

I shrugged. "I know what you mean. It's going to be strange going back to normal life."

"Especially for your mom."

I nodded to show Jack that I agreed with him, but to say it out loud felt like a betrayal. My mother's increasing isolation was a constant worry for both Kate and I, but loyalty was expected. It wasn't done to complain and I definitely didn't want our family to seem as vulnerable as we were. Especially with Jack's father sniffing around our farm, and after the slap this morning, and the Rosie and Ruth story, which I still didn't fully understand. I made my voice light and said, "Ma will be fine," but I was not at all certain this was true.

"I'll check in on her when you're gone," Jack said.

I nudged his thigh with mine. "Thanks."

"It'll be strange for me too, not having you around all the time."

I looked at his face hoping to find more meaning than his words conveyed, but his eyes were closed. I imagined that he was picturing this familiar space, the willow, the reeds, the blue-grey gums with their bitter leaves, just as I was in that moment – entirely silent, without either of us here, disturbed only by the flick of a returning kingfisher or a leaf drifting down to float away on the current. I stretched out alongside him and allowed my arm to roll open until the back of my hand came to rest against his side. The sun was warm on my cheeks, my arms, my thighs and belly, and yet all my awareness was concentrated on the few square centimetres that pulsed against Jack's skin.

"You are lucky though," Jack said in a quiet voice.

"Why?" I asked even as I knew what he was saying. I'd come to understand things about the Turners I had not known before. Reasons Jack might prefer to be away at boarding school. Even the memory of my father seemed preferable to the presence of his. I willed myself not to glance back at his broken fingers and searched instead for a silver lining. "Boarding school is not so great. There are too many rules. You've got a lot more freedom here."

"Freedom." Jack expelled a puff of air with the word, and his body flinched in disagreement.

"You'll see what it's like when you join the Air Force and you can't just do whatever you want all the time."

Jack pushed himself onto his elbows to check on his fishing line. The float continued to bob, unmolested, in the water.

I laced my fingers across my belly, stroking the hot patch of skin on the back of my hand, and squinted up at his shoulder and the underside of his jaw.

"Doesn't look like that's going to happen now."

"Why not?"

"My father wants me here."

I knew that Jack was talking about his father's plan to take over our farm. Part of me wanted to understand how much Jack had to do with the portion of the plan that included him and Kate getting married, but another part was too afraid to ask. Too afraid to get confirmation and maybe see excitement from him.

"Tell him you don't want to be a farmer. Ma told me your dad liked being a soldier. He should understand."

Jack didn't respond. He sat up, faced the river, and hooked his arms over his knees.

"Just talk to him," I said. "You never know."

He moved his shoulders in a short, resigned shrug. The muscles worked behind his jaw.

I'd seen enough to grasp that for me to suggest that Jack "just talk" to his father might not be as simple for him as it had been for me. The temptation to tell him that I'd seen his father at the barn the day of my father's funeral pressed against my tongue, but I recalled the desperate sound his father had made, and the words would not come. Instead, I rested my open hand on Jack's lower back. He drew in a deep breath that expanded his ribs, and his shoulders softened as he sighed it out. He plucked a stalk of wild grass and used the thin stem to scratch under his bandage.

"Fish aren't biting," he said.

"It's too hot."

We both looked up at the sky. Not a single cloud interrupted the wash of blue.

I was still resting my hand on Jack's back. The moment of offering him comfort had passed, but I didn't know how to remove it without drawing attention to it still being there. Also, I liked what it suggested, that I could easily touch him, as if he were mine. I moved my fingers slowly inwards and out again against his skin. "What are the girls like at your school?"

Jack rolled the grass stalk into a soft bundle and flicked it away. He leaned back on his elbows and I pulled my arm out of the way. His forearm butted up against mine and his knee dropped against my thigh. I lay very still and closed my eyes.

"I never noticed," he said. I heard the movement of his head in the shift of his voice and peeped out from beneath my eyelashes. I followed his eyes as they moved down my body and my legs, until he was facing the river again.

"I don't believe you."

"It's true. I don't notice other girls."

All my senses leapt like puppies at a chew toy at the word "other". Other girls? Girls who weren't me?

"Anyway, what's got you so interested? Are you writing a book?" He lay back with his arms bent behind his head and closed his eyes.

Jack's breathing slowed and grew even. It was hot in the sun, but I didn't want to move in case I disturbed him, or our closeness. A fly buzzed across my ear and settled on my cheek. I shook my head and it hummed into the distance. Light folded in a bright geometry behind my lids and my limbs grew heavy. My thoughts thickened and grew quiet, and I allowed myself to drift towards sleep.

I was standing in a parched riverbed that ran through a brittle veld. The shrill song of insects surrounded me as a single sensation of screaming heat. On the bank, under the pale shade of a lone acacia tree, its lower branches pruned into a distinctive umbrella shape by grazing giraffes, squatted a San hunter. He was naked apart from a short leather loincloth. His brown skin hung soft on his bones, and his eyes squinted against the glare from within the folds of his old face. He addressed me in the soft

whistles and clicks of his ancient language, and the unknown sounds formed familiar words. "A secret is like a dead fish, it will always float to the surface." At my feet, a large silver fish slipped and flopped on the dry sand. Its eye was white. I pushed my fingers into the dust, until the sand darkened and became cold. Cradling the fish, I angled it into the wet ground. It flicked its tail and swam into the earth.

I woke to a rhythmic plop of something landing alongside my head, then being dragged away. Landing again, and slowly being drawn back. Jack was not lying next to me. I opened my eyes. A small bunch of forget-me-nots, with tiny, pale purple petals, landed on the towel alongside my head. The wild bouquet was knotted with a grass stalk and hooked at the end of Jack's line. He was casting from the water's edge, up to where I lay, putting the flowers next to my shoulder, then reeling them back. I caught the bouquet and stopped the line from travelling.

Jack reeled in, following the shortening line until he was next to me.

"Myosotis," I said, rubbing a small, furred petal between my fingers. "It means mouse's ear, in Greek."

Jack was wet, as if he'd just walked out of the river. He knelt next to me on the towel and unhooked the bouquet.

I sat up, and when he didn't move away, I leaned towards him.

It was my first kiss. When he parted his lips, I did the same, eager to appear experienced and unafraid, even as my entire body thrummed with blood and nerves. His skin was cool but his mouth was hot, and it took me a moment to organise what it was I was touching; his lips, mine, my tongue, then his. I was surprised at how alive and insistent it was, and that I could be heartbroken and happy at the same time.

A sudden bark from the path, and Jack jumped up and into a

low crouch before I could even turn my head. Mr Turner blustered through the willow fronds into the clearing with Bantu.

"Jack!"

Jack scrambled to his feet and positioned himself with his back to the trunk of the tree and his knees slightly bent, like a cat facing down a dog.

The hand of Mr Turner's limp left arm was tucked into his short's pocket, and in his right hand he brandished his sjambok. He waved it over the small sandy beach and our swimming hole and turned slowly in the low space. "So, this is where you come to hide?"

"I'm not hiding," Jack said.

"You sure?" Mr Turner made a grab at his son, which Jack dodged, moving behind his father, so the larger man had to swing around to face him. I was reminded again of a dog worrying a cat. The cat is quicker and nimbler, but knows that to turn and run will give the dog some advantage, so it holds its ground, maintains eye contact, and makes sure the dog remembers it has claws. I moved up the bank and pulled my dress over my bathing suit. I was afraid for Jack, for what his father might do to him, for the fact I was here to see his shame. At the same time my spirit spat with rage. Tommy Turner would never, *never*, have behaved this way if my father was around. Brazenly confronting his son on my father's farm, in front of me. He was the worst kind of bully, a cowardly one. My hand folded around my father's pocket knife.

"I told you I wanted you to drive me home from town. Where were you?"

"I forgot."

"Don't lie to me, boytjie." Mr Turner raised his voice and his sjambok, pointing it at the fishing rod, the last crumbs of tart, and the towel where Jack and I had just been sitting. "I had to find a ride and missed lunch with my Legion pals. All so you could sit outside in the sunshine having a bloody tea party."

Almost as tall as his father, though not yet as broad, the shape of

Jack's chest and the way he held his ground suggested that soon he would be. He jutted his chin out and held steady.

Mr Turner aimed himself at me. "And you? Did you tell him what your mother did?"

Jack put himself between me and his father. "We were only swimming."

"Swimming, eh?" Mr Turner laughed a high, mocking bark, which he turned on me, allowing his eyes to move up and down my body before he faced his son again. "Is that what the kids are calling it these days?"

The muscles in Jack's jaw clenched. He met his father's eye, his face dark with emotion.

"Well, you're *swimming* with the wrong sister, my boy. Get home now, or you're going to get it." Mr Turner shouldered past Jack and knocked him back a few steps. He opened the tree's fronds like a curtain and gestured with his sjambok. "Go. Now."

Without looking back at me, Jack ducked out of the willow shade, but he didn't run. He walked down the path, his head steady, his back rigid.

Tommy Turner looked me up and down again. "What would your father think, Eve?"

He turned to leave and rage rose in me as courage and defiance. "What would he think of you?" I shouted at his back.

Mr Turner stopped. My throat thickened. The river was still, the birds were quiet, and the wind held its breath. Jack returned a few steps back down the path. Mr Turner leaned down to scratch Bantu who waited, ears cocked, on the path. "Good boy," he said, then continued through the willow fronds. They disappeared together through the trees.

My chest and head pounded with the force of my heartbeat. How dare he invoke my father as a way of humiliating me. Fear, embarrassment for Jack, for his father's ugliness exposed in this way, threatened behind my eyes. I squeezed my eyelids closed and swallowed, determined not to give him any power over me.

Only when both the Turners and the dog had vanished did I rise from my crouch. Blood tingled behind my knees and under my arms, and tears made silent tracks on my cheeks. The shock of Mr Turner's unwelcome intrusion braided like coarse wool through the silken strands of the afternoon with Jack. His skin, his touch, the promise of his mouth. Jack had left his shirt behind. It smelled of him, of cold water and warm air. I pulled it on over my dress. Before I left the clearing, I searched around until I found the small purple bouquet.

Back at the house, the stoep was quiet, and the thin remains of the abandoned tea still lay spread across the table under the tree. The kitchen smelled of frying onions. My mother was seated at the kitchen table, feeding George, while Kate stirred something on the stove. Rosie was nowhere to be seen. I slipped the bouquet into my pocket.

"Where have you been?" my mother said. The terse enquiry told me she already knew.

"At the river." I avoided eye contact with her. I'd decided on the way home not to mention how Mr Turner had burst into our afternoon. My mother had enough to worry about, but I resolved to do everything I could to make sure he did not get his hands on our farm. I focused instead on a cloth bank bag that my mother held, and that I knew was filled with orange paper wage-envelopes. "Where's Rosie?"

"It's Friday," my mother said, holding up the fabric bank bag, as if it was my responsibility to remember that it was payday. "Tommy Turner went to the bank for us. I completely forgot." Emotion shimmered across her face.

From the yard came the raised voices of the farm staff, who waited for their pay, but had clearly begun celebrating the weekend with their beer allotment.

My mother pushed the bank bag across the table towards me. "Take this out to Petrus, and tell him to make sure everyone gets one." She tucked George into her neck, stood, and began to pull the bobby pins out of her hair, dropping them one by one onto the floor. She passed me at the door.

"And Eve."

"Yes, Ma?"

She plucked at the collar of Jack's shirt. "I don't want you entertaining Jack on your own."

"He's my friend."

"He's a boy. I know what they're like." She left the kitchen and went up the passage and into her bedroom. The door clicked closed.

Kate turned from her task with the wooden spoon in her hand. "You should have come home with me."

"Did you tell him we were at the river?"

Kate turned back the stove and lifted a chopping board. Using the spoon, she scraped chopped carrots and celery into the onions and continued to stir.

"Kate!"

"Yes, Eve, I told him you were there."

"Well, thanks to you, he found us." I explained to my sister what had happened, detailing Mr Turner's unpredictability and his rage. "He's dangerous, Kate. I'm sure he hurts Jack. We cannot sell that man our farm." I couldn't stand the thought of Tommy Turner and his sjambok being in charge of my father's staff. Kind, hard-working people like Petrus, and Moses, and all the loyal men and women who'd worked for our family for all the years I'd been alive. "You can't marry Jack."

"Oh, you'd like that wouldn't you?" She put the lid on the pot and turned to face me.

"What are you talking about?"

"I'm not stupid, Eve." She leaned back against the counter and crossed her arms over her chest. Her eyes looked tired.

"This is not about Jack, Kate. It's about his father. I hate him."

"But you love Jack."

I made a dismissive noise and looked away. I couldn't reply, afraid anything I said would reveal how much I wanted the very thing I was not allowed to have. My mind replayed the moment on the riverbank with Jack with such clarity, that I was sure Kate would see everything I was thinking if I met her eye. I busied myself folding a pile of dishtowels next to the sink.

"You're wearing his shirt, Eve."

"He left it behind," my voice rose, "because of his father! You're missing the point."

"You smell like the river." Kate wrinkled her nose as she passed me on her way to the fridge, where she took out a cooked chicken carcass with meat still on its bones. She carried it to the stove and began slicing off pieces and dropping them into the pot. "Soup will be ready in half an hour."

A coldness spread through me. How was this the same day that had begun so hopefully, with my mother coming outside to sit in the sun with George? With Kate and I lazing warm and dozy under the tree, and with Rosie making tea in our kitchen?

"Where's Rosie?"

"She's gone." Kate poured a jug of chicken stock into the pot and wiped her face.

"Gone to the compound? Or gone, gone?"

"All I know is that she wasn't here when I got back. You better get the wage packets to Petrus, and when you're done with that, you can clear the table outside."

Chapter Fifteen

Mouse's Ear | *April 1960*

Kneeling on the floor of the sun room, I lay two sheets of blotting paper onto the open pages of *A Boy's Guide to the Wilderness*. The heavy, hardcover book had been a gift from my father on my 9th birthday. He'd apologised for the title. He'd tried to find a similar Girls Guide, but it seemed there was no such thing, and anyway, he said, it didn't matter because it wasn't as if the wilderness knew the difference. The book offered instructions on the correct way to stack firewood and light it with a flint, how to build a raft, whittle a slingshot, and gut a fish. How to pluck a chicken, string a bow and feather an arrow. For a couple of years, it had been my prized possession, one that Jack and I had referred to like a favoured parent.

I arranged the purple mouse-ear bouquet between the blotting paper. Thinking of Jack's mouth, I flattened each petal with my fingertips before closing the book to press the flowers. There was nothing in *A Boy's Guide to the Wilderness* about how to behave when your father died. How to protect your home. How to comfort your mother. How to comfort yourself. I stacked the book at the bottom of volumes A to J of the Encyclopedia Britannica, then looked up at the tall book shelf of files, recipe books, magazines, and paperbacks.

It was Saturday morning, and Kate had driven my mother to town that morning. It was the first time my mother had left the farm since my father's funeral. Persuaded by Kate's invitation to dinner at the Turners, she'd insisted they shop for a new dress. I had dressed to go with them but changed my mind at the last minute. Without Rosie around, I was completely alone. Even the dogs had wandered away to wait out the morning in the shade somewhere. I planned to use the time to go through my father's files with the hope of finding the deed to the farm. I didn't know what I'd do with it, only that I needed something that could delay the sale to Mr Turner. At breakfast that morning, my mother had talked to Kate about agreeing to a price with Tommy and a time frame for the exchange. She'd also suggested that Kate stay on the farm when I returned to school after Easter. "There is a wedding to plan, after all." Kate dismissed her with her usual argument: "Ma! He hasn't asked me yet," and the dark snake stirred up my spine. I'd excused myself from the table. I couldn't support their willingness to follow Mr Turner's plans or the easy assumption of Jack's compliance.

I stood and pulled the first file off the shelf and opened it on my mother's desk. File dividers labelled in my father's angled scrawl were interspersed with others in my mother's neat print: *Accounts. Staff. Leave Roster. Milk Log.* All related to the running of the dairy. I put it back and selected another. In the third file I found the divider labelled *Lasswade*, and behind that, the white A4 sheet with "Certificate of Title" printed on it in black ink. Elaborate cursive below the heading described the extent of our property's borders. It was notarised with an embossed stamp and a green ribbon. Soft wings of excitement and worry fluttered in my belly as I slipped the certificate free of the twine ties, folded it in half and tucked it into the waistband of my shorts. I celebrated with a silent, thrilled shiver and pushed the file back into place.

Framed photographs of my family's faces were dotted around the shelves. My very young parents leaned against a car I did not recognise. My clean-shaven father held a cigarette between the fingers of one hand, his arm draped around my mother's shoulders. She looked about the same age as Kate was now, and peered shyly under her eyebrows. There was one of them on their wedding day. My mother was a bit older, more confident, and smiled directly at the camera while my father turned to look down at her beautiful face. Another black and white picture showed my mother on their honeymoon, standing on the boardwalk in Durban. She wore a pale dress and smiled towards the camera, holding her hand as a shield against the bright sun. There were pictures of my mother holding Kate, and later, me. Both of us were wearing the same long, embroidered christening robe. In a third picture, my mother held an infant, her head bent low over the little scrunched face. I could not tell if it was Kate or me in the picture, but something about my mother's expression caught my attention. She seemed happy. In the photos of Kate and my christenings, she looked distracted. Her mouth formed a smile but her eyes were flat. There was no connection between her and the babies in her arms. We could have been anyone's children. A stranger's infant she'd been asked to hold while its mother was occupied with a task.

I took the frame down and unclipped the stand, lifted the backing out, and released the thin piece of cardboard that held the photograph in place. It was smaller than the frame, sized to fit by a mount which had been taped in place. I peeled back the sticky tape that had become brittle and yellow with time and slid the photo out of the mount. A curl of blonde hair was taped to the back alongside a stamp with the photographer's name, and a date: April 1939. Beneath the stamp, written in faded sepia ink were the words "*Susan with John at 2 months.*" John. I read and reread the inscription. John. The small gravestone Jack had uncovered when we'd run through the cemetery in the summertime reared into my mind, along with my mother's words the night of my father's funeral. "*When you bury someone you love in a place, it becomes impossible to leave.*"

My mouth filled with saliva, and pinpricks of light sparked in my peripheral vision. The clock that hung on the wall in the entrance hall toned ten times. The bell reverberated through the house, then settled like dust sheets over the furniture in all the unoccupied rooms. With shaking fingers, I layered the glass, the mount, the photo and the cardboard back in the frame, pushed the metal clips into the wood, and balanced the picture on the shelf. The replaced photo dipped at an angle inside the mount. I sank to the floor and held myself as still as I could, not wanting to allow the possibilities of my discovery to unfold and solidify. Another child. A small grave. A secret. How many of the adults in my life must have conspired to keep this from us? Or did Kate know? Was it just me? I couldn't bear that. To be the only ignorant one. Did the Turners know? Did Jack? Rosie and Moses?

Sounds from the house – a settling beam, a turtle dove calling outside, the clock ticking in the hall – drifted into my consciousness, and I became aware of the brush and whisper of my limbs against my body. I held my breath, screwed my eyes shut and pressed my palms against my ears as hard as I could. Still, there was a hum. The hum of my own self. My blood and my brain and the pressure of my skin against my own skin.

I wished Kate was home. She and I had grown up under our overprotective but absent mother's wing. Both of us were regularly reminded that in Africa, you keep your babies close, because life is cheap and children die all the time. According to our mother, danger lurked everywhere, in the form of disease, extreme weather, and people. She insisted our milk was boiled before we drank it, no matter how much we complained about the disgusting skin that formed on top. Whenever a thunderstorm rolled overhead, Moses would be sent outside to sprinkle dry mielie meal on the ground as an offering to appease the gods, while our mother gathered me and Kate into her bed, pulled the covers over our heads, and in a loud voice intended to drown out the storm, told us stories about British children in boarding schools, bluebell-lined brooks that babbled through villages and were home to swans and silver fish – gentle images harvested from her own childhood in England. It was a place

I knew about only from books and songs and my mother's words, and which was so different and far superior to the yellow veld: the dust, the heat, the blackjack seeds that stuck to my socks and my shorts, and the powerful thunderstorms that crashed through our summer afternoons. But, my mother would remind us, we should all count our blessings. "At least I'm not Mrs van Breda," she'd say. A local Afrikaans woman who'd lost all five of her children to polio in one year. They'd been buried like naval seamen asleep in their bunks in a submarine – one atop the other – one grave, one headstone, five names.

I opened my eyes and released my hands from my ears. The house was so quiet. Too quiet. I'd been by myself so often throughout my life, but for the first time I understood what it meant to be alone. Accompanied only by ticking clocks and walls and dust and the lazy mope of air moving through and across it all. My temples thrummed like bees in honeysuckle. If I'd had to guess, I would have said that being alone would feel like a vastness; a huge space that widened and stretched away, leaving you out of contact and exposed. Now I understood that being alone was a closeness, a pressure, as if every molecule of air had taken weight. I pushed myself to my feet. I was suddenly suffocated by the closed windows and the silent, empty rooms. I went through the kitchen and out the back door into the yard, and blinked into the bleached heat of the day. I kept walking. Away from the house. Away from the closeness of being by myself. My feet stepped on the grass and onto the dirt drive in front of the garage. Sparrows chitted to each other in the trees, and a locust clicked through the yard.

The image of a toddler directing a hand-carved wooden horse on wheels around a track smoothed into the driveway leapt fully formed in my mind, singing as he went in a high, child's voice. He was blonde like me.

John. Johnny.

My father's name for me. Except there had been a boy and it was his name. My chest tightened with the sudden fear that John was their first choice and I was a poor replacement. I felt the sensation of a presence behind me, like small fingers at the nape of my neck. I spun around.

"There's no one here," I said out loud.

Had my father loved me as much as he had loved the boy? When he called me Johnny it made me feel special. My mother had objected, telling my father it was inappropriate. I'd always thought her objection was with me, not the name. I thought she meant that I was the thing that was wrong. That I wasn't girly enough to satisfy her, or boyish enough to satisfy my father. Rather, something in between. Trying and failing to be all things to everyone at once.

The sound of an axe against wood broke the quiet and I followed the smell of wood smoke round the back of the garage, where I found Moses feeding the fire below the water tank. When he went to the woodpile for more fuel, I pulled the title certificate out of my waistband and tossed it into the fire. The green ribbon curled and the paper caught, flared, and blackened around the edges. I poked at it with a stick, stirring what remained into the week's worth of ash. I watched until there was nothing left. Johnny was gone. My father was gone. Rosie was gone. I wasn't going to let our house be taken from us too.

The photo of my mother holding John had always been there, on display for Kate and I to see every single day if we'd only known what to look for. The lock of hair was deliberately tucked away behind it. Not mislaid or forgotten. I stepped closer to the fire, allowing the heat to burn my skin and the smoke to sting my eyes until they overflowed.

It was almost lunchtime, and my mother and Kate had still not returned from their shopping trip. I sat on the stoep steps and peeled a naartjie, waiting for the sound of the car to arrive down the drive, simultaneously wanting and dreading my mother's arrival. I was still in two minds about confronting her. Embarrassed in case I was the only one who didn't know, furious that she and my father had kept a secret from me, also afraid that I'd got it all wrong and burned the deed in a rush of misplaced anger.

A bee landed on a segment of naartjie and poked around looking for a sweet drink. I transferred the small creature onto my finger and stood to carry it down the steps where I edged it onto a lavender flower.

"Careful it doesn't sting you." Jack stood on the lawn behind me. He was dressed in long trousers and a collared shirt, and wore shoes. Very unlike his usual shorts, khaki shirt and bare feet. Since his father had exploded into our afternoon at the river a few days before, there was a fresh bruise on Jack's upper lip, which was slightly swollen. The bee ran each sticky leg across its long tongue.

"They don't sting for no reason," I said.

"Is Kate here?"

"So that's why you're all dressed up." A pinch of irritation at Jack's interest in Kate's whereabouts, layered on the emotion of the morning, made me prickly and mean.

His tone shifted to defence. "I'm not dressed up."

I walked away from him. "You're wasting your time. My sister isn't interested in farm boys." I tossed the words over my shoulder hoping they would land hard. They did.

"What the hell's the matter with you?" His voice was clenched. He followed me around the side of the house and we faced one another beneath the sun room window.

"What's the matter with you?" I gritted my teeth to mimic his tone.

"Did I do something wrong?"

"What happened to your lip?"

Jack tucked his lips together in a thin line and turned his head.

My mind flashed on his father's fists and his mother's plump hands. "Why doesn't she stop him?"

"He can't help it," Jack said.

"He's your father, he shouldn't hurt you."

"He's not a bad person."

"I know, he's just a bad drunk." I repeated the words I'd heard my father say so often about his oldest friend and with the immediacy of a punch, I recognised my father's complicity. "Did he know?"

"What? No. My dad would never..." Jack wiped his face. "What happened at the willow tree the other day… he would never have done that, not before."

"He should have been the one that died," I spat out the words that had sat on my tongue as bitter as dandelion leaves for the past few weeks, and let them float between us like the seeds of the same plant.

Jack matched my look. There was a coldness in his expression I'd never seen before. He aimed a kick at a stone, sending it skittering through the flower bed. It cracked against the brick wall of the farmhouse.

There was a sharp rap on the window. We jumped apart like fighting dogs sprayed with a hose. My mother was leaning into the window. She waved to me to come inside and mouthed "*now*" behind the glass.

"Jesus," Jack said.

I was breathing hard, as if I'd had been running. I hadn't heard the car. I shouldered past Jack, but he grabbed my hand.

"Wait. Please. Let's go for a walk." He took a small yellow box from his pocket and held it in his palm like a peace offering. When he shook it, matches rattled inside. "Can you get a cigarette?"

I glanced at the window of my mother's sunroom, then back to Jack. The alternative was to stay and have lunch with my mother and my sister, pretending everything was normal.

Jack raised his eyebrows and shook the box again.

"Meet me at the barn," I said.

My mother waited in the passage outside the kitchen, not even trying to hide her disapproval. "Evelyn, I told you not to entertain Jack here on your own. It's inappropriate."

"I can't tell Jack what to do, Ma." I wasn't even angry, just blunted and numb and uninterested in anything she had to say.

She faltered, and I could see she was taken aback at my insolence. "You know your sister has been invited there for dinner."

"What has that got to do with me?"

"Don't act dumb, Eve." She dismissed my words with a flick of her wrist. "Come and have some lunch. We're not finished with this conversation."

"I'll be there just now." I waited while my mother went into the kitchen and opened the fridge to bring out a roast chicken and salad, then ran down the passage into the sunroom. I opened her desk drawer, flicked open the silver box and helped myself to a cigarette. My mother's copy of *Lady Chatterley's Lover*, wrapped in brown paper, lay at the back of the drawer. I snatched the book and left the house via the front door, avoiding what was left of my family.

I read out loud:

"Ours is essentially a tragic age, so we refuse to take it tragically. The cataclysm has happened, we are among the ruins, we start to build up new little habitats, to have new little hopes. It is rather hard work: there is now no smooth road into the future: but we go round, or scramble over the obstacles. We've got to live, no matter how many skies have fallen."

"Find the good bits," Jack said.

Far away from our mothers and our responsibilities, and concealed by stacks of hay bales, Jack and I lay on our backs in the barn, passing a cigarette back and forth. Slats of sky could be seen in the gaps where the high corrugated-iron roof met the wooden beams my father had built.

I flicked through the novel and scanned the pages. I could not bring myself to read the words *balls* or *penis* in front of Jack, so I read on a bit to myself, then aloud:

"*There fell a complete silence. Connie was half listening, and threading in the hair at the root of his belly a few forget-me-nots that she had gathered on the way to the hut. Outside, the world had gone still, and a little icy.*" My eyes flicked to Jack as I thought of the wild bouquet I'd carried home from the river and pressed between the pages of *A Boy's Guide to the Wilderness* that morning. I continued: "*"You've got four kinds of hair," she said to him. "On your chest it's nearly black, and your hair isn't dark on your head: but your moustache is hard and dark red, and your hair here, your love-hair, is like a bush of bright red-gold mistletoe. It's the loveliest of all!"*"

"Love-hair? Jesus," Jack laughed.

"Scandalous," I lay the book face down on the hay as Jack passed me the cigarette. He was teaching me to blow smoke rings and I made an O with my lips and puffed the smoke out in short bursts. All I managed was a loose incomplete oval, which faded fast and drifted away.

"Almost." Jack took the cigarette from me and sucked it down to the filter. He puffed out a string of tight circles, then ground the stompie hard into the dirt, ensuring not a single ember remained.

We lay in silence, our bodies mirroring one another's. Legs and arms starred. My right hand touched Jack's left, and his left foot rested against my right ankle. We resembled paper cutouts that, if repeated, would form a chain of bodies, toe-to-toe, finger-to-finger, the negative space between us as essential to the pattern as the positive shapes of our bodies.

I picked up the book and carried on reading aloud. "*She was nearly at the wide riding when he came up and flung his naked arm round her soft, naked-wet middle. She gave a shriek and straightened herself, and the heap of her soft, chill flesh came up against his body. He pressed it all up against him, madly, the heap of soft chilled female flesh that became quickly warm as flame, in contact. The rain streamed on them till they smoked. He gathered her lovely, heavy posteriors…,"* I had to stop. My cheeks were on fire.

"Did your ma say anything about what happened at my house the other day?"

Jack paused as if deciding how much to say. "She said your ma is losing her senses since your dad passed and keeps a baby monkey in her bra."

I could see he wanted to laugh but despite my feelings about my mother, I couldn't give Anne-Liese Turner the last word. "Well, she's talking kak. Ma is sad, but fine." I took a few breaths and calmed my voice before continuing. "Did she say anything about Rosie?"

He rolled his head towards me. "She told Pa that Rosie's daughter is staying at the compound. That there's a problem about her being there."

"Did she say why?"

He shook his head and was distracted by a plane droning over the barn.

"The Germans painted the bottom of their fighter planes blue, like the sky, or very light grey," he said, "to make them harder to see from the ground. They painted the top in earth colours, greens and browns, to camouflage them from the top."

"Did they paint them black to fly at night?" I was trying to be funny, but Jack answered earnestly.

"That's actually worse, because it makes an empty shape against the stars." He flew his hands, flat and open-palmed, over us as he spoke. "But they did paint some planes white, to fly in the snow."

"How do you know about this stuff?"

"I'm not just a farm boy, you know." Jack propped himself up on his elbows. His neck was exposed, taut and smooth, as he followed the plane's arc across the bowl of the sky. The patches along his jawline where he had started to shave were mottled with tiny red spots. He flipped onto his stomach. "And I didn't come to your house today to see your sister."

He leaned closer until I could make out each dark lash around his eyes. I turned my face, and he closed the space between us. His mouth tasted smoky and I could feel the hard tender rise of the swelling on his lip, which made him flinch as I drew it into my mouth, but he did not pull away. Instead, he shifted closer until his full weight was pressed along the length of my body. The sensation was both comforting and exciting. I lifted a knee to angle myself towards him and slipped my arms around him. His back moved under the thin cotton of his shirt, and the memory of his skin beneath my hand at the river was immediate and vivid. I tugged up his shirt and he made a sound in his throat, somewhere between a groan and a gasp, and I understood my power. I wanted to make him make that sound again. I pressed my fingers into the rise of flesh low on his back where his belted trousers hung on his hips, and he said my name, "Eve," like a breath into my mouth. I did not think about my father or the boy they called John. I did not want to think about my sister and her need for a new dress. I thought of perfect purple petals and the soft impact of the bouquet being cast onto the river sand. I was glad to defy my mother. Mostly, I just wanted Jack, and I wanted him like this, breathing my name, choosing me. He reached under my skirt, and all my senses tracked his hand up my thigh and over the soft rise of my cotton knickers. He rested his finger there and I pushed against him, surprising myself with my need and my willingness to show it. I undid his belt. When he lifted my skirt, I raised my hips to help him. When he pushed against me, I let him.

Chapter Sixteen

The Dung Beetle | *April 1960*

I left Jack at the barn, conscious of the hot, wet pain between my legs, but instead of going home, I headed straight to the river, stripped off my dress, and plunged naked into the swimming hole. The water was freezing, but I forced myself to stay submerged as I rubbed at the blood between my legs. When I was dressed and drying, I followed the path that Jack and I had taken from the river to the compound all those years ago. My feet left wet marks in the red dust, a neat line of heels linked by a thin bridge to the ball, each topped with five toes. The day had grown cooler. I could feel autumn in the air and in the crisp snap of the grass beneath my feet. Startled by a locust's crimson wings as it leapt from the grassy verge and flew across my path, I ducked slightly. "It's nothing," I reassured myself. "It's just a fat grasshopper."

As I approached the poplars I began to whistle, keeping myself company and my father near. Each morning, as I emerged into consciousness, my brain reminded me: he is dead. I'd believe I was living with the truth of knowing, and then something – a distant whistle, a car arriving down the drive, an ashtray at the centre of the table – would make my father present again. I'd wait for him to walk through the kitchen door, throw his hat onto the sideboard, toe his boots off on the mat. Then I'd re-remember: he is dead, and have to adjust all over again. My betrayal at the discovery of the photograph had darkened and deepened my grief, like I was looking at the world from inside a well.

At the graveyard, I cleared grass and leaves from around the stone and traced my fingers through the letters. J-O-H-N. This time, I paid more attention to the dates. February 1939 - August 1940. Only a baby. The stone was cold under my fingertips, and my thoughts pushed through it; through the sand and grit, through the decayed leaf matter, the earthworms, the compact mud, and the translucent roots that would find a path into those tight layers, to the hole with its sheer sides and the box that lay there in the quiet. It was a delicious torture, this determination to meet the details and decay of death face-to-face. I thought again of my mother's words, and the desperate grab of her fingers across the dining room table. *"Don't bury me, love. Don't tie yourself to this place."* We hadn't yet scattered my father's ashes. That image was harder to summon. I could not interrogate what it would feel like to hold his remains in my hand. I hoped they would be smooth and powdery, but guessed they might contain bone. Fingers crawled against my skin again and I shuddered. I faced the path that would lead me to the compound. Rosie. I needed her to tell me what had happened.

Remembering the dogs from my last visit with Jack, I paused on the hill and looked back the way I'd come. The sun was low in the sky, and the poplars' shadows lay long and flat. The day I'd visited the compound with Jack, that same row of trees had held sentry, showing me the path back to the refuge of the farm. Now, they seemed to mark a divide between the way things had been and the way they were. A jackal yipped in the distance. Blood thudded in my ears and knocked my heart against my chest bone so hard that I began to wonder if it was possible for a sixteen-year-old to have a heart attack. I made a shushing noise, both to calm myself and against the possible threat of the dogs. The rhythm was comforting, and it slowed my breathing enough that I could gather myself and settle in my body. I pushed my bare toes into the soft sand. A dog barked somewhere in the distance. "Rosie." The word came out in a whisper. I took a few cautious steps farther down the path towards the fire pit. "Rosie." Louder this time. The fire was not burning, but the large logs, still white hot from a recent burn, had been dragged out, and the coals at the centre had been left to cool. The dogs did not come. Every house remained quiet. Four closed doors and four dark windows.

I took a log from the wood pile and rested it on the warm coals, then squatted at the fire's edge and blew a few long, slow breaths, until the coals flared, flamed, and caught the wood. I swallowed over a dry throat. My eyes itched with fatigue and emotion. I sat cross-legged in front of the fire and leaned my head on my hands. I wondered if my mother still listened for her little boy's laugh.

"Miss Eve?" Petrus was carrying an armful of firewood. "Miss Eve?" He said my name again, as if unable to believe it was me sitting in the compound on a Saturday evening. Other members of the staff moved across the clearing towards the small houses, glancing over, but giving me and the fire pit a wide berth.

I stood. "It's me, Petrus." I said, as if I needed the words to bring myself into being.

"Is Madam alright? Do you need me at the house?"

"She's fine."

"Come, I'll take you home."

"No. I came to see Rosie."

"Aikona. Rosie is gone away."

"Gone where, Petrus?"

"Your mother…"

"I won't tell, I promise. I need to speak to her."

Petrus shook his head, "You must go home."

"No."

Petrus sighed deeply and looked over to one of the houses. I knew he couldn't force me to leave, and my comfort in my authority as the Baas's daughter made me brave. Even if the Baas was no longer alive,

I still had some status. I sat down, faced the fire and threw a handful of kindling onto the flames. Dry seed pods cracked and spat. "I can wait."

Petrus's footsteps moved away behind me, and I heard the creak of a door opening and closing. Muffled sounds and voices, a man's, then a woman's, came from inside the small house. Things grew quiet again and I added more fuel to the fire. I could feel that I was not welcome, but my need to see Rosie fought my discomfort. There was a whisper of movement in the sand. The feet next to me were dusty and bare. Multiple strings of tiny coloured beads interspersed with seed pods were wound around both ankles, and they rattled gently when they moved. I looked up at a tall, slim woman in her mid-twenties. She had dark skin and Rosie's brown eyes in a round face. Her hair was uncombed and uncovered, and she wore a grey blanket wrapped around her middle.

"You want my mother?"

I stood to greet her. "I'm Eve."

"I know. The last born."

"I wasn't sure if you ..."

She didn't let me finish. "My mother is at my uncle's house," Ruth indicated loosely to the south.

I followed the direction of her gesture and we stood together gazing over the veld. I had no way of knowing if Ruth was telling the truth. Where her uncle's house was, or if an uncle even existed. This was Rosie's home. The last time I'd seen her, she'd been trying to persuade my mother to allow Ruth to stay. Why would she go now, and leave her daughter here alone?

"I need to speak to her, Ruth."

"I can give her a message."

Curtains twitched in the window of the house behind her. I sighed, trying to convey how unconvinced I was by her story. "There's no message, I need to ask her something. It's important."

"I'm sorry about your father. He was a good man, always fair."

She had a gentle voice and the unexpected pressure of tears prevented me from responding. I rubbed my eyes with the heel of my hand and nodded.

Ruth stepped towards the path. "Come. I'll walk you home."

I stayed where I was. "I don't need a guide, Ruth. I need to talk to your mother." I could not go home without the confirmation of my suspicions about the boy called John. I needed to know who he was and what had happened to him.

Ruth regarded me for a while, then waved me towards her. "I think your questions are for your own mother." She pointed in the direction of our farmhouse. "Come now."

With one last look around all the closed doors and blank windows in the compound, I kicked sand on the fire and followed Ruth. We walked single-file on the narrow path through the veld. The seeded grasses grazed my bare legs.

"What are you looking for, Last Born?"

"I found something but I need Rosie to help me understand."

She stopped and turned to face me. "Why not your own mother?"

I shook my head. It seemed impossible to ask my mother. I was afraid of what I might learn about the photograph – that John was my mother's child, and that she had concealed him from us all our lives – but I was also afraid of what I'd learn about my mother. Who was that young woman in the photograph? That happy, attentive stranger that would choose a dead son over two living daughters? My confusion was stirred in with real physical pain, a loss so complete that I worried my chest would collapse. I wanted the story from Rosie, because any information from her would come with comfort. If I asked my mother for the story, I would be the one who would have to comfort her.

"Never mind," I said, overtaking Ruth on the path. "I'll come back another time."

"Your mother thinks it is my fault that he died," Ruth said.

I spun to face her. An abrupt tightness in my chest made it hard to get the words out in more than a whisper. "You knew him? You were there?"

"I used to come and help my mother in the kitchen. Your mother was always busy, busy, busy somewhere in the house." She made her voice high and flapped her hands as she spoke, indicating a disdain for any busy work that might have preoccupied my mother, when she knew how much actual work occupied hers. "He had just started walking, still a baby. He was usually left in the kitchen with my mother."

"John?"

"John."

"He was my mother's child? My parents' child?"

"Yes."

"What did he look like?"

"He had yellow hair and blue eyes, like you. He liked to play outside, to put his fingers in everything. Shongololos, lizards, spiders. Eating snails." She wrinkled her nose.

A dung beetle pushed a ball of cow dung across the path at our feet. Balanced on its front legs, it pedalled its back legs against the ball, rolling it along the ground like a circus act.

"This is why you want my mother?" Ruth said.

I crouched over the beetle and nodded. "Nobody ever told me about him. I saw the grave a few years ago, and I found his name on the back of a photograph this morning. It was taken at his baptism, I think."

Ruth knelt next to me and together we watched the dung beetle.

"These inkuba are smart. At night, they can use the stars to find their way." Ruth plucked a blade of grass and laid it across the beetle's path. The insect stopped, moved this way and that, then climbed onto the ball of dung and lifted his head and front legs into the air as if sniffing for a clue. Satisfied with the scope of the obstacle, the beetle deftly circumnavigated the grass stalk and returned to the exact trajectory he had followed before.

"Why does she blame you?"

"It's better that you talk to your mother."

"You must have been a child when it happened."

"Yes, a child." Ruth ran her finger through the dust.

"I'm sorry."

"Sorry for what, Last Born?" Ruth laughed and we both stood.

"I don't know." It had become a habit. Stepping in for my mother. The distant jackal yelped again, and in the still evening, the sound seemed to come from everywhere.

My father and I had found a jackal trapped in a hunting snare once. Its leg had been bloodied and raw where it had chewed on itself, trying to escape. My father had covered the animal's face with his jacket and released the snare, and the terrified creature had escaped into the bush. I ran my tongue over my teeth. It was thick and dry. "I can't see how we all fit together anymore." Two weeks ago we'd been a family. Four stars in a single constellation linked by love and light. Since my father's death, my mother, my sister, me, and even Rosie, had become satellites, thrust from the centre, each in our own orbit. "They shouldn't have sent you away."

Ruth shrugged and snapped her tongue against the roof of her mouth.

"My mother has never been well." A part of me was hoping for forgiveness from Ruth, for my mother's sake. An acknowledgement that although Ruth had been wronged, my mother had suffered too.

"Your mother lost a child, so she decided my mother should also lose her child."

I thought of Rosie carrying me around on her back as she worked in our house.

"My mother's not unkind, she's…"

Ruth shook her head and lifted her hands up to stop me. "You say you want to ask for our story, but really, you want to tell us your story."

"No…" My thoughts jumbled.

"White people are the earth and black people are the moon. We show you one face and you think that is all we are."

"It's not what I meant." I didn't know what I meant. Or what she meant. My head felt like cotton wool.

"So, why are you here, Last Born?"

"I want Rosie to come home."

She planted her heels and lifted her face to the sky and howled with laughter. Not joyful, but unrestrained, cutting, aimed to humiliate. The jackal howled a reply. "Miss Eve, my mother is home."

"I want to know what happened to John."

"Your mother is what happened to John. He was her son." She clapped her hands at me as if she was trying to wake me up or chase me away, like an unwelcome dog trying to steal meat off her plate.

I took a step back. "I'm not afraid of you." I was reminded of Ruth as a teenager, standing over me where I lay in the dirt beneath the tyre swing. I remembered now that I'd swung too high and fallen off and winded myself. She hadn't helped me, and had the same expression on her face this evening as she'd had back then: a blank disregard for my discomfort. I could see why she wouldn't want to help me, then or now. I was the child her mother took care of. The child Rosie fed, washed, cleaned up after, tucked into bed at night and woke up with a cup of sweet, milky tea in the morning. I relied on her mother's comfort. I expected it. It was always available to me. Even when my own mother wasn't.

"Go home, Last Born." Ruth tossed her final words at me and left in the direction of the compound.

I waited until the shush and tick of her beaded ankles faded before I turned and followed the path back to the farmhouse. It was almost dark and my skin pricked and tingled with the heat of watchful eyes and the breath of ghosts. Every muscle twitched with the urge to run. I pressed my fingertips against my thumb one by one, hoping to reignite the sting of the thorn pricks I'd made at my father's wake. A fist of anger clenched and unclenched in my chest. Anger at my father, for dying without first diffusing this powder keg he and my mother had buried, without any concern for what might happen if it was one of their daughters who dug it up. Kate and I deserved as much consideration for staying alive as John did for dying. Anger at my mother. At Rosie, who had known but never told. The fist unclenched as I thought of Rosie. It didn't seem fair to be angry with her for keeping their secret.

According to my mother's worldview, one that I had accepted without question so far, in order for someone to be right, the other person must be wrong. If my mother was suffering, Ruth, and by association, Rosie, must have done something to hurt her. But if Rosie had suffered because of choices my mother had made, and my mother held all the power, did that make my mother wrong too? It occurred to me that life was not as simple as I'd thought it to be – that there was always another side.

Chapter Seventeen

A Dragonfly's Wings | *April 1960*

I woke late on Sunday morning. The house was quiet, but my mother's car was parked in the driveway. The dogs were lying with their bellies flat on the stoep's cool concrete. They opened their eyes to watch me go past and twitched their ears towards the French doors, alert to the threat of being shooed out of the shade. I found Kate in the kitchen pouring hot water over a tea strainer into a cup. She was wearing her church dress, but had left her shoes on the doormat. I sat at the table but avoided my sister's eyes. I was certain she would see Jack on my skin like a bruise.

"You missed church." She put a cup of tea in front of me and sat to face me.

"Where's Ma?"

"You also missed her taking George to church this morning." Kate shook her head. "Luckily he slept through the service. I just don't understand her. We couldn't persuade her out of bed for weeks and now she's gallivanting around with a vervet monkey like she's introducing the town to a visiting dignitary."

"I need to speak to her."

She sipped her tea and uncertainty fluttered behind her eyes as she heard the note in my voice. "She went for a walk. To the river, I think."

"This is important, Katie."

Kate put the tea cup down. "What's wrong?"

"Come." I didn't give her a chance to object or argue, but headed out the back door and through the yard. Out on the farm track, the day was stunned with heat. The sand shimmered, and sunlight flashed against the whitewashed walls of the farm buildings and sparked in the windows. Kate was a few steps behind me on the river path and I spotted my mother. She was standing quite still, staring across the river, wearing a cornflower-blue shift dress with a matching short-sleeved jacket, but like Kate and me, she was barefoot. George crouched on her shoulder. She turned at our approach and lifted a finger to her lips, indicating with a nod of her head towards the opposite bank.

Being Sunday, the usual animal and machine noise of the farm was absent, and a distant singing carried up to the three of us like leaves on the breeze. On the other side of the river, the trees thinned to reveal an outdoor church service on a shallow stretch along the bank. A crowd of black men and woman, dressed in the khaki, green, and yellow uniforms of the Zionist Christian Church, were gathered on the bank. Among the loose circle of worshippers, I recognised Petrus's smooth, hatless head, and Rosie's, wrapped in the dark green doek. Alongside Rosie stood the tall, slim shape of Ruth with her bold halo of dark hair.

"Ruth." My mother confirmed the young woman's presence in a whisper and I felt her stiffen.

The congregation sang and swayed in unison. Socks and shoes were arranged tidily at the water's edge. The group opened to reveal a girl being led into the water by the minister. She looked about thirteen, and wore a white, sleeveless shift. As she moved deeper into the water the skirt of her dress bellied up with trapped air. The minister turned her to face the congregation. The girl tilted her head back and kept her eyes on the sky, either in fear or reverence, or perhaps in keeping with the formality of the service. The minister addressed his small flock, and snatched phrases in Zulu and English rose to reach us on the opposite bank. He punctuated his sermon with firm upward thrusts of his right hand, in which he clasped a wooden staff, sanded smooth and painted white. His left hand supported the girl. Over his dark trousers and a long-sleeved white shirt, he wore a bright purple tunic, starched and emblazoned with a white cross, the shaft of which ran the full length of the tunic, front and back. He tapped his staff on the girl's forehead and dipped her backwards into the river. As her face disappeared beneath the surface, the girl stiffened, arched her back, and her arms shot up. Her fingers splayed like the helpless frogs I lifted out of the reservoir.

"Father, surround this child with your love, protect her from evil."

When the prayer finished, he lifted her up. Water flowed down her face, across her tightly closed eyes, and glistened in the knotted rows of her hair. In a gasp of relief that we heard on the path, the girl sucked in a breath, but just as she found her footing she was pushed back under. Her fingers clawed the air as the congregation prayed. When the minister released her, she gasped to the surface. Again, he touched the staff to her forehead. Again, she was tipped beneath the surface. Again, she arched and clawed.

I found I was holding my breath.

The minister played extravagantly to his audience. His final "amen" was repeated by the congregation, and the baptised girl was released, choking and limp, to scramble up the bank.

"She doesn't seem to be enjoying it very much," Kate said.

"Well, you know they don't like water," my mother said.

The young girl was back on solid ground. Her dress was soaked and her small breasts showed darkly through the white fabric.

My mother tugged on my hand. "Stop staring."

I obeyed, and Kate and I followed our mother in silence with George glaring at us over her shoulder until we reached the swimming hole. A large dragonfly hovered an inch above the water. It dipped on the wing to kiss the surface, then skimmed away.

"Where have you been?" I asked my mother. I had a million

questions for her, but I did not want to let my emotions overwhelm me before I could ask them. It was difficult for me to demand answers from my mother. What I wanted was a conversation that would reveal the secret she had kept from us, but before it had even begun it felt like a confrontation. Especially when I already knew the truth, as if I was daring her to lie.

"I went for a walk.."

My mother never went for walks around the farm. I imagined her sneaking off to put flowers on the grave. "By yourself?" The emotion in my voice was audible.

"With George," she said, as if the monkey was obvious company and enough of an explanation, then seeing Kate and my expressions, she sighed. "I was looking for a suitable place to scatter your father's ashes, before the sale goes through."

"How do you bear it?" I felt the fist bunch in my chest. Now that I knew the things I knew, it was impossible to imagine how my mother could look at Kate and I without feeling guilt every day.

She frowned at my tone, but assumed I was talking about the loss of my father. She took a deep breath and sighed it out, drifting away behind her eyes, to that place deep inside her. "Well, one has no choice but to keep going. One foot in front of the other," she said. "Once you've survived the unimaginable, you have to find some meaning in loss. There are worse things."

Unimaginable things. Worse things. "Losing Dad is the worst thing that ever happened to me," I said.

She came fully into herself and looked me in the eye. "I know."

"Do you miss him?"

"Johnny, what's going on?" Kate's voice carried a note of caution as if she could feel the tension in me. She put her hand on my arm.

I shook her off. "That's not my name." Even though it was not Kate I was angry with, my emotions demanded expression.

"Of course I miss him," my mother said, "every moment of every day, but I'm comforted by the thought that he…" She stopped talking and made a gesture in the direction of the poplars, to the old graveyard.

"I'm not talking about Dad."

"Eve?" Kate dug her fingers into my arm.

"What *are* you talking about, Eve?" My mother straightened her back, sensing that she might need the ballast.

"I'm talking about John, Ma. Do you miss John?"

My mother took a sharp breath and her eyes left mine for a moment and flicked towards the poplars. She sank into herself for a bit, seeking refuge from my question, then seemed to struggle back to the surface again. She regained her composure and turned her attention back to me. Her voice was quiet. "What do you want to say to me, Eve?"

"I know."

"Know what?" Kate was tugging on my arm now, trying to turn me to face her. "What's happened?"

I grabbed my mother's hand. She'd lost weight – her bones were pronounced, and her engagement and wedding rings shifted around her finger behind her knuckle. "I know about John."

She snatched her hand away. "Kate, take me home." George had begun to shimmy and chirrup on her shoulder, expressing my mother's distress.

I grabbed her wrist. "No, Ma. You owe us. If you don't tell us now, I'm going to tell Kate what you did."

Kate had started to cry. "What's happening? Someone talk to me."

Our mother walked away from us towards the water. We followed her.

"Ma?"

She replied with a sound rather than a word, but didn't look up.

"Why don't you like Rosie's daughter?"

She lifted her head and looked at me.

"Does it have to do with John?" I said.

"You know what that is, Eve. John was your father's nickname for you. He wanted a boy, and—"

I didn't let her finish, "I know that's not all it was, Ma."

She backtracked up the bank, trying to shake us off, but we stuck to her like flies. Where the sand ended, she began to pluck wild grass, gathering the soft green stalks with their furred seeds and delicate flowers in one hand. I waited one step behind her, but she wouldn't turn around.

"I found the photograph of you and him, and the lock of hair you hid in the frame."

My mother made a quiet sound, like the opening twist of a soda bottle. Her face lit with a moment of recognition.

"And I've seen the grave. I know you take roses there," I said.

My mother stood up and sighed, long and low, as if she wanted to blow all the breath out of her body and into the air – a lifetime of holding her breath – until she was completely empty. She walked back down the bank, and when her toes touched the water's edge, she stopped. When she inhaled again, it was deep and purposeful, as if she was doing it for the first time. She reached for Kate's hand, and when she spoke, the words travelled on this renewed breath. "John was our son. He died before either of you were born. I was nineteen."

Relief at my mother's confession flowed through me, but all the tension I'd been carrying seemed to transfer into Kate's body with the shock of hearing this news for the first time. Kate was nineteen. I tried to picture my sister having a baby, and then losing it. *The unimaginable.*

"What..." Kate looked from my mother, to me, and back to my mother, "...are you talking about?"

My mother dangled the bouquet of grasses loosely in one hand. "I only remember fragments of that day. But the things I do remember, I recall with such clarity it's as if they happened yesterday. I do remember that we'd had a great deal of rain. Days and days of rain. The gutter outside the kitchen door dripped constantly on the step. Drip, drip, drip. It was unusual for October, but apart from that, it was a day like any other day. And then it wasn't."

The dragonfly returned on shimmering wings, skirting the edges of the water, but staying just out of arm's reach. A cloud of midges skittered chaotically between the reeds. A kingfisher called downstream.

"It's the sounds I remember most vividly." My mother stilled herself as if tuning into the echoes of that day. "The usual sounds of a farmhouse morning – dogs barking in the driveway, chickens in the yard, a chair scraping on the kitchen floor, the broom knocking against the table legs, Moses pouring coal into the stove, and Rosie's low voice guiding Ruth through her chores. Ruth sometimes came and helped her mother. I thought she was too young, that she should be in school, but Rosie would laugh when I asked any questions, saying, 'She's a girl.' You know, it doesn't matter to them, and it was none of my business. She was a good playmate for John." Her eyes glazed and a smile edged her lips. "I remember John's laugh. The kind that makes everyone who hears it smile. And then nothing. Quiet. Only the sun against the windows."

"Where was Dad?"

"He was in Tobruk. The war had started, and he and Tommy left for Egypt with the Transvaal Scottish. John was eighteen months old. I was pregnant with Kate." At this she touched Kate's cheek. "Anne-Liese was pregnant with Jack. We imagined the men would be home soon. The North African campaign was in the bag. Or so we thought, until the Italians arrived. It was a miserable, hateful time."

"What happened to John?"

"I left him with Rosie and Ruth. It was Ruth's job to feed the chickens, and she often did it with him while I went up to the dairy to update the milk logs. It all fell to me while your father was away. That morning, I was doing the accounts in the sun room. I heard them first – Ruth's voice, John's high reply, the chicken's clucking – before the two of them appeared around the side of the house. The little girl with her bare feet and unruly hair, and John, still chubby with puppy fat. They were followed by the chickens, pecking at the earth around their feet." As she spoke, my mother clustered her fingers together and made a downward pecking motion. She smiled at the images in her head.

"How old was Ruth?"

"I don't know, nine? Maybe ten? Maybe younger." My mother's eyes shuttered and greyed. "They were children, playing at chores. She was teaching him how to spread the feed in a thin layer on the ground, with an arcing throw. But he was too little. He kept lifting both hands above his head and throwing his hardest, sending panicked chickens racing from the shrapnel of corn and seed. This little procession travelled beneath the sunroom window and disappeared in the direction of the yard. That was the last time I saw him alive."

I walked down to the water's edge and waded in up to my thighs. Kate was crying and taking short, shallow breaths.

"And then the dogs began to bark. Well, not immediately. I must have spent some part of morning answering letters, because I know I wrote to Granny May. She and Grandad had moved back to England by then. I included that lock of John's hair in the envelope. A single, soft curl. I was so grateful afterwards that I never got to post that letter." She took a breath before she could continue. "The dogs were not usually excitable, but they were yapping and howling in the yard, so I took it that the postman had come with a letter from your father. He always brought those down to the house. He knew how valuable they were to me. I went through to the kitchen. The door was open and the earth had that distinct after-rain smell, sort of metallic and fresh at the same time."

She looked to me for confirmation. I nodded.

"Ruth was alone, sweeping ashes out of the fire grate. I can picture her as if she's standing right here." She pointed to a spot a few feet in front of herself. "Her head was covered in a pale yellow doek, tightly wound and knotted at the nape of her neck. She never covered her head. I knew Rosie had asked her to do it because I'd complained to her about Ruth looking scruffy, and for a moment I felt sorry for the little girl, as if I'd taken something from her." She ran a hand over her face. "The barking became harsh and repetitive, increasingly urgent. I was so distracted by their noise, that although I noticed John wasn't with Ruth, I didn't think much of it, until Rosie came into the kitchen with the dirty linen in her arms and he wasn't with her either."

My mother came down the bank and filtered the tall grasses and wildflowers through her fingers, allowing them to drop, one by one, to the water's surface. Each followed the current downstream.

"I asked Rosie, is John with you? And she spoke to Ruth in Zulu. Of course, in those days, it meant as much to me as birdsong, but there was one word I did know: *umfaan*, the boy. Ruth shook her head, she pointed at the fire, then to her bucket of ashes. I realised that neither of them knew where he was, and this coldness took root in me." She gripped the bodice of her dress in her fist, just above her heart. "I said to the younger girl, quite firmly, I said, Ruth, where is John? And she shrugged her shoulders. 'I didn't see him,' she said. Just like that, so casual. I remember those words. *I didn't see him.*" My mother's voice broke and Kate placed a hand on her back. "Rosie dropped the linen and I ran. I didn't know where I was running to or why, I just understood that I had to move. A mother's instinct, maybe? The ground in the yard was soft, and had been churned to mud by the dogs running back and forth from the back door to the chicken coop, and I kicked off my heels. Everything tasted coppery. Then I saw him. In the base of the chicken coop. Rainwater was trapped inside the wooden frame. It had pooled into a few inches of water that was milky with dust and feathers and straw and the small body of a hatchling, and next to it, my boy, lying in the muck. It was him, of course, but I was thinking, it's too still, too still to be John. I saw the white shirt I'd dressed him in that morning and the blue shorts I'd pulled up over the deep creases at the back of his knees, but still it felt unreal. I think I must have fallen over a dog – they were rough and pushing around my legs – because I was crawling when I reached him. I bargained with God to go back in time. Back to the sunroom. Back to the kitchen. To breakfast. To my bed that morning. I was saying out loud: 'God, if John is alright, I'll keep him close, always. I'll never let him out of my sight again.'" She clenched her fists and waved them at the sky. "But when I reached him, his skin was already cold. I tried to clean his face, but my hands were covered in mud, so I used the hem of my skirt to wipe mud off his eyebrows and scoop it out of his eye sockets. When I moved him, his arm flopped outwards, and chicken feed leaked out from between his fingers. Ruth stood in the kitchen doorway, and this rage rose in me. I wanted to kill her. I wanted to have her take his place. As if I could exchange one child for another. I started screaming at her: 'What have you done? What have you done?' over and over again. 'What have you done?' Rosie took Ruth's hand and ran. They left me alone in the mud with John." Tears streamed down my mother's face. "I tried to cover him. I wrapped him up in my skirt. I think in my muddled mind I believed that if I couldn't see him, it wouldn't be true. But when I tried to stand and lift him, I couldn't do it. Something inside me tore. I heard it. A sound like bark being ripped from a tree." She stood for a while, just shaking her head, looking at the water. "My life was split in two at that moment. There was time before that sound and time after. What was most shocking, was that the world went on." She met my look with wide, questioning eyes, as if the mystery of that fact had still not been solved for her.

I took both her hands in mine. "Why didn't you tell us?"

She kept shaking her head. "I don't know, Evie. I was young, and grief-stricken. I was alone. Kate arrived six months later, and when your father came home, we could barely address it. I worried that he blamed me, and he felt guilty for not being here. You arrived soon after, and once you were both old enough to understand, we had grown used to not talking about it. It was so painful. I hadn't kept anything of his, which was a mistake. I gave it all away. All his little socks and knitted cardigans, his toys, his blankets. Rosie came back eventually and she dealt with all that stuff. I couldn't bear to give anything to the women at the compound. I couldn't stand the thought of his clothes being worn by other children here on the farm. So I insisted she donate his things to the church. It was easier to start fresh, like we were being given another chance."

"And Ruth?"

"I sent her away. I told Rosie her whole family would have to leave the farm, unless Ruth went." She covered her face with her hands. "She was only a child. I was in so much pain and it made me cruel."

We stood by quietly while she cried. There was one more thing I needed to understand. "Why did Dad call me Johnny?"

"I'm so sorry, Evie. God knows what he was thinking. I tried to make him stop, but, like so much else, with time it became normal."

I carried on deeper into the water until it was up to my hips, my waist, and then my chest. The surface rippled from my disturbance and the sun caught each small crest in a blinding flare. I kept moving until my whole head was underwater. I sank into silence.

One of the myths my family was built on was that I was my father's child and Kate was my mother's. I was gifted the story of a farmer's son. A child with an interest in nature, in being outdoors, who was a fast runner, and who was nicknamed Johnny – qualities that put me firmly in my father's outdoor camp, while my mother occupied the silent indoors. I'd built an identity on this storyline, and the facts, as they were presented, were that I had nothing in common with my mother. But now I understood that this was only one version of me. A retold version of another child's story. It was John's story. The boy who had not lived to embody my parents' hopes for his life. When I'd found the photograph this morning, a crack had appeared in this version, which another truth now shone through: this woman, my mother, barefoot in the shallows with her hair twisted into a bun at her neck, had stepped out of the carefully curated image she'd designed of herself, and taken the more honest shape of a young mother twisted by grief, struggling to make sense of an unkind world. For all these years, I had searched for a glimpse of myself in my mother, but I couldn't find it, because my mother had been playing a role. While I, in turn, played the role my father's grief had allocated to me – as Johnny, the son who never was. I'd never been able to find myself in my mother, because my mother had never truly been there. And so, neither had I.

I surfaced in a rush of bubbles and air. Kate was holding George and waited with our mother at the water's edge. I went up to my family.

My mother spoke in an urgent whisper. "Stand still."

I stood with my feet slightly apart on the soft riverbed and my mother's hand brushed across my shoulder.

"It was sitting on your back. Isn't that lucky?"

I slipped my fingers into the gap between my mother's cupped hands and opened them to reveal an insect's bright turquoise body. The translucent wings were folded upright like a sail and pulsed with a calm throb of movement. It made no effort to fly away.

"A dragonfly," my mother said.

"It's a damselfly." I touched the tip of my finger to the creature's wings. "See, its wings are folded together. A dragonfly's lie flat."

I slid a finger under the insect's legs. It rested there for a few moments then flew into the light.

Chapter Eighteen

Barbel & Bream | *April 1960*

In the yard, I watched the glow behind my mother's curtained window dim and go dark. The moon was full and high. I sat on the bare square of concrete that I now knew to be the remains of the chicken coop where John had drowned. My father had torn it down when he'd returned from the war, and the chickens had been moved to the other side of the garage. I sat there until the only sounds were night sounds, and I could see my shadow in the moonlight.

Mr Turner had picked Kate up at five to take her back to the Turners' farm for dinner, promising as he turned his car around in our drive that she wouldn't be home late. Kate had waved from the passenger seat, a mixture of excitement and trepidation in her eyes. Mr Turner was true to his word. Kate had not been late at all. By the time she'd arrived at the Turners' farmhouse, Jack had been missing for hours. Mrs Turner made excuses about a problem with the herd, then a problem with the truck, then she'd said he wasn't feeling well, and finally, unable to cover for their absent son anymore, Mr Turner had taken his bottle of brandy and phoned around town, becoming increasingly belligerent with each new disappointment. When Tommy finished the bottle and shouted to his wife to bring him the details of the army barracks in Pretoria, Kate had asked Mrs Turner to take her home. After telling us what had happened, she'd crawled into bed with our mother, too exhausted to cry.

I went through the house, locking windows and doors and drawing curtains. I filled the kettle and checked we had fresh milk and bread, then swept the kitchen grate, laid fresh logs, and wadded up newspaper in the fireplace, ready to light in the morning. I was supposed to begin packing for school, and wondered if my uniform was clean and ironed, and my shoes polished. For about the hundredth time that day, for a million different reasons, I wished Rosie was there.

The first time I was aware of Jack running away from home, I had been about seven. A farmworker from the Turners had appeared at the back door at breakfast time. After a brief conversation with the man in Zulu, my father had grabbed his hat and headed out to the yard, saying to my mother: "The boy has run away again." The second time, when he'd made it as far as our primary school and was found sitting alone on a seesaw in the playground, I'd been old enough to join the search. When he was twelve, I'd been the one who had found him in the old barn. I'd gone in alone, felt a shift in the air and looked up at Jack's bare feet dangling from a rafter. I had turned back to my father, who was parked outside with his truck engine running and shook my head, "not here," as I hopped into the cab and pulled the door closed.

I didn't even bother to undress for bed. I flopped on the covers in the clothes that I'd put on in the morning – the same dress I'd worn into the river – and fell into a restless sleep.

As soon as it was light enough to see, I tiptoed out of the sleeping house, ran across the lawn, through my mother's English rose garden, and onto the farm track. I raced the sun's rays to the river, where I found evidence of a small wood fire. Jack was there. He stood in the water in the stillness of the emerging day with his trousers rolled to his knees. His fishing line curved from the tip of his rod to an orange float that drifted hopefully over the deepest part of the river. The line swayed, caught the light, and gleamed.

A grey loerie cried its distinctive *go away* warning call at my arrival, causing Jack to look upriver towards me. Under the broad brim of his hat, I couldn't tell if he could see me on the shaded bank where the sun's rays had not yet found their way through the branches. I lifted my hand in greeting and made to walk towards him but he turned back to his line and I faltered, suddenly conscious of myself, barefoot, in yesterday's dress, but essentially naked in my intentions. I couldn't be alone in this. I'd felt brave sneaking out of the house, but now that I'd seen him, I had to admit I was being selfish. If he welcomed me then at least we were complicit, and me being here didn't feel so disloyal. I needed Jack's participation to make it alright. I stumbled on the rocks, exposed in my desire for him – that dark, animal side of me that required feeding, and a rough rub behind the ears.

Without looking up, he spoke. "You're up early."

I started forward. "Catch anything?"

"Only barbel, but I'm hoping for bream."

I waded through the water until I was alongside him. "Everyone is looking for you."His usually sharp blue eyes were blunted to grey, like smoke from a veld fire drifting across the summer sky, and I wondered if he was pleased that I'd come.

"I needed time to think. The dinner last night, the engagement..." He paused, and glanced at me. This was the first time I'd heard him say the word, had any acknowledgement from him that he knew what was being asked of him and Kate, and in a different way, me. After what had happened between us at the barn the day before, I knew this would all have to change, that Jack must have run away to give himself time to figure out what to tell his father. I kept my expression neutral. He continued, "... Taking over your farm, none of it was my idea. I'm sick of him telling me what to do."

"Kate was upset."

He shook his head. "That's not what I wanted."

A plane arced overhead, and we both looked up to watch it flash through the trees. The water chuckled and gargled around the rocks.

Jack's line ticked over each turn of the reel. I moved my foot until it butted against his in the water.

He tugged sharply on the fishing rod, but his line came up empty.

"I'm not having much luck, Evie."

"I know."

Jack leaned across and kissed me on the mouth. We kept our hands by our sides, feet facing forward, as if not touching made it more chaste. When I pulled his bottom lip deeply into my mouth, a small groan escaped him, and he pressed his hand into the small of my back where it burned like a brand. He pulled my body into his with a pressure that felt like desperation and just as abruptly, let go.

He reeled in his line, then cast it out with a hard toss of the rod. The float swung on the momentum and landed with a light splash.

"You don't have to worry about any of that. I burned the deed. My mother won't be able to sell the farm without it."

"You did what?"

"I found the deed to our property. I threw it into the fire." I smiled at him, anticipating his pleasure and approval.

"Eve." Jack shook his head, this time with frustration rather than regret. "That's not going to change anything." He reeled in his line and cast out again. "Anyway, I've made up my mind."

"Good. It's for the best, and Kate will understand," I said.

Jack tugged on the line and it snagged. A bright silver shape spun on his hook.

"No, Eve." He angled his shoulder slightly away from me as he reeled in the line and grabbed for the fish. "I'm going to marry her. I'm going to stay."

I stepped backwards out of the water and onto dry land. The kiss had not been a beginning, it had been a farewell.

Chapter Nineteen

Feathers & Fire | *April 1960*

After lunch, I lay on my belly in the shade with my cheek on the grass. It wasn't comfortable, but I'd resigned myself to the itch of the green blades. The yard was quiet, apart from the sharp tick of a passing locust's wings, and the occasional sound of my mother's voice coming from inside the house. She was in the sunroom, going through the files, looking for the deed to the farm. I pictured the green ribbon twisting in the flames, and dug my fingers between the hardy stems of the kikuyu grass to feel the grit under my nails. A flicker of movement caught my eye. A tiny segmented leg, or possibly a wing. Adjusting my focus, I discovered the distraction. A minute and industrious ant stopped and waved its antennae as it followed a scent trail. Then a bird appeared, only a shadow as it streamed overhead, and another ant to follow the first. The world teemed with life, even as everything I loved slipped away.

I rolled onto my back. A ladybird landed on my hand. I was the only person in the whole world, in all the time that had been and all the time that might come, who could see this bug, smaller than my fingernail, sitting on my skin. The ladybird extended its hard, spotted wings to free the softer wings beneath and flew into the air. "*Ladybird, ladybird fly away home, your house is on fire, your children are gone.*" I recited the nursery rhyme, closed my eyes, and with a full belly in the afternoon sun, slipped into sleep.

I was standing in a parched riverbed that ran through a brittle veld. The shrill song of insects surrounded me as a single sensation of screaming heat. On the bank, under the pale shade of a lone acacia tree, its lower branches pruned into a distinctive umbrella shape by grazing giraffes, squatted a San hunter. He was naked apart from a short leather loincloth. His brown skin hung soft on his bones and his eyes squinted against the glare from within the folds of his old face. He addressed me in the soft whistles and clicks of his ancient language and the unknown sounds formed familiar words. "He is not yours." A man walked towards me through the haze of the rising heat in the river bed. He wore a broad-brimmed hat and carried a fishing rod in one hand, with a clutch of silver fish hanging inertly from the other.

"I know," I said.

Something settled on my face. I blew my cheeks out and puffed. It lifted, but then, like the kiss of an eyelash, it settled on my arm. The ladybird, or a fly. I shook it off. Persistent, it landed again, tickling the inside of my elbow. I swatted it away and half opened an eye. Something as directionless as a feather rose and fell, then twisted and turned in the air. Another followed, and awake now, I opened both eyes and moved my hand to catch one of the shapes. It was light and papery, and when I closed my fingers it disintegrated into grey ash. Thin leaves, propelled by heat rather than any breeze, were being deposited across the lawn, landing on the flowers and dropping onto the roof of the house. In the same moment that I realised what I was seeing, I smelled the burning.

A wave of panic lifted me to my feet and I was running across the lawn and up the steps to the stoep of the farmhouse from where I could see over the property. A grey cloud – lit from beneath by an orange glow – swirled like a swarm of insects on the horizon.

"Fire!" I shouted, "Ma! Fire!"

Like a vortex, the fire drew all surrounding energy to it, and it seemed that the whole farm was suddenly alive to the worst of all threats. The noise of the response came first: a low hum of awareness that underscored the shouting voices, slamming doors, and car engines. Men whistled. Dogs barked. Birds wheeled through the air, squawking their alarm. A team of black farm labourers roared past the house, balanced on the open bed of a truck. Every face was alert and focused on the cloud in the distance. The afternoon milking had been abandoned.

I met my mother on the stoep.

"Someone must go and warn the Turners." She shook the car keys in my direction. We both glanced towards the oak tree where the car was parked.

"Where's Kate?" I said.

"Hurry, Eve."

"I can't drive." I shook my head. The suggestion was absurd.

"But we have to do something!"

"Yes, Ma, you must go."

She stepped back into the house. She called Kate's name, then again, louder, leaning out into the yard. "Kate!"

"Send Moses." Panic expanded through my body. The fire would be spreading. All my mother's rules about where she could and couldn't go seemed like a choice, and now that choice was dangerous.

"He's gone already. It looks like it's at the barn." My mother thrust the keys towards me, holding them between her thumb and forefinger, as if they were hot. "You have to go." She tossed the car keys in my direction, as if the responsibility would pass to me with the object. I made no attempt to catch them, allowing the sharp jangle of metal to hit me on the collarbone. The impact burned through my skin and found my bloodstream, where it ignited the fear and anger that was already there. I boiled. I picked them up and threw them back at her across the threshold where they landed on the mat at her feet.

"Eve, I'm sorry." My mother reached for me.

I swatted her hand away. "I'm going to the fire."

"It's too dangerous."

I plotted the fastest route in my mind. Smoke caught in my throat. I could taste eucalyptus. I cleared the steps in a single leap, ran across the lawn, out of the gate and onto the farm track, which had been churned to dust in the wake of the passing traffic. Ignoring my mother's calls, I ran, eyes stinging, towards the heat and smoke. I took a shortcut across the top pasture, and as I approached the barn, the air grew increasingly thick with smoke, shouting voices, and the crackling laugh of the fire. Mr Turner was already there. He stood, facing the flames in a row of men, with his handkerchief held over his nose. The fire spun and danced. It flashed across the hay and cartwheeled through the wooden frame like an acrobat, throwing sparks into the dry veld like fireworks, as if in celebration of its own power and beauty. Through the flames, I could make out the shifting shapes of men, like otherworldly creatures made of flesh and fire as they battled the flames on the other side of the burn.

Mr Turner looked towards the pasture and shouted to his men. "Watch the trees!"

Only the gum trees, with their dry peeling bark, formed a thin barrier between the burning barn and the pasture, where my father's herd of Friesians milled around with a growing unrest. The fire flirted, lifted, and flicked its yellow skirt to reveal flashes of red and orange petticoats. A finger of flame reached from the barn and twisted around a eucalyptus branch. The dry outer leaves popped and hissed in surrender. The tall gums began to sway in the fire's wind as more flames followed the path of the first.

"The trees!" I shouted.

Mr Turner looked down the row of men and strode towards me.

"For God's sake! What are you doing here?" He spun me by the shoulders in the direction of our farmhouse, where I'd left my mother paralysed in the doorway. Smoke from the fire stretched above our heads, all the way to the main road. "Go home!"

I twisted out of his grip and jumped up onto the back of the truck where Petrus was handing empty grain sacks to the men. They each took one to soak in the cattle trough, using the heavy wet hessian to beat at the sparks landing on the veld. Petrus's shirt was wrapped around his face. He made space for me.

"Make sure she stays up there," Mr Turner said to Petrus as he helped himself to one of the sacks, then addressed me. "Do you know where Jack is?"

"No, Mr Turner." It would feel like a betrayal to tell him that I'd seen Jack at the river this morning. I was conscious that my mother didn't know where Kate was either, and the fear they were together spat into my mind like venom.

Mr Turner swore under his breath and shouted to the team of men in a mix of Afrikaans and Zulu. "Keep it out of Baas Hunter's pasture. Kom manne! Hamba!"

Determined to be useful, I dragged a stack of sacks to the edge of the truck to pass to the waiting men. The hessian was rough against my palms. Even from this distance I could feel the throb of heat. The men pushed as much of the sacks and themselves into the trough as they could. They shouted and called out spontaneous exclamations, some laughed in short humourless barks to reassure one another.

"How did it start?" I called to Petrus. "It's not even the dry season yet."

Winter was the time for fires, when there was no rain and the Highveld dried to tinder. Then, to prevent the veld catching alight, we'd deliberately scorch dark firebreaks onto our land, directing thin lines of flame across the veld. The veld grass would burn down to spiked clumps, sharp underfoot but easily crushed to ash, and for a few months afterwards, the world smelled of charred earth.

Petrus shrugged. "Maybe it was a campfire? Or a cigarette?"

We flinched and shut our eyes against a blast of smoke. We all understood the risk of fire. It was bred into us like walking, like language. My father and his labourers made a careful and deliberate habit of extinguishing every stompie between their fingers before disposing of their roll-ups. We would never leave hot coals unattended, and were taught to pick up broken glass wherever we found it. It was unimaginable that anyone who lived on the farm would be so irresponsible. Petrus jumped to the ground and leaned into the truck to drag a sack off the diminishing pile.

"Maybe those boys from the mines." He lifted the sack over his head and headed towards the flames.

My father had found evidence in the past of small cooking fires down at the river. Men looking for work on the mines would leave their families in the rural areas and travel to Johannesburg, traversing old paths through local farms, sometimes asking for a few eggs or some water, often just helping themselves.

The row of men beating back the flames sang to maintain the rhythm of the work. "*Shosholoza*," a man called and the team lifted and landed their sacks on the reply: "*Kulezo ntaba*," working in unison on the beat of the song. "*Stimela siphume South Africa*."

Mr Turner had a homemade trailer hitched to his truck. Welded to an old tractor axle were three pieces of metal, arranged in a triangle. On this base sat three sixty-gallon barrels and a hand pump. One of his farm boys shoved a hose into the open mouth of the first water barrel and started to drive the hand pump, pushing water through the hose, which another boy directed at the flames.

"Keep it in the barn," Mr Turner called to his men as he waved his good arm towards our farm. "There's only veld between here and the house."

Like the features of an old friend, I could picture each turn in the road back to our farmhouse. I knew where the barbed wire fence was stretched enough to climb through, and where the ground was pebbled or sandy underfoot. I knew how the smell changed en route, from the minty eucalyptus gums, to the sharp uric smell closer to the dairy, and the marshy wetness of the river. The fire would have one fallow field to navigate before it met the lucerne, and then it was a short hop to the bamboo fence strung together with thin wire around our yard. That brittle fence – erected by my father when I was barely walking and now weathered to grey – would offer no defence against a fire. It would eat quickly through my mother's flowers, and then it would be at the house. The house where I was born, with its wooden beams across every ceiling, wooden frames in all the doors and windows. I knew each groove and warp in the yellowwood floorboards. All kindling. The pomegranates would cook and pop. The chickens in the garage, their feathers singed. My mother. George. The barn, stacked to the ceiling with hay bales, mice running in the beams, the cats and kittens that hunted there. At the dairy, the cattle were in the stone-walled kraal waiting to be milked. When I was younger, my father would sometimes squirt a hot stream of milk directly into my mouth while he milked a cow. I swallowed against a dry throat. My face burned.

Mr Turner pulled the trailer along the length of the barn, while his boys directed the hose in a steady arc, back and forth to dampen the grass in a broad fire break. The water came in waves with each pump of the handle, slopping out hard and sucking back to be driven out again.

Through the smoke, Jack appeared at a full sprint on the path from our farmhouse. He was breathing hard and his cheeks were red, although behind the exertion, his face was pale. He passed the truck where I stood and I caught his eye.

"Jack!" His father's voice roared over the boil of noise. "Where the hell've you been? Get up there!"

Jack pulled himself onto the truck and shouldered the boy off the pump.

"Pump!" Mr Turner shouted up to his son, who scowled but did not have the breath to reply. His shoulder bunched and released like a fist beneath his skin. A team of men formed a line behind the truck and advanced on the fire, crushing any landing sparks under the damp weight of their sacks.

A loud crack split a branch as the sap boiled and screamed in the gums. Seeing the fire reach the full height of the trees raised the level of urgency among the men.

"Over there!" Mr Turner shouted as he accelerated, pulling the home-crafted firefighting cart to arrest this new burn in the tree line.

They fought the fire all afternoon. It burned out in the trees and left the barn a dark husk, but with the labourers' help and the Turners' pump, they managed to dampen enough of the land to prevent the fire from spreading. The boys shovelled soil onto the last thin strip of flames. The fire would be left to slowly suffocate on its own relentless appetite.

Exhausted men sat in small groups on the ground, mostly silent apart from occasional coughing as they hacked and spat the smoke out of their lungs. They were covered in sweat, ash and dust, their eyes red and streaming.

Mr Turner climbed on the flat bed next to me and craned his neck to see beyond the burned trees to my father's pasture. The cows still stood there, blinking dumbly in our direction.

"We're lucky the wind didn't shift." He waited for me to nod before he dropped to the ground. "I'm sorry about the trees, and the barn." His voice was gruff but kind. He nodded once and walked towards the smoke, pulling his handkerchief up with his right hand to wipe his face.

On the road, dust rose behind my mother's car as it drove from our farmhouse. I looked down at the smudges on my dress, which had been blue this morning but was now uniformly grey. My arms and legs streaked black. I pulled my hair across my face. It reeked of smoke.

Kate drove with Moses in the back seat. A canvas bag plump with drinking water was strung across the radiator with moisture beading on the grey-green fabric. A large basket was unloaded from the trunk and Moses handed enamel mugs to the waiting boys, who filled them with water from a tap in the corner of the canvas bag. Kate handed out thick-cut white bread sandwiches, smeared with peanut butter and jam. There were pork sausages piled in a dish under a tea towel, and a bowl of tomatoes fresh from the garden, which were eaten like apples in quick bites by the hungry men.

I jumped off the truck, took a cup of water from Moses, and offered to help with the food.

Kate stopped me. "Don't touch anything. You're absolutely filthy." She took the enamel cup from me, saying, "Those are for the workers," and handed me a glass.

I carried my sandwich to where the blackened edge of grass still smoked. The men, satisfied by food and water and with the fire finally under control, had begun to relax. Lying or sitting together in the grass, their conversation occasionally spilled over into laughter as they discussed umlilo, the fire with the devil's breath. What was left of the barn smouldered under a dust of ash as the few remaining flames exhausted themselves, petering out one by one with a resigned puff of white smoke. It was hard to imagine that this gentle ending had its origin in the spitting, flashing fury from a few hours earlier. I took a bite of the sandwich, but could not swallow. Diminished knots of old weaver nests clung to the blackened gum trees. Pins of light shifted in front of my eyes, and the land shimmered and lifted on the haze. I sat on the ground and pressed my fingers into my eyes.

"You alright?" Jack sat next to me.

I made a loose gesture towards the pile of smouldering wood and corrugated iron that had been the barn. "It's all gone."

Jack's pale blue eyes were red-rimmed and watery and shone against the dirt on his face. We sat shoulder to shoulder, watching the men load up the vehicles with shovels and sacks before following their tools into the trucks. A few words of instruction were shouted by his father.

"Is your dad angry with you?" I said.

"Usually." Jack shrugged a tired, resigned lift of his shoulders. "I'm sure I'll hear about it later."

"Where were you?"

Jack didn't answer.

"Didn't you see the smoke?"

Jack's eyes had settled on Kate, who watched us from the car. When she saw him looking her way, she came over with a sandwich, sliced tomatoes, and a couple of pork sausages on a plate. Jack stood to meet her, and Kate smiled and offered him her hand. A gold ring with a solitaire diamond caught the light and gleamed.

It made sense, the two of them together. I'd seen it all my life, and more recently at the river: their mutual ease in one another's company. I felt foolish for even thinking otherwise, for thinking Jack would ever choose me over my beautiful, older sister. I wanted to pinch that stupid girl who'd stolen a cigarette and gone to the compound with Jack. Pinch her for lying alongside him at the swimming hole, wooed by a bunch of wildflowers, for reading that book with him up and the barn and allowing what followed to happen, for going to the river this morning. I had been so foolish, so obvious, so embarrassing in my intentions. I hated Jack for allowing me to think he felt the same way, and Kate for being the "right" sister. I fought the urge to slap the plate with its evenly sliced tomatoes out of her hands. I pushed myself to my feet and started to run. Past the tired men, past Moses handing out sandwiches and pouring water into cups, past Mr Turner, exhausted by worry and relief, standing where my father should be standing, and back home, to my mother.

George was curled asleep in my mother's lap, his belly full. I stood in front of her, aware of my dirty feet on the carpet. "I couldn't stay here and do nothing," I said.

"It's not nothing to stay safe. Think, Eve, what it might be like for us if something happened to you? After your father..." She couldn't finish the sentence, and I met her eye for the first time.

Our earlier fight and the fire had been frightening, and back with my mother, emotion swelled in my chest and tugged at the muscles around my jaw, turning my lips down. The tears I'd been fighting ever since I'd seen Jack and Kate, and the ring on her finger, filled my eyes. I thought of Jack's tired, red-rimmed eyes, and the way she'd looked at him. My shame and sadness shifted to resentment. I wanted to bundle up my pain and throw it at them, smearing my hurt across their smug faces. I wiped the back of my hand across my eyes.

"It was Jack, Ma."

"What was Jack?"

"He started the fire." As soon as I said the words, I wanted to swallow them.

"Why would he do something like that?" My mother sat upright in her chair, disturbing George from his sleep. Her face was pale. "What have you done, Eve? I thought I told you not to be alone with Jack."

"He doesn't want to farm, or marry Kate. He wants to join the Air Force and fly planes." He wants me, I wanted to add.

"Enough of this, Eve. It's done. They're engaged. The farm is sold."

"You can't sell the farm without the deed."

My mother stood, and George climbed onto her shoulder, blinking his little eyes in the light. Something altered in the way my mother looked at me, as if she were looking at a stranger lifting her dress in a public park. "What do you know about the deed, Evelyn?"

I lifted my fingers to my mouth. I wanted to tell my mother about Jack, about the kiss, about how much I loved him. I wanted to tell her about Tommy Turner at the barn with his pistol and under the willow tree. I wanted to confess about the title deed, how I'd thrown it into the fire. I wanted her to understand, to see how afraid I was to lose my home. I wanted her to comfort me.

"Haven't we lost enough?" My mother straightened to her full height. She carried George across the living room and stopped at the threshold, looking through the open French doors at the garden. Her body was silhouetted against the remains of the smoke being blown to the horizon, which were slowly being replaced by purple storm clouds.

"I just want something to be mine."

She turned back into the room. "Holding tight onto things does not make them stay."

"Kate gets to stay. She gets everything."

"And you get to leave, Eve. What a gift that is."

She emphasised gift, making fists with her hands as she said the word, and I could see she believed she was giving me something of great value. Something she'd always wanted for herself.

"When John died, I thought that if I stayed very still I could prevent another tragedy. If I sailed through life avoiding storms and keeping to the shadows, I could just hold on until the relief of my own death. But it's impossible and arrogant to think a hurricane will not blow your way again. Your father's death made me realise that I failed you and your sister. I believed my inaction would keep you both safe, but instead it made us all vulnerable. Selling the farm, seeing Kate married, and giving you some money to get an education is the best I can offer you both now. I don't want you to make the same mistakes I did, Eve. The point is not to maintain an even keel, it's to move forward, and keep moving forward despite the wind and the waves. You can't avoid life. It must be lived." The smell of rain sweetened the air, and my mother went back to the open doors and lifted her face. "And I have never been alive on this farm."

Heavy drops bounced against the corrugated-iron roof. Slowly at first, but soon loud enough to drum out the sound of my sniffling and short gulps. After a few minutes, my mother turned back into the room. She started when she saw me, as if she'd forgotten I was there. "Go and wash your face."

Chapter Twenty

Succulents | *May 1960* | Johannesburg

A puff of dandelion seeds lifted on the gust and gasp of the arriving train, chased down the platform, and settled as the engine calmed, at my feet. The seed head brushed across the polished toes of my school shoes, before catching another flurry and dancing away through the feet of the other passengers.

The first time I'd seen a dandelion seed alive on the empty air, I'd thought it was a fairy. I'd been at the age when the existence of fairies was as certain as the existence of Father Christmas, or the tooth mouse, who collected baby teeth from beneath children's pillows at night and built castles and roads and entire cities with the neat enamel bricks. My mother had taught us how to tell time by blowing the seeds from a dandelion. She'd taught us to fold agapanthus petals into fairy slippers, and to squeeze the sides of snapdragon flowers so they opened and closed in bright-lipped conversation. She'd warn us: "If you swallow a dandelion, you will float away."

My mother and I had said our goodbyes at the house, and Kate had left me at the station on my own. She'd decided not to return to school. Instead, she would go to secretarial college and get a job. I stowed my bag on the metal rack above me. The conductor blew his whistle, and the engine hissed in response, jerked forward an inch and stopped hard, then gathered itself and slowly heaved out of the station. No one sat across from me, so I unlaced my shoes and rested my socked feet on the opposite bench. It was against school rules, but I shrugged off my blazer, took off my hat, and curled my tie into my top pocket. I adjusted the shoe box of succulents which I'd potted to take back to school with me on my lap, and settled deeper into the window seat, resting my cheek against the glass. Over the course of the next hour, the horizons crept closer and closer. The open landscape, spotted with grazing cows, was replaced by sprawling shanty towns, which were soon replaced by grey-blue buildingscapes lit by street lights and neon signs and billboards for OMO washing powder, inviting commuters to make their whites whiter and their colours brighter. Although it had always been the plan for me to return to school, I couldn't shake the feeling that I had been sent away. As the world stripped past, I longed for a stomach full of dandelions to lift me up and out of the train.

When the train exhaled to a stop at Johannesburg station, a man travelling in the same carriage stood to retrieve his bag from the luggage rack. There was something about the way he moved – the particular shape of his shoulder running from his neck beneath the collar of his shirt – along with a glimpse of his red-brown beard, that for a cruel moment, he looked like my father. I opened my mouth, "*Dad*," and lunged forward, almost standing, before I remembered. My movement was so decisive that a lady sitting in the next row looked up from her book and over her shoulder to see who I knew. I converted my momentum into a full-body stretch, then gestured out the window as if to say, this is me.

I was the first one from my dorm room back at the boarding house. It was a Sunday, and since all my roommates lived in the Johannesburg suburbs, they weren't concerned with train timetables and usually arrived back at school around dinnertime. I unpacked my biology textbook, *A Boy's Guide to the Wilderness*, a new notepad, and some stationery I'd brought from home. I stood the framed photographs of my youthful parents leaning against the car and my mother with the infant John on my bedside table. I hung my blazer and my winter uniform in the wardrobe, with my hockey takkies and school shoes below, and put my socks and underwear into a drawer. Finally, I arranged my succulents along the windowsill, lined up in the soft afternoon light. All the time I was busy, I anticipated a hollow thud of impact and expected, if I glanced up, to see the faint oily remains of a bird-shaped print on the window. It was less than a month since my father had died and everything had changed. The girl I'd been that March Sunday was a stranger who shared my memories. A girl whose biggest concerns were memorizing biology terms, having a flat chest, and not being as sophisticated as her city friend. A girl who assumed life would always be safe and kind, and include a mother *and* a father. That a childhood friendship could easily turn to love. A girl I no longer knew.

I spun a pot to maximise the African violet's exposure to the sun, and considered how plants protect themselves with thorns and poison and bitter sap. In Greek mythology, Daphne, the naiad-nymph, was transformed by her father, the river god Peneus, into a laurel tree. He did this at her request, to protect her from an unwelcome love. I lay on my bed and closed my eyes. I imagined my skin cells merging and growing firm, from the soles of my feet to my fingernails, my shoulders, over my eyelids and into my mouth. The metamorphosis continued up my neck, behind my ears, and across my scalp as my pale dermis darkened and thickened into bark. My new, rough edges scratched against the cotton sheets. My eyes fused, my back grew rigid, and I throbbed; blind, mute, and deaf, within.

16th May, 1960

Dearest Evie,

How's school? How're all the girls? Do they miss me? Please tell Margaret I say hello. I left some bits and pieces in my dorm room and I've written to ask her to pack them up and give them to you to bring home. Please don't forget! I hope you've settled in and it didn't feel too strange going back alone. Ma says getting back to some form of normality will help keep your mind off things. She also asked me to say congrats on making the first hockey team. If she can manage it, I may drive her out one weekend to watch one of your matches.

We're doing fine here. (As fine as can be expected.) There's so much work to do. Organising the house feels like a mountain that needs to be dug down to size rather than climbed. Ma and I are taking it on, room by room, but it's extraordinary how much junk she and Dad accumulated over the years. Of course, Jack and I are going to need the furniture, so at least that can stay. Ma made the (un)fortunate discovery that Jack fits into Dad's clothes, and keeps foisting his things on him. It makes sense, most of it is in good shape, but it's very strange for me. I'm not ready for her to be emptying Dad's closets, and not ready to see his boots on Jack's feet. But she's hellbent on "getting things done", so I've told him to help himself to whatever he wants.

I started a short-hand, typing, and bookkeeping course in town, two mornings a week. Ma can't imagine why, since she insists I won't have time to work off the farm, but I'm enjoying it and it's always going to be useful.

Nothing is firm yet, but we're considering a small engagement party towards the end of the year. I'll let you have the dates as soon as they're confirmed.

Apart from that, there's not much news, except a bit of excitement last week when a lion cub fell into the swimming pool at the tennis club. It's been so dry that the female brought her litter down the kloof to drink from the pool. One of them toppled off the edge and into the water and was too small to climb out. The Murray boys were there, fortunately, and David kept the mother at bay by shouting and banging two racquets together, whilst Patrick and Shaun jumped into the water and fished the poor little thing out using a garden chair, all while its mother stalked around looking furious. Luckily, they got it out and the little family ran off unharmed. Although I saw Mrs Murray in town and she tells me that Patrick now "has a devil of a cold", but I suppose it's the season for it.

Please write back. Hope to see you home for a weekend sometime soon. Let me know if you'd like me to wire some money for a train ticket.

With love,
Kate x

Added afterwards in a different colour pen, was: *PS: Ma says to tell you that George says hi!*

June 1960

The skaters slid and shone across the ice. So trusting, I thought, on what was essentially water, transformed. I'd never seen such an expanse of ice before. On mid-winter mornings on the farm, the water in the dogs' bowls froze overnight, and a transparent crust had to be broken in the cattle troughs, while between the reeds, the river's muddy edges iced to a crystal sheen. But the Wembley Ice Rink in Johannesburg was as big as a frozen soccer field. I'd expected a surface like glass, but the ice sprayed, melted, and mowed into sugary lines behind the skaters, who twisted and spun, athletic and balletic, brave and fast, cutting tracks behind them. In contrast, I felt like a dog in socks. The rented skates had been laced too tight around my ankles and I had to scrunch my toes to inspire blood flow.

Outside, the winter day was crisp and blue, but inside, I wore Libby's winter coat from last season and two pairs of socks, as well as gloves, which all skaters must wear, according to the list of safety rules detailed on a board in the lobby. The gloves were more than a barrier against the cold; they were to protect naked fingers from the metal blades in case of a fall. I wondered how effective hand-knitted gloves would be against the sharp skates, and tugged each a little higher up my wrists. Some of the skaters moved around the oval course in couples, linking hands or elbows as they sailed over the chill. Each with a grip on the elusive magic that allowed them to trust each other, the ice, the thin freedom of their blades.

"Come on, Evie," Libby waved as she glided by with Jonty paddling in her wake.

I took a tentative step onto the ice, then another, bowed at the waist with my hands held out in front of me, palms in, as if worshipping the god of balance. I kept my knees and ankles firmly together as I'd been instructed by Libby, and a bit ungraceful but very focused, pushed away from the gate. I stayed close to the barrier and circuited the rink once, twice, and by the third time was managing to propel myself with backwards thrusts of my right leg. Libby swung by and took my hand. Reassured by my friend's ballast, I moved faster, picking up the beat of *Hit the Road, Jack* that sang through the speakers.

Libby laughed. "I told you," she said, "I told you you'd love it."

The outing to the ice rink had been Mrs Peele's idea. Libby's mother sat on the bench beneath the exit sign. She smoked a cigarette through a tortoiseshell cigarette holder, and flicked through *The Rand Daily Mail*, looking up to wave or wink at us whenever we swung past. I waved back, hoping people would assume Mrs Peele was my mother too, and that Libby and I were sisters. Libby had invited Jonty, and Jonty had brought Greg, who was also a student at WITS and Jonty's good friend. Libby had introduced me to Greg after I'd told her what had happened between me and Jack when I'd been back home. "He'll help you to take your mind off Jack," she'd promised. The neatness of our coupling – Jonty's best friend with Libby's – appealed to Libby's idea of being in a grown-up relationship. Most of this idea was informed by American magazines and their depictions of double dates; couples ice skating, dancing to rock 'n roll music, sipping a shared soda through straws at a counter in a diner like Archie and Veronica. I didn't like Greg very much. I wasn't drawn to his clean-cut, broad-shouldered, dimple-chinned version of handsome, or the self-assurance that came with it. Nevertheless, he seemed to like me, and so I went along with Libby's plan, grateful to be part of something.

Libby turned her body with a quick spin of her skates, and, moving backwards, led me around the rink with small observations and instructions about how I should angle my ankles to drive forward, and position my feet to slow down. Greg raced alongside us with short running steps. "You're doing well, Eve, for your first time."

Libby let go of me to link arms with Jonty.

"Thanks." I tried to straighten up and look more relaxed, but immediately lost my balance and landed on the ice, spinning in a slow circle with my legs out in front of me.

"Sorry, hey," Greg said. He slipped his hands under my arms and began to tug at me, to try to lift me up, but his skates made it hard to find purchase. That, and me making my body deliberately limp and heavy. He slipped and struggled a bit, then let go.

"I'm heavier than I look." I offered him an excuse.

"Sorry," Greg said again.

"You didn't make me fall."

"I know," he said, leaning over to take hold of my upper arm.

"It's easier if I just do it myself," I said and waited for him to release me.

I got to my knees, pulled one skate up, then the other, until I crouched with my palms resting on the ice. My gloved hand splayed next to the boots and the sudden image of a skate cleaving the tips off all my fingers in a neat stripe to reveal four blunt ends of bone, ringed by red flesh and skin, flared in my mind. When I felt stable, I stood. I was not accustomed to being clumsy. I was used to being fleet of feet and at home in my skin, capable and reliable, like when I was running on the farm or wielding a stick on the hockey field. Being unsteady, like a newborn calf finding its legs, particularly under Greg's attention, made me self-conscious. I was hot in the coat, and I pushed my hair out of my eyes and back under the barrette I'd borrowed from Libby. My skin pricked under all the layers.

A week earlier, Jonty and Greg had come to our school to watch our hockey team play, and win, our match. Afterwards, outside the change room, chatting and celebrating with the team, Greg had put his arm around me and tried to kiss my cheek. I'd ducked away and made some excuse about being sweaty. The same sense of claustrophobia clung to me now as he reached for my arm. I shifted away.

"I'm alright," I said, with a bit more of an edge than I intended, and made my way to the side of the rink.

Greg skated close behind me. When I reached the side, he put his hands on either side of me and pushed his full weight along the length of my body, pressing me firmly into the plastic barrier.

"Don't you like boys?" His breath was hot and smelled of peanuts.

I didn't push back. I allowed myself to sink into helplessness under his superior strength. The abandon felt good, like slipping into sleep. I experienced the same calm sensation as I did when Libby chose an outfit for me to wear, or when Kate braided my hair, or when Jack shaped animals out of river clay, his fingers encouraging sharp hips and shoulders and horns from the mud. I wondered what Jack was doing right this moment, whether he and Kate were together. I closed my eyes and exhaustion washed through my bones. Greg interpreted this as capitulation and pressed his mouth against mine, so hard that my lips ground on my teeth. His mouth felt nothing like Jack's. I thought again of skates slicing neatly through flesh, and let my mind go blank, shrinking myself into the tree bark skin that offered me security and comfort, and from where the world receded. There, I could watch myself like I was a character in a black and white, silent movie. I had no control and no responsibility; I only had to follow directions and play the role of a living girl. I wondered if this was the same borderless realm my mother disappeared into at will. If she too found comfort in the disconnection. When I turned my head, Greg pushed himself off the barrier and skated away.

I began another slow circuit around the rink, trying my best to distract myself with the demands of staying upright. I avoided small children with no concept of space, fast-moving teenagers, and all eye contact with Greg. By pushing my heels towards each other, then letting my toes meet – heels again, then toes – I made gentle progress, waving a pattern in the ice as I went. I knew the ice was machine-made, but still imagined dark fathoms beneath the skaters, and seen from below, the scream and scratch of quick shadows passing overhead, muted laughter, and the dull thud of music.

Libby was behind me. She put her hands on my hips, and with Jonty behind her, we formed a short conga line with me as the unsteady lead. Greg slipped in at the front, holding my hands on his hips. I stopped moving my legs and allowed myself to be pulled by Greg and pushed by Libby, giving myself over completely to be a part of them. I focused on my feet, the push and glide of Greg's skates, and the rhythm of the circular course – effort on the straights, slow on the turns, effort, flow, effort, flow – until bodies blurred into shapes and movement and traveling air, and all I could hear was my breath.

4th June 1960

Dear Eve,

We haven't heard from you, but I know how busy things can be. Kate did try to call on the weekend, but the girls in the boarding house couldn't track you down. They said you were out for the weekend. Staying with Libby, I assume? I wish you'd let us know.

It's still awfully dry, with no hope of rain until the spring. With the loss of the feed that was stored in the barn, it's been a bit of a struggle, and enormously reassuring to have the Turners to help keep things on track. You'll be pleased to know that Rosie came back to work. I swallowed my pride and went to the compound, where she and I had a good talk and papered over all the old cracks. Ruth is still there, and I've had to make peace with that. Too much was lost for too long, and anyway, this is a time of new beginnings.

Speaking of which, the October date is sealed for the engagement party. Kate is excited, and of course Anne-Liese is behaving as if it's her daughter getting married and she is the last word on wedding planning. Hasn't she heard that the mother of the groom has only two jobs? Wear cream and keep your mouth shut!

One of the cats got bitten by a puff adder, and its entire head swelled to at least double its usual size, but it didn't die. I learned something I didn't know, and that is that domestic cats can resist the venom. I got Petrus and some of the boys to clear all the old tools and rubbish out of the garage, where I'm certain it has been living. Petrus chopped its head off with a swift strike of a spade and that was that!

Anyway, my girl, I must be off. Work hard, and call us on Sunday if you find the time.

With love,
Ma

8th June, 1960

Dearest Evie,

I wish you would write and tell us how you are. Ma worries about you so much. I know you're still upset about her selling the farm, but you can't keep punishing her this way. It's all for the best and we must all move on.

I'm writing because I want to ask you if you will be my bridesmaid at my wedding. It would mean the world to me to have you stand up there with me, and Jack agrees. He's here with me now and says to say "hello".

Ma seems to be doing a bit better. She's driving again, and even went into town on her own the other day, to pick up fabric and thread to sew herself a wedding outfit. In fact, a warning, she's talking about making you a dress too! You might want to have some say in the style in case you end up looking like a pink meringue. Haha.

Did she tell you she went to get Rosie? Thank God. I don't know what I'd do without her, honestly.

Will you be home for the July holiday? It would be good to have you here. I miss having you to talk to at bedtime. Everything feels a bit strange, like we're living this half-life, waiting for more change. It's a good change, I suppose, but a part of me doesn't welcome it. I long for things to go back to normal, whatever that means.

Please come home in July. I don't think I can wait until October!

Love,
Kate xx

July 1960

I folded the two letters into my homework planner with a spike of guilt that I hadn't written back or returned Kate's phone calls. The resentment I'd felt towards my mother and my sister when I got back to school had taken on the dimensions of an enormous, chainmail blanket that I could not crawl out from under. I wanted to acknowledge my mother's letters, but each time I sat down, I could not summon the words.

The geography classroom was cold, and I tucked my blazer around my legs to get a layer between my bare thighs and the wooden bench. My hands were mottled and purple and my skin was dry. Another hour before lunch, and although I was not at all hungry, I willed away the time that stretched between me and my bed.

The geography worksheet lay on the desk in front of me. We were only supposed to label each of the ten Bantustans in a different colour, but instead, I was carefully outlining and colouring each one in. Brown for KwaZulu, yellow for Venda, Transkei in purple, Ciskei in orange, a pale green for Bophuthatswana. The repetition was restful, and I could drift away as I did it. I sharpened just the tip of a coloured pencil in the same colour as the outline around Lebowa, letting the shavings drop onto the page, and then rubbing them into each piece of land with the tip of my finger. Some were easy to colour, single, continuous bodies, while others were scattered clusters, like dark sun spots on the pink hand that was South Africa.

"The Bantustans have been organised on the basis of ethnic and linguistic groupings," our geography teacher, Mrs Casey, said from the front of the class. She used a long stick to point to a map of South Africa that hung over the blackboard. "Each tribe has been given their own territory, where the same type of people can self-govern, live and work together."

KwaZulu was for the Zulus, who were separate from Xhosas, who lived with other Xhosas in the Transkei. Northern Ndebeles lived in Lebowa, and Bophuthatswana was for the Tswanas. And so it went, each tribe sliced up and apart from the others, and all of them kept apart from the white people.

"Homelands work," Mrs Casey emphasised with a tap on the map, "because people are happier living among their own kind."

"Rubbish," Libby said under her breath. I could see that she had written one large label across the whole map – SOUTH AFRICA – and was roughly colouring everything in green, from coast to coast, ignoring the borders.

"You have something to add, Miss Peele?"

"Yes," Libby said, she sat up straight and put on her most grown-up voice. "Tribalism is a weak justification for Apartheid."

The class giggled, both impressed and shocked by Libby's daring. Libby was known as a 'liberal' in our school. A girl who was anti-Apartheid, who believed in one-man-one-vote, and that all South Africans deserved the same opportunities. She liked to argue with our more conservative students and teachers about the race situation in South Africa. She was confident and articulate enough to do it well, and benefitted from what she learned through her mother's growing involvement with the Progressive Party.

Mrs Casey tapped her stick on the board to shush the titters of unrest.

"Birds of a feather flock together," she said, and went on to explain to the class of high school girls, that if whites and blacks mixed with one another and had children, the black genes would soon overwhelm the white genes and in time, all South African children would be brown-eyed and dark-skinned. She raised her eyebrows and nodded sagely, allowing the weight of her caution to sink in. "It's biological."

"It's the same questionable science that argues that a woman's brain is smaller than a man's, Mrs Casey." Libby spoke up again. "Is that what you believe? That women are not as smart as men?"

"That's an entirely different argument, Miss Peele. And since you've wasted our class time with your disruptions, you can all finish your labelling for homework."

There was a universal groan through the room and a few hard stares directed at Libby. She winked at me as she shoved her books into her satchel.

"Racist old cow," she said. "By the way, Jonty has invited us all to go camping in the Magaliesberg with his family during July break. My mom will only let me go if you go too. You think your mom'll let you?"

"I'll ask her," I said, knowing that I wouldn't. "I'm sure it will be fine."

July 1960

Jonty's parents drove Jonty, Libby, Greg, and me to the Magaliesberg to camp for a few nights. We hiked, climbed the kloofs and gullies, and although it was too cold to swim, explored around the natural rock pools, which flowed from a mountain spring with crisp water clear enough to drink.

After a lunch of braaied boerewors and potatoes baked in the coals by Jonty's father, the four of us followed a path made by animals into the mountain. The boys ran ahead, jostling one another and hopping from rock to rock, while Libby and I walked behind. The world remained blunted and distant, as if I was accompanying my body wherever it wanted to go, and experiencing everything from just off centre. I had become good at responding to difficult questions, sometimes only hearing them about a second after they were asked, with a smile and a reassuring, "I'm fine, just tired." Since anyone who was interested in my well-being knew I'd recently lost my father, they accepted my explanation, not really wanting to drill much deeper. I walked through my days repeating, "I'm fine, I'm fine, I'm fine," in my head like a mantra, willing myself to believe it.

We climbed around a granite outcrop and looked down on a rock pool that was bordered on three sides by tall, slick rock walls. The pool was almost a perfect square, as if God had taken a sharp trowel and sliced four even vertical cuts into the earth. A stream of water gushed over the smooth stone, white and bubbling in the eddies, to fall about thirty feet into the pool below. Jonty kicked a rock over the edge and we watched it drop and be swallowed by the dark green-black water.

"Let's jump," Greg said.

"Too high," Jonty said. "We can get down this way."

He'd found a path that zig-zagged down the steep slope and took the four of us closer to the pool. I stood at the top, staring down the valley. The relief I found being back in nature, where horizon lines stretched for miles and I was surrounded by the calming hum of grass and wildflowers, felt like being barefoot after wearing thick, hot socks, and shoes that were too tight.

"Eve," Libby called from below and waved to me. I followed them down the path.

We lay fully clothed in the sun, like a family of lizards warming ourselves on a rock. Greg felt for my hand and wove his fingers through mine. I was exhausted by his persistence, and when Libby and Jonty went for a walk, I allowed him to roll on top of me and kiss me, his fingers pressing into my skin and reaching into my clothes. Greg did not ignite the warm pleasure in my body that Jack did. I closed my eyes, and tried to pretend, but when he slipped his hand into my bra and I felt his fingers against my nipple, a jolt of revulsion shot through me. I pulled my head back and pushed his hand away. Our noses were an inch apart. Most of the girls who knew him thought Greg was good-looking. He was a good sportsman, and embodied a wholesomeness that translated to trustworthiness. He often joked that parents loved him, revealing in himself the need to project something lovable, and that the facade was necessary.

"I'm sorry, Greg, but you're just not my type," I said to the tip of his nose.

"That's okay," he said but didn't move off me. "You're not really my type either." He leaned in but I turned my face away and he rolled off me and rearranged his shorts. "We're just having fun, Hunter. Not everything has to be serious."

I sat up and buttoned my blouse.

"I'm only going with you because Jonty asked me to."

"Gosh, you're such a gentleman," I said with an edge, but I wasn't really angry. I was with Greg to make Libby happy, which was much the same thing, and yet, it was hard to hear.

"What? You didn't really think I fancied you, did you?" He scoffed, as if the idea was unthinkable.

"No, I didn't, but you don't have to say it out loud."

"Anyway, everyone knows you're in love with your sister's fiancé." My skin flushed and I resolved to kill Libby when she got back.

"I don't think you're a very nice person, Greg."

"What?" He seemed genuinely surprised. "You said I wasn't your type first." I glared at him. "I don't know what your problem is, Hunter. You're always in such a bad mood. If you smiled occasionally, you could be quite pretty."

"Go to hell, Greg."

"I mean, we could have fun together, but you never want to do anything. You just sit around like you're bored or miserable all the time."

"I am miserable all the time, you idiot." It had taken every ounce of energy I had to be on this weekend. To participate and be polite to Jonty's parents, eat dinner in a group, make and hold conversations with people who didn't know me. I'd come because Libby had asked me to. To make my friend happy. And I'd kissed Greg to make him happy, because it was easier than causing a fuss. I'd given up Jack to make my mother and my sister happy. I'd been Johnny for my entire childhood to make my father happy. When did I get a turn?

"You could at least make an effort."

"You know what, Greg? You're absolutely right." I pushed myself to my feet and went around the edge of the rock pool, to find the zig-zag path that had brought us down the kloof. I headed back up. When I reached the top, I looked down on Greg standing on the pool's edge, and at the thirty-foot drop into the water. My body vibrated, scared and excited, as I positioned my feet with my toes hanging over the lip of the rock face.

"What are you doing?" Greg called up to me.

"I'm making an effort," I shouted. I knew this unpredictability would make him uncomfortable. I was not feminine enough, not demure enough. "Eve blows hot and cold," he'd once complained to Libby. I watched his expression as I lifted my arms out from my sides, and got a shot of delight when his eyes grew wide and his mouth dropped open.

"What are you doing? I didn't mean what I said."

I almost laughed out loud. He was so arrogant that he thought this had to do with him. His lips continued to move, but I tuned him out and tuned into the song of the wind through the ocean of veld that ran over and down the mountainside. A sustained note of exhilaration. I lifted myself onto my toes.

"Hunter, come down! It's too high."

I felt like myself in a way I had not felt for a while, but that I recalled like a familiar smell. The smell of summer and river water and Jack. The smell of running through the fields on the farm, through the blue gums, past the cattle, ducking under the willow into the opening at the swimming hole and sucking down fresh air in deep, rich gulps, with the satisfaction of drinking cold water from a tap on a hot day. The smell of wet earth, and roses, and hot dust after an afternoon thunderstorm. Lavender and cigarettes. Musty monkey finger pads. Tobacco. Hot hay and burning feathers. I tensed my jaw. I wanted to feel again, all of it. Layers and layers of thrill and pain and love.

The disconnection that had frayed my edges for these past few months shifted and re-centred. For a second, the world came into focus. I saw myself in full colour. I smiled. Greg flinched. How must I look to him? Poised on the edge of something terrifying, grinning. I pulled back my lips and showed him my teeth.

"Libby?" he shouted, "Jonty!"

My friend came around the rock as I bent my knees.

Three voices shouted various combinations of "No," and my name, and "Don't do it," but I was airborne. The rock walls and the hardy ferns that grew out of them rushed by me in streaks of green. I spiralled my arms, working to keep my body upright, and pointed my toes towards the water. I fell for longer than I anticipated, and a moment of panic rose with my momentum before my feet hit the surface and it exploded. I sucked in a breath. The water, shockingly cold and immediately wet, closed around me. I sank until I felt the muddy bed, stilled my body and allowed it to float in place. I opened my eyes. Pale light streaked through the water in yellow rays. I screamed my name as loud as I could, "Evelyn Roberta Hunter," and watched as it was borne away in the bubbles of my breath to break on the surface. I kicked hard and rose.

27th August, 1960

Dear Eve,

Thank you for your letter. How nice that you were able to get away for a few days. Please let me have Jonty's mother's details so I can drop her a thank-you note.

I would like you back for the engagement party please. The silent treatment has gone on long enough. It's been a hard year, but now it's time to chin up and do what's best for the family. It's been months since you were home and your sister could use your support.

I have been going to church group on Wednesdays and for Sunday service. I was so taken with the young minister who conducted your father's service, and he's turning out to be a wonderful addition to the community. The only bit of unfortunate news is that Tommy Turner rear-ended the old librarian, Mrs de Waal's station wagon on Main Road last week. Mrs de Waal told Mrs Abelheira that he reeked of brandy. Honestly, I think he's getting worse. I almost feel sorry for Anne-Liese these days, and I've noticed Jack spends more and more time here, sleeping in the sunroom, which is fine since he'll be living here after the wedding anyway.

I've been in touch with an old school friend of mine from London days, Iris Banfield. She lives in Surrey now. Her husband, Harold, died last year, and when she heard about your father's passing, she invited me to come over and stay with her, as a sort of shared convalescence. I think it will do me good to go, and at the same time, give Kate and Jack time to settle down here. We can talk about it when we see each other in October.

Ma x

Chapter Twenty-One

Baby's Breath | *October 1960* | Lasswade

I sat cross-legged at the foot of my sister's bed and watched Kate's reflection in the mirror that hung above the dressing table. She concentrated on applying nail polish to her fingernails. We'd been practicing hairstyles for Jack and Kate's engagement party, which would be held on our front lawn the next day, and a few bright white blossoms of gypsophila still lay like confetti in her hair.

She lifted her hand for me to admire. She'd applied a pretty coral polish to each of her nails, leaving a pale moon at the cuticle and the nail tip bare. "It's called a moon manicure. I saw a picture in *Woman's Weekly*."

"Can you do mine?" I asked, admiring the curved bottle of Coral Caress that had travelled over seven thousand miles by boat from Scotland, an engagement gift for Kate from some distant aunt in Edinburgh. The bottle had been wrapped in layers of pink and white tissue paper and tucked snuggly into a box that was covered with brown paper, secured with string, and finished with a wax seal. Kate had opened it with all the childhood excitement of a round of pass the parcel.

"They make nail polish from the same paint they use to paint cars," I said.

"Unlikely, Eve. I've never seen a coral-coloured car."

"Well not this jar specifically, Kate." I shook my head.

Kate twisted in her seat to face me. She waved her hands from her wrists to dry the polish, pausing occasionally to blow on her nails. "I'll only do your toenails," she said, "I don't want us to match."

I scooted to the edge of the bed and offered my bare feet to my sister.

Coming home had been like stepping into a familiar pair of shoes. The smell of floor polish, coffee and wood fire baked into the kitchen walls; the silent drifting light in the bedrooms; the reliable weight of cupboard doors, and the creaks and clicks of window latches were an ongoing conversation that I was welcome to rejoin. The house remembered me. It remembered my first cry, my footsteps, my father's voice. When Kate had driven me back from the station a couple days before and I'd walked through the kitchen door, and into Rosie's warm arms, all the memories had echoed in greeting.

Outside the bedroom window, a team of farm labourers called to one another. Their banter was interrupted by an occasional Zulu word of instruction from Tommy Turner, as they worked to erect a white marquee tent on our front lawn. The smell of Rosie's baking, vanilla, and sugar, and heat, floated through the house. My mother's old wedding dress, adjusted to fit Kate, was hanging on the back of the door.

"Why don't you just get married tomorrow? It seems like a lot of work to do this now and then again in a few months' time."

"I know, and it's all so expensive."

"So why bother?"

"Well, Ma wanted to do things *properly*." She flicked two fingers on both hands to make air brackets around the word. "And Tommy likes the show, and any excuse for a party really." She glanced at me knowingly and her eyes filled. "I wish Dad was here."

"If Dad was here, none of this would be happening." I couldn't keep the bitter spit out of my voice.

She busied herself with my final few toenails.

"Do you like the dress?" I said.

Kate's eyes flickered across to the slim cream shape hanging on the door and she nodded.

"Are you nervous?" I asked the top of my sister's head.

She shrugged. "Not really."

"Excited?"

"Something in between."

"Are you sure you want to marry him, Katie?" I said.

Kate glanced up at me and gave my toes an affectionate squeeze. "Stop worrying about me. Jack and I have known each other all our lives."

"Knowing what your life is going to look like doesn't mean it's the one you'd choose." Any concerns I had for my sister were undermined by the fact that I knew, and she probably suspected, that I loved the man she was about to become engaged to. I had no idea if Jack had confessed to my sister what had happened between him and I up at the barn in April, and would never have the courage to ask. It was better forgotten. Another secret to replace the ones that had been revealed. Kate marrying Jack and the two of them living together in this house, so soon after my father's death, felt like they were high-stepping over their youth and into our parents' lives. It might be the best life my mother and the Turners could offer their eldest children – a life that looked like theirs. To me, it was settling for the comfort of the known over the discomfort of change. For duty over love. It felt like pretending. Like a black and white photograph that has the colour painted onto it after it's developed.

"I don't mind. I can't wait to have a family, to brighten this house up with children playing about the place."

Kate's idea of a family did not sound like the one we'd grown up in. My thoughts ran to my mother at the river the day we'd learned about how John had died. I wondered if Kate thought about him too, and about what kind of mother she would be.

"And we do love each other." Kate sat back on her stool as she finished the last toe on my first foot. "So pretty." She started on the next one.

I pointed, then flexed my painted toes. My feet were transformed by the coral enamel. I looked over Kate's head at my reflection in the mirror. I'd had my hair bobbed at Libby's hairdresser before I left Johannesburg, and wore it parted to the right, hanging straight to just below my jaw and then cut bluntly in an asymmetrical line which shortened towards the back. My mother thought it was too severe, but I liked the more sophisticated style, as well as the way it enhanced my eyes. I was pleased with my outward appearance. Pleased to appear more adult even while my true feelings still stung like the iRhawurhawu wild spinach that Rosie picked to make tea whenever I'd had a sore tummy when I was little.

"Stop wriggling." Kate tugged on my baby toe.

An old photograph of Jack, Kate, and me must have been dug out in the big clean-up, and was framed and displayed on Kate's dressing table: the three of us as children, perched on the reservoir wall. A collection of pale elbows and knobbly knees, wet hair, and oversized, mismatched, toothy smiles. In it, Kate smiled at the camera, but Jack smiled at me.

"I don't think I'll ever get married," I said.

"First you have to find someone who'll marry you," Kate teased.

I crushed one of the gypsophila flowers between my thumb and forefinger and sprinkled the dust over her hair.

"Let me see the dress on you."

"Maybe later."

"Please, Katie. I want to see."

"My nails are still wet."

"I'll do the fastenings."

I made to stand up but Kate jumped to her feet. "I'll get it." She took the dress off the hanger and sat at the dressing table to unbutton each tiny button down the back. "Isn't it bad luck?" she said.

"Only if the groom sees you."

The intermittent hammering and noise of industry in the garden paused, like a communal intake of breath. Then, a single call was answered by a roar of exertion, and the full spread of the marquee's white fabric sailed into view beyond the bedroom window. It billowed outwards before the strain of the ropes caught, swinging the tent back slowly until the top line snapped firm, and the heavy sheets sighed and settled into place. Short shots of regular hammer blows rang out as each guide rope was tightened and secured.

Kate untied her dressing gown and moved in front of her mirror to step into the dress. I crossed to the open window, balancing on my heels to keep my wet toenails curled off the floor. The small marquee the Turners had rented shone a brilliant white against the backdrop of the blue sky and the distant grey of the hills. The sides were lifted and folded back around the poles, creating elegant entrances and exits with views out across the fields. Beneath the tent, a few men adjusted the legs of folding chairs and arranged the trestle tables my mother had borrowed from the church. Mr Turner stood on the lawn with my mother, who had George balanced on her shoulder, overseeing the work. He waved someone over and Jack appeared around the corner of the house. It was the first time I'd seen him since I got back and I held my breath as my heart sped up, as excited as if he was there for me.

"How does it look?" Kate said.

"Beautiful," I said.

My mother greeted Jack warmly and he kissed her on the cheek. He seemed skittish and unsettled, running his fingers through his hair and shifting his feet, leaning first on one leg, then the other. His father did most of the talking, occasionally touching his son's arm as if to draw him into the conversation.

"Eve?" Kate faced the mirror with her back to me. The satin of our mother's old wedding dress draped down her body in creamy folds and as she moved, the fabric pulled across her breasts and her hips, shifting with her thighs to offer a suggestion of her form beneath.

"Kate, you look gorgeous." I was pleased to finally feel a sincere moment of excitement and joy for my sister.

She flushed and closed her eyes. "Do me up?"

I stood behind my beautiful sister and began to refasten the line of tiny, silk-covered beads that snaked up from her hips to her shoulder blades. Seeing Kate in my mother's dress put me firmly in my place. I was outclassed, there was no doubt about it. Of course Jack would rather be with her. The first couple of buttons slotted into their opposite elastic eye quite easily, but fastening them became increasingly difficult as I moved up into Kate's waist. I tugged on one and squeezed the button through with some effort. The next was even more difficult and the next didn't reach at all.

"It won't go." I pulled against the fabric, trying to make it meet in the middle, but a thin strip of Kate's slip still showed in the gap. "Did Ma let this out for you?"

Kate didn't reply and I looked at her face in the mirror. Her eyes were wide. She was pale. The expression showed both expectation and dread. Her fingers were interlaced across her middle. Beneath them, a small belly swelled.

"Katie?" Realisation landed immediately, but even though I could see the state my sister was in, I tugged again, trying, hoping, wanting so badly for the two sides to meet.

By the time the guests arrived on Saturday afternoon, the engagement party had turned into a wedding. My mother and the Turners had reacted to the unexpected news of Kate's pregnancy by rolling through the same series of emotions at the same time, at the same speed, with the same degree of surprise, shock, horror, anger, resignation, and finally, acceptance, which led to immediate action. The young minister my mother so admired was persuaded to step in, and agreed to shift some appointments around so he could accommodate the occasion that afternoon. Since a church wedding was now out of the question, it was agreed that the ceremony be conducted under a canopy in our garden

It was a perfect spring day. I was bathed and dressed, and had finished setting the tables under the marquee. I went to the kitchen to see if Rosie needed another hand and helped myself to a syrupy, twisted koeksister from a platter she was arranging on the kitchen table. She batted my hand away. "Those are for the guests."

My mother found me with my mouth full, being swatted around the kitchen by Rosie's tea towel.

"Nice that you two have time to play around on a day like today. Eve, I need you to go with Jack to pick up the cakes from Mrs Turner and bring them back here." She nudged me down the back steps as she spoke. "He's waiting in the drive." She stepped back into the kitchen and immediately popped her head back out. "Don't think I haven't noticed your toenails, young lady. You'll have to take that off before the ceremony!"

Excited to see Jack, I ran to the driveway and jumped into the cab of his father's truck as he engaged the gears. He reversed into the driveway. His knuckles were white, he looked pale, and his hairline was damp. He pushed the vehicle into gear and headed towards the main road.

"Are you alright?"

He managed a weak smile, which didn't quite reach his eyes. "Mmhmm."

"You don't look well."

He shrugged and rolled down his window.

We continued in silence, bouncing through the uneven ruts which split the dirt track. Jack brought the truck to an abrupt halt and we both jerked forward in our seats. In the same movement, he threw open his door and heaved wetly into the dust. His back arched with each spasm, and the curve of his ribs expanded and contracted under his shirt. I longed to put my hand there, to offer him comfort, but also to feel his body beneath my palm. Instead, I waited until the violence in him subsided and his breathing steadied. When he sat back in the seat, his eyes were moist.

"You don't seem alright," I said.

Jack wiped his mouth on his sleeve. "I just need to sit for a bit." He turned off the ignition. Birdsong, insects, and light filled the space the truck's engine had occupied.

"Are you sick?"

"It's just nerves." He leaned against the steering wheel and stared out the windscreen. The Lasswade gate was open onto the main road.

"I hope you're not thinking of running away," I said, half in jest.

He met my eye and offered me an apologetic shrug. "I can't say it hasn't crossed my mind."

His face was leaner, with pronounced bones where a previous softness had been discarded. I took note of how neatly put together he was: his pressed shirt and trousers, his clean-shaven face, his hair trimmed close to his scalp, and his boots polished to a high sheen. I'd gone over and over the imaginary conversation I would have with Jack the next time I saw him. Now, here he was, the actual physical person, and although it had been easy to imagine what I'd say, I hadn't accounted for how I would feel. Being near him turned a current on in my body. I was aware of every movement he made, every swallow, the way he licked his lips, his fingers knuckling in his lap, his shoulders moving beneath his shirt. I almost expected the air in the cab to crackle and buzz between us, and wondered if Jack was as conscious of my body as I was of his. I wasn't certain if it was attraction or just the undercurrent of words unsaid, the possibility of a life not lived. I unstuck my tongue from the roof of my mouth.

"Are you okay to drive?"

"Yes. I'm fine."

"Good, because then I can give you this." I wound my arm back and punched him hard on the shoulder.

He grabbed his arm and glared at me. "What the hell, Eve?"

"I can't believe you got Kate pregnant. You're so bloody stupid."

"It was an accident."

"An accident! Didn't your mommy teach you about the birds and the bees?"

He rubbed his shoulder. "Jesus, Eve. That hurt."

"Good."

"To think I was looking forward to seeing you." He gave me a half smile.

"Don't change the subject."

"Please change the subject. It happened. It's happening. I'm not going to talk about it with you."

"Why are you doing this?"

"Don't start, Eve." He shook his head as he spoke the words and slumped back against the seat.

"I need to know what made you change your mind. All you ever did was talk about flying planes and joining the Air Force. I still don't understand." It seemed impossible to me that I was the only one who felt any sense of fear and panic at the possibility of wasted lives. If we didn't act now, things would never be the same and could never be fixed. My mother had confessed to me that she did not feel alive on the farm. She'd lost her son and her husband here, and yet she was happy to offer her daughter her life. Jack could not fill my father's shoes, and neither did he want to, yet here we were. "Only you can stop this from happening."

Jack exhaled harshly. "What if I don't want to?"

"Don't you? Can you look me in the eye and tell me this," I waved my arm to take in the fields around us, "the farm, this life, being married at nineteen, is what you want?"

"It doesn't matter if I want it, Eve." He slammed both hands onto the steering wheel. "I accept it." He took a breath. I could see the muscle working behind his jaw. He rubbed his hands over his face, then shifted in his seat to look at me. "You talk like someone who has a choice."

"I do! You do! We all have choices."

"You're wrong. Some of us have responsibilities. If I didn't step up, where would that leave your mother, Eve? And Kate? I'll tell you where, it would leave them with my father. He would take over your farm slowly but surely, doing things his way. Your mother would let it happen. You know she would. At least this way, he paid a fair price for it and I will be managing the land. Your mom can go back to England if she wants, and Kate can have a home and a family. I'll take care of her, I promise."

"But you don't even love her."

"I do love her, Eve." His voice was strained.

"What about me?" I slapped the seat between us, sounding and feeling like a child who can't get her own way.

"You get to choose your life."

"What if I choose you?"

Jack shook his head. His eyes were hooded but the colour was back in his cheeks. He pulled his door closed and turned the key. The engine coughed to life. My hand still lay on the seat between us, and he covered it with his and squeezed my fingers. My entire nervous system chased to his touch like a school of silver fish after a lure.

"I'm glad you're here," he said.

"I won't be for long," I said, and pulled my hand away.

Chapter Twenty-Two

Wild Dogs | *October 1960* | Lasswade

After the ceremony out on the lawn, the guests gathered in the marquee for the reception. The sun performed magnificently for the occasion with a vivid display of purples, pinks and oranges, returning for an encore of pale rays that streamed through the folds of the hills long after the first act was over. Candles on every table cast the scene in a quiet, flickering glow.

Moses carried a tray of full champagne flutes over to the top table, and I helped myself to a glass. The drink was unexpectedly dry, and the bubbles burst at the back of my nose. I spluttered.

Kate laughed and took a glass for herself. "Wait for the toast."

Further down the table, Moses handed Jack a glass and dipped between the Turners to put a glass in front of each of them. Mrs Turner flinched from Moses theatrically and Mr Turner dismissed him with a wave.

"What's their problem?" I asked Kate.

"Jack's dad thinks Moses is...you know?" She shimmied her shoulders. "*Unnatural.*"

I felt a blush of pride as my mother stood and rested a hand on Moses' shoulder, pointedly helped herself to a glass from his tray, thanking him as she did. She called for the guests' attention with a clink of her fork against her glass.

"Thank you all for coming. If Robert were here..." She paused to compose herself. "I know he'd agree that tonight is truly a case of gaining a son rather than losing a daughter. Jack has been a part of our family since he was a boy, and I'm proud to call you son." She raised her glass. "To the newlyweds, Jack and Kate."

The guests stood in a rustle of evening wear and agreement. A few calls of "hear, hear," followed the toast, and a group of Jack's school friends sang "For He's A Jolly Good Fellow".

When everyone had quietened down, Jack stood and offered Kate his hand. She took it and stood alongside him with a complacent elegance. The pale colour of the dress, almost white but with a hint of gold, blended with her skin so beautifully that she seemed to glow. Gypsophila lay sprinkled in her hair, waiting – I imagined in torturous detail – for Jack to lift out later, one by one.

"I am not a man of many words," Jack began his speech, "instead, I made a gift for Kate…" he stopped and smiled, "for my wife."

Moses came forward and handed Jack a cloth-covered parcel, which he placed on the table in front of Kate. He nodded to her and she lifted the cloth. There was a collective intake of appreciation as Kate revealed an intricately hand-carved wooden bird. It was a pied kingfisher, like the one that lived in the river bank. Each detailed feather had been painstakingly drawn from the wood. The tufted lift of its crest and the dark stripe across the bird's chest were apparent in the careful staining. Two delicate nostrils had been chiseled into its long black beak, which held the curved shape of a fish. The bird's eyes almost seemed alert.

Kate thanked Jack with a kiss and the tent erupted in cheers and applause. He draped his arm around his new wife's hips and offered a small bow. Framing the couple, my mother and the Turners stood on either side of Jack and Kate, holding their glasses aloft and completing the tableau. My father's absence was an empty outline cut from a family photo.

My eyes filled with a rush of loss and sentiment, and I slipped out of the bright activity of the tent into the quiet garden. I'd abandoned my shoes beneath the table, and left dark footprints on the dampening grass. I went through the old gate, onto the driveway and leaned against the oak tree that stood sentry outside our farmhouse. Under the marquee, Mr Turner had found himself in a circle of men, whose conversation erupted in regular roars of laughter as they raised their glasses of scotch to whatever deserved a toast: the green hills of Scotland, the Empire, the Queen. My mother, Mrs Turner, and other women from the church and the tennis club sat around the top table, finishing off the last of the wedding cake and nodding their heads in perpetual, social agreement.

"I remember your ma in that dress," Rosie said. I thought I was alone and turned with a jerk of surprise. She was wearing the black maid's uniform and white apron my mother had bought for the occasion. "They are a pretty couple, eh Miss Eve?"

I nodded. Even I could admit that, while at the same time feeling that something had been taken from me. Even I could be wooed by the scene of the lovely young couple lit up in front of me. Despite knowing that most of what I was watching was a well-choreographed act performed with some love, I had been assured, but done mostly for tradition and responsibility and appearances. All these things had to be maintained at any cost, even happiness, it seemed.

Perhaps, I hoped, as I watched my sister and Jack link arms and head to the dance floor, Kate did understand that Jack was marrying her out of a sense of responsibility. It was more comforting to me to imagine that my sister had agreed on the arrangement, knowing exactly what she was getting into. Perhaps the real act of love tonight was Kate's commitment to Jack's unwanted responsibility.

The newly weds moved slowly around the dance floor, leaning into one another. Kate rested her head on her new husband's chest as Jack rubbed a restless hand up and down her back.

"He carved that gift special for her," Rosie said.

Nobody would go to so much trouble for someone they didn't love. I pushed myself off the tree trunk to stand next to Rosie. "I just hope she's happy."

"Being a mama will make her happy." Rosie nodded sagely, like she was holding some future image of Kate with a baby in her mind's eye, "but it's not easy, and they are too young."

The familiar slither of jealousy began to coil through my insides, not because I dreamed of being a mother, but because I wanted to be the one up there with Jack, opening the dancing to "The Way You Look Tonight". I felt only relief not to be pregnant, and with that realisation, the magnitude of my sister's new adult life, its burden's and responsibilities, revealed itself to me and I felt my throat catch at the weight of it.

"Will you stay when Ma goes back to England, Rosie?"

Rosie shrugged and hugged her tray across her body. "I'm getting old now, Miss Eve, I can't work so hard anymore, up and down, and back and forth. There's lots of girls who can do that. But if Miss Kate needs me to help with the baby, I'll stay."

"Please do. I'm sure she'd love that."

"Or maybe Ruth can come and help?"

I glanced over to see if she was making a dark joke or if she was sincere. Her brown eyes sparkled.

"Rosie, you're getting naughty in your old age."

She chuckled and leaned into me in a moment of recognition and affection. Together we watched the rest of my family – the old and the new – moving around the dance floor. Mr Turner danced with my mother, Jack with his, and Kate with the young minister.

"There's been so much change this year, Rosie."

"Hau, too much change. God is trying to catch our attention." She whistled and clicked her fingers a few times like she did when she called for George. "If we don't listen, then God will start to…" she clapped her hand hard against the back of the tray, "and then, if we still don't come, He will start to shout." She raised a fist. "It's better that we listen."

It was the way they held themselves that alerted me to the menace in the rough circle of men standing in the yard. There were six of them, bristling like hunting dogs around a cornered rabbit.

I was carrying a stack of plates, sticky with the fruity remains of wedding cake and marzipan, to the kitchen door. Gas lanterns had been hung along the stoep and in the trees, each casting a dim sphere of yellow light. As I rounded the corner into the yard, I heard a barked laugh. I stopped and peered beyond the lamplight. Slowly, out of the dimness, they emerged. Six men in a loose circle around a shape on the ground.

I recognised Tommy Turner immediately even though he stood with his back to me. His shoulders twitched and flexed under his dress shirt, straining against an unclear threat. His injured arm hung at his side. As my eyes grew accustomed to the light, I recognised the local milk inspector. A quietly spoken, shapeless man who used to bring extra milk board pencils to leave with me and Kate on his monthly visits when we were younger. His usually gentle face was ruddy, his eyes unfocused and his soft mouth twisted into an expression of lascivious pleasure that I didn't recognise but that made me flinch. Mr Turner moved around until I could see his face. He leered across the circle with Bantu crouched darkly at his feet. Bantu growled and bared his teeth, and Mr Turner laughed.

"Even the dog knows you're unnatural," he said, and poked at the shape on the ground with the toe of his boot.

The milk inspector giggled, a high, nervous sound. Emboldened by Mr Turner's gesture, a couple of the men stepped closer into the circle, breaking ranks just enough to allow a thin finger of light to fall across the cowering shape at the centre. It was Moses.

Fear ignited every one of my extremities. My hands shook with a sudden flare of adrenaline that put my whole body on high alert. The shadows lengthened, as if the night itself was posturing, pushing its chest against the light.

Moses was crouched on his haunches, collecting the broken

shards of a white china platter. The remains of a haunch of lamb and roast potatoes lay spewed at his feet. I glanced down the length of the porch. The sound of music and conversation travelled from the garden on the warm night air. I heard the tones of my mother's voice and a bright peal of laughter in response. Glasses clinked in celebration. I willed my mother to come around the corner.

"Are you?" Mr Turner directed his question at Moses. Moses kept his head down. He slowly reached towards another piece of the broken platter, dragging it through the dirt and wet mess towards himself, as if gathering them all would offer him protection. Mr Turner crouched to Moses' eye level.

"Boy," he spoke softly. "I asked you a question. Are. You. Unnatural?" He enunciated each word as if he was speaking to a child. Bantu growled deep in his chest.

Moses made no reply.

"Maybe he's deaf?" one of the men suggested, causing a low ripple of amused agreement through the group.

I looked up as the kitchen door opened and threw a hopeful rectangle of light onto the concrete floor at my feet. A young kitchen maid who I knew worked for the Turners stepped out. She carried a tray loosely in her hand and seeing me there, smiled. "Miss Eve," she said, and dipped her head.

I gestured to the scene in the yard and whispered urgently. "Go and fetch my mother."

The girl squinted beyond the lamplight. It took her a moment before recognition dawned across her young face. Six white men, flushed with drink, standing over the defeated form of a black man who was smeared with food and kneeling in the dirt. Like a buck watching a stalking lion, she backed towards the kitchen. Inside, she carefully closed the door and with a soft click, the bright rectangle of light disappeared.

With the shift in the glow, a few of the men glanced towards the kitchen. Sensing a pause in the tension, I took a deep breath and called out cheerfully, "Mr Turner? Is that you?" The light lift of my voice cut through the weight of aggression, and the group broke apart, blinking at me as if coming up through water. Two of the men, who I recognised as Mrs Murray's teenage sons, slunk off quickly into the shadows. A third guest looked first to Mr Turner, then back to me, and then followed them.

"Hello?" I continued affecting innocence. "It's too dark. I can't see." In an exaggerated gesture, I leaned out over the porch wall, squinting towards the remaining men. "What are you doing? You're missing the party."

Mr Turner did not reply but stared at me with unblinking eyes. His lips were parted, and his chest rose and fell deeply, as if he was panting. He came across the fractured circle, walking deliberately close to Moses's stooped form. Close enough to nudge him forcefully in the cheek with his knee, knocking Moses into a hard seat on the dirt. The milk inspector giggled, and bile rose in my throat. I shifted my thumb to secure a cake fork that shook tinnily on the plates in my hand.

"Ahh, Eve's here," Mr Turner announced as if I had just arrived at a party. "Usually found following Jack around like a puppy." His eyes were red and moist with excess.

Jack came running around the corner into the yard and I said a little prayer of thanks for the kitchen maid. His father opened his good arm as if to welcome his son. As if Jack had arrived to support him.

Jack stood at his father's shoulder. "What's going on?"

Although Jack's eyes were kinder, I was struck again by how similar the two men were. They shared the same broad shoulders and loose posture, which appeared as swagger on Jack, but had hardened into menace in his father. They also shared the same square chin, which had thickened with age and a nightly whiskey on Mr Turner, and the same blue eyes, which once upon a time, might have been as clear and hopeful as his son's.

"Moses." I pointed, directing Jack's attention to the man crouched on the ground.

"Kate is looking for you," Jack said to me, trying to communicate with his eyes that I should leave.

"We were just talking to your kitchen help, Eve." Mr Turner jerked his head towards Moses's crumpled form. "It looks like he's been stealing your father's whiskey."

"Thank you," I said trying to keep the fury out of my voice at his blatant lie. "I can sort it out."

Mr Turner barked his joyless laugh and spoke to me in a high, taunting voice, "You think you're the Madam here?"

"Pa, leave it." Jack put his hand on his father's shoulder and tried to turn him back to the party. Mr Turner shook him off, but was so unsteady that the movement made him stumble. Jack grabbed his father's upper arm.

"Let go of me." Mr Turner took a directionless swing at Jack, which his son comfortably sidestepped.

"Pa," he said, his voice calm. "It's time for you to go."

"You can't tell me to go. Who do you think you are?" Mr Turner swung his good arm around Jack's neck and got him in a chokehold.

I was about to scream at him to let Jack go, but was struck by the look on Jack's face. Instead of fear, or panic, he looked tired, resigned even, but totally unafraid. He grabbed his father's arm, and twisted himself out of the older man's grip, moving behind him in one quick movement until he had his father's good arm twisted behind his back. Now his eyes held menace. He hissed into his father's ear. "I told you, it's time for you to go."

His father struggled, but quickly realised he was outmatched.

"And if you ever hit me again," Jack continued, "I'll kill you." He released his father with a push.

Mr Turner stumbled, then recovered and laughed lightly, dusting himself down. Behaving as if he was still in control. He lifted his hand up in mocking surrender. "Okay, my boy. I think you've made your point. Come on, it's a party." He took a few steps towards the music and the laughter, then turned. Looking me directly in the eye, he said to his son, "Let's go find that pretty little wife of yours."

I watched the men round the house towards the sounds of the party. Mr Turner strode ahead with Jack at his shoulder, the milk inspector jogging behind. A warm roar of acceptance greeted their return, like arriving heroes.

I balanced the plates on the stoep wall and rushed down the steps. Moses was still cleaning up the broken pieces of the china platter, and I bent to help him, but hesitated when I saw the thin stream of tears darkening his cheeks. Like Rosie, Moses had worked for my family since before I was born. He was a dignified man of high standards in his work and his appearance. Tonight, he seemed diminished. I was ashamed. For Moses's humiliation, for my own discomfort, but mostly for my association with the man who'd done this to him, and that my mother had essentially handed us all into his grip.

"Are you alright?" I asked. The question was wholly inadequate in the face of Moses's split lip and his obviously swollen cheekbone. His face and hair gleamed with the oily smear of gravy, bits of potato and white chunks of lamb fat that lay like maggots on his dark skin. The fleshy mess continued into the neckline of his collared shirt, staining the white cotton. A few of his buttons were missing.

"It was your mother's favourite," Moses said, lifting a shard of what remained of the serving platter.

"What happened?" I took the china out of his hand and indicated to the meat and gravy pooling on the sand.

Moses, still on his hands and knees, would not meet my eye. "I dropped the plate," he said.

Rosie appeared carrying a metal pail. She handed it to Moses, speaking quickly to him in Zulu. Using his hands, he began to scoop the meat and bits of plate and mess off the ground and into the bucket.

"Leave it, Miss Eve." Rosie clicked her tongue on the roof of her mouth, pulling me to my feet with a strong hand on my upper arm.

A small team of the black staff gathered in the yard. Some assisted Moses to his feet while others helped with the cleaning.

"I'm going to call my mother," I said, clearing the steps up to the kitchen in a single leap.

"No!"

Something in the tone of Rosie's voice stopped me. The circle of staff faced me, their eyes expressionless.

"Miss Eve, it's better you leave it."

The staff returned to their task. Quietly fussing, each knew their role – clean up the mess, keep your eyes down, don't give anything away. They folded the injured Moses into their group and led him into the dark. The young kitchen maid carried away the pail, filled with broken pieces of the china serving platter, while Rosie called the dogs out to lick up the remains of the food.

For the first time since I'd caught the train from Johannesburg a week before, I thought about being back at school. Spending time with Libby, going out with our friends, worrying about what to wear to parties, or if we'd covered enough material for our next exam. Even Greg crossed my mind. I could have fun with him if I tried. If I wasn't always wondering if another, better option waited for me on the farm. A door closed inside of me and another one opened. Kate and Jack were going to have a baby and start a grown-up life. Greg and Jonty were at university, and Libby was talking about what she wanted to study after school. I'd never thought beyond my life here on the farm, and it had become more and more apparent that that life did not exist anymore. God was trying to attract my attention, and I had started to listen. I picked up the stack of plates as the evidence of the night's confrontation sank away in silence around me, taken by the dogs, the soil, and the dark. All that remained was an empty bottle of Scotch whiskey that was left where it had fallen, for someone else to tidy up.

Chapter Twenty-Three

Cuttings | *Christmas Eve, December 1960* | Lasswade

I checked and rechecked the small green tartan Christmas gift in my lap. Beneath folds of red and white tissue paper was a grey felt rabbit with visible yellow stitching along its oversized ears. Suitable for either a boy or a girl, an infant who would grow into a toddler with fat knees, playing in the yard, picking flowers, catching goggas with small sticky fingers. Would their child be fair like Jack, or dark like Kate?

Beyond the train window, the cool grey and blue shades of the city neutralised and warmed into the sand-hued, earthy tones of home. Billboards gave way to trees, pedestrians to cattle, and smog shifted to wood smoke. A light summer rainfall laid horizontal rivulets across the glass. School was over for the December holidays. It was summer, a time of the year I usually loved, but this year was different. This year I was coming home to Kate and Jack's house. I felt a twinge of loneliness at the thought that neither of my parents would be at the farm when I arrived. After my father died, I'd assumed that his absence would feel like emptiness, a hollow space where he had once existed. But instead, I found myself preoccupied with a tangible rock of grief – some days a pebble, other days a boulder – that I carried with me all the time. Almost everything reminded me of him. The liquid freshness of morning air, the shadow of a bird flying overhead, the golden light in the afternoon, the dimensions of a passing stranger, the smell of tobacco, of dust, of my father.

My mother, who seemed to rediscover life after my father's death, had caught a plane to London almost as soon as the wedding marquee's final tent peg had been pulled out of the ground. She'd spent the last few months of the year touring around the British Isles with an old friend. I hoped that apart from my parents' absence and Kate's pregnancy, everything else would feel the same. I looked forward to seeing my father's dogs run alongside the car as we travelled to the farmhouse from the main road, and being in Rosie's kitchen, with its cool concrete floor and smell of burned coffee grounds.

The train slowed into the station. I used my mother's most recent postcard, featuring a sepia print of Edinburgh Castle, to mark my place in my book. It was hard to reconcile the isolated woman of my childhood with the one who visited Arthur's Seat and shopped on Princes Street, who travelled around England meeting long-lost cousins and catching up with childhood friends. I could hear her voice in her written words, efficient clips of information that dealt only with the facts. *Arrived safely in Southampton. Weather is mild for the season. London is less smoggy than I recall, but far more expensive! The cousins send their regards. Delighted to be back in Edinburgh. P.S. Call your sister.*

I could admit to myself that my father had always been my favourite, and so it surprised me to discover that I missed my mother more. Perhaps the fact of my father never being there again made it easier to accept. My mother *could* be at home, but chose not to be. If she was suddenly going to be capable and independent, it was Kate and I who should benefit from the change, not distant strangers who knew nothing about our lives in South Africa. "You should be here," I wanted to tell my mother, who would soon become a grandmother. "We need you here."

It was still raining when the train sighed to a stop, but the sky was bright enough to suggest it wouldn't last long. The conductor blew his whistle, and I reached for my weekend bag on the overhead storage rack. I saw Jack before he saw me, leaning against my father's truck and smoking a cigarette. He was wearing sunglasses, something I'd never seen him do before, and the affectation made me uncomfortable even as I acknowledged the effort I'd made in selecting my own outfit this morning. The flared jeans and stack-heeled boots I'd borrowed from Libby in an attempt to appear fashionable and independent seemed over the top now that I was standing in the doorway of the station house. I was wondering if I had time to change my shoes when Jack looked up. He flicked his stompie away and crossed the small car park.

"Monkey's wedding," he said, pointing up at the sunshine through the light rainfall. He reached for my bag. "Is this all?"

"I'm only staying for a few days. I'm leaving after Christmas."

"Kate will be disappointed." Maybe sharing some of the discomfort I was feeling, he took the sunglasses off and slipped them into his shirt pocket. Pale creases fanned out from the edges of his eyes as he squinted into the light. He seemed changed. Resigned. Like a man used to not getting his way. "She's expecting you for the whole week."

"I have to get back." I did have to get back, but the suggestion that it was out of my hands was not altogether correct. The truth was, I wanted to get back. Libby's parents had invited me to travel with them to Durban for a few days over New Year's. I'd never been to the coast before, never stayed in a hotel, and I was excited to go, especially since Jonty and some of his university friends would be staying nearby in Ballito Bay. I might even persuade myself to look forward to seeing Greg again.

"She misses you," Jack said.

And you? Do you miss me? I wondered. As if he could read my mind, Jack pulled me into a hug. I felt instantly calm, like the sheet of my mind had been unpegged and shaken out in the fresh air. He smelled the same as he always did, of light and dust, and I wanted to lean into that familiar feeling of coming home. We stood together for a beat longer than a normal 'hello' hug required, and I pushed out of the embrace. "Let's not waste any time, then," I said, and led the way to the truck.

On the drive from the station, Jack caught me up on what was going on in town and on the farm, but he did not mention Kate. When I asked him about the pregnancy, he crossed his fingers, telling me not to jinx it. "It's early days yet."

"How're your parents?"

"Ma is overexcited. She's at the house every five minutes with soup and honey, ginger tea and other mumbo jumbo voodoo remedies she gets from the girls at the compound. Either to help Kate relax, or the baby to grow, who knows."

"Your dad?"

"I see him at the dairy most days. He doesn't really come to the house."

I pulled off my boots and socks and discarded them in the footwell, then scrunched my toes and stretched my calves. The summer day fizzed with heat. People crossed the street in shorts and light dresses, carrying shopping bags, licking ice lollies, and wearing sandals. Strings of lights had been hung and linked together in even loops from the lamp posts all along the main road. Christmas decorations had turned the town into an incongruous winter wonderland in a place that, in all the years I'd had been alive, had never experienced snow. Shop windows featured winter scenes of cotton wool snow and cardboard snowflakes, shiny with glass glitter. Ornamental robin redbreasts were perched stiffly on bare branches while wary snowmen with carrot noses looked out at the bright blue sky.

Jack pushed his sleeves up to his elbows, and each time he pressed on the clutch to shift gears, his muscles tensed and released. He tapped the gold band on his ring finger against the steering wheel. With the thumb of my right hand, I stroked the thin skin between the fingers on my left. On the open road beyond town limits, he sped up. He rolled down his window, lit a cigarette, and passed it to me.

"How's school?"

"Fine."

"What were your results like?"

"Good, I passed."

"So, Matric next year, hey?" He squinted through a thread of smoke as he lit a second cigarette for himself.

"Yes."

"How's Libby?"

"She's fine."

"You got lots of friends?"

"No one special." I looked over at him with an eyebrow comically raised, wondering if his almost parental enquiry was deliberate. Is that how he saw himself now? As a father figure to me? "Dad."

"What? I don't mean..." He grimaced, then laughed. "Sorry, I do sound a bit like a dad. It's just, we don't get the chance to talk much, you know. We haven't had much time together since..."

Since April? When you kissed me at the river on the same morning you decided to marry my sister? Or since October? When you went through with marrying my sister? I'd arrived less than an hour ago and I was already thinking of leaving.

Jack continued. "...I don't even know since when? We used to talk all the time. I want to know what's going on with you. We're still friends, aren't we?"

"Do we feel like friends?"

"More than friends. We're family now."

I rolled my eyes and looked out my window. "I'm fine. School is fine. Everything is fine."

We turned into Lasswade. Across the top pasture, the blackened frame of the burned barn could be seen over the rise. The old truck bucked and struggled over the uneven farm road. Jack slowed down.

"We've had a lot of rain," he explained, as the truck rocked through another donga. The dirt road was pocked and sunken from water that had pooled, dried in the thirsty soil, and churned to mud again. My father would have smoothed it over by now.

"Would you like me to drive?" I said.

"Since when do you drive?"

"I can drive!"

"Aren't I doing a good enough job?"

As he asked the question, we bounced through a pothole and I had to grab the dashboard to steady myself.

"Well…" I rocked my open hand from side to side indicating that my opinion on his abilities may go either way. "But it is my father's truck, and it's my farm."

"It's my farm too, Eve." Jack's tone was defensive, and the skin across his cheekbones flushed.

I realised, with a spike of satisfaction, that I'd hurt his feelings.

"Everything looks the same, but it feels totally different," I lied, aiming to drive the spike deeper.

"You're always welcome here, you know." Jack parked under the oak tree and pulled the brake up.

"It's my home, Jack. It's not for you to invite me."

I left my bag for him to carry and pushed through the gate into the front garden. Rosie waited for me on the front stoep. She clapped as I ran up the path. Kate came out the front door with a warm smile, a noticeable belly, and George perched on her shoulder.

After dinner, while Rosie cleared the dishes away, Kate and I trimmed the Christmas tree with our mother's ornaments and sent Jack to the garage to dig out the box of lights. Kate wound tinsel through the branches, stopping occasionally to lure George out of the tree with a corner of shortbread or a honeyed-almond. She wore an old dress of my mother's that she'd let out to accommodate her growing bump. She'd also begun wearing her hair knotted at her neck in a loose chignon. A flush covered her chest and ran up into two bright flashes on both cheeks. Her skin was otherwise pale and a sheen of sweat covered her forehead. She'd barely eaten anything at dinner.

"How're you, Katie?" I asked, twisting a glass bauble's wire to a spiked branch.

She pushed her fists into her lower back and stretched, accentuating her belly. "A bit uncomfortable."

"I mean generally. Are you alright?"

Kate ran her hand around the back of her neck. "I'm struggling with morning sickness. I can't keep anything down and I'm so tired all the time. And my ankles are so fat!" She lifted her feet one at a time to show me.

"And Jack?"

"Jack works hard. He's always busy around the farm, doing this and that."

"I don't mean that, Kate. I'm asking if you're happy, you know, with him?"

"I'll be happy when this baby is out of me." Kate busied herself selecting another decoration from the box. She chose a little angel with a ceramic face, wearing a white cotton dress with row upon row of down feathers stitched to the fabric. "Remember this, Evie? Ma made the dress from chicken feathers."

I took the ornament from Kate and studied the cherubic face with its pink cheeks and a single ceramic curl in the middle of its forehead. My mother made the dress after I dropped the ornament and its original ceramic dress and gold painted wings shattered into a hundred sharp shards that were too fine to be repaired. Only the head remained intact. The ornament had been my grandmother's, and, my mother explained to me, had "sentimental value". Something I did not understand at the time, except that it could not easily be replaced. My mother had cleaned up the little head, and sanded down the sharp break at the neck. She twisted cotton into a cone and glued the narrow end to the angel's head. I'd collected the chicken feathers she'd hand-stitched onto the cone as a kind of penance. She'd made the repair without speaking to me, even as I delivered handful after handful of feathers. That's how I knew she didn't forgive me. I'd dropped the ornament after she'd told me not to play with it. But I'd wanted to see if it was a boy or a girl. I'd taken it off the tree, and turned it upside down. A tiny porcelain ball had hung on a string inside the dress, and if you shook it lightly, it chimed. An angelic little bell.

I turned the repaired angel upside down in my hands and looked up its feathered dress. It was empty. I balanced it in the branches.

"I wish she was here," Kate said.

"Jack says his mom is helpful."

"She likes to be needed."

"The garden has lost Ma's military edges."

"Yes, there's so much to do. It's hard to get around to everything."

"No, I like it, actually." I'd noticed on my way in that a trellis had broken from the fence and dropped forward, so the rambling rose that clung to it spread along the ground and flowered in the grass. The sharp English edges my mother liked to maintain in her rose garden had softened in her absence, and there was something charming about it. The disarray held romance and mystery, and the possibility of faerie folk with elvish faces and pointed ears making their homes around the damp roots of the trees. I remembered childhood easter egg hunts, when I would reach into the dark secret spots in the garden to snatch out painted eggs, anticipating the tiny fingers that might snatch back.

"Jack has all the men who aren't needed at the dairy working on the barn, which we have to rebuild before the winter. I'll get into the garden when I'm feeling a bit better."

I tried again. "But are you happy, Katie?"

She didn't answer at first, and I could see that she was thinking. Kate was good at thinking before she spoke, not like me, who had to say almost everything I thought and felt while I was in the throes of thinking and feeling. I was worse when I was younger. I hoped I'd learned some of the self-control my mother valued.

"You're always worried about my happiness, Evie, but is it ever that simple? There's a whole life that needs to be taken care of. Lots of people who rely on us." She hung another ornament with her delicate fingers. "The baby will make me happy. It'll be good when we're a family."

I scooped George out of the tree, and he hissed at me and scrambled into Kate's arms. "I saved your life," I scolded him. "Ungrateful creature."

"He likes to be babied." Kate stroked the monkey's forehead.

I gave her a smile which I knew didn't extend to my eyes. She wasn't herself.

"I'm just tired, Eve," Kate said, reading my expression. "Stop looking at me like that."

"Found them." Jack stood in the doorway. He was carrying a cardboard box with the words *Christmas Lights* written on the side in our mother's handwriting.

I drew back the curtains and pushed up the sash windows in my parents' old bedroom as far as they would go, allowing the early morning air in to blow away the coppery smell of blood and loss.

A patchwork quilt covered the unmade sheets. Knowing what it concealed, Rosie and I stood on opposite sides of the bed and each took a corner. A mutual pause revealed our reluctance, then, working together, we tugged it back. Kate's blood had dried in a dark circle. I tried not to look and kept my eyes on Rosie's face instead, following her lead. We tore the sheets from the bed. Each new layer exposed a fresh stain, right down to the mattress where it squatted like a taunt.

"We can clean it," Rosie said.

I was grateful for Rosie's confidence, although I had no idea what manner of detergent could remove the blood. I imagined vinegar, salt, and battery acid. Something acerbic that bubbled.

"Just burn the sheets," I said, knowing she wouldn't, but wanting it gone. Not only the physical indicators of loss, but the emotional sadness that accompanied them. Rosie carried the stained linen to the kitchen, where a tin bath of cold water waited, while I stripped the pillowcases from the pillows and folded the quilt.

There were many things about Kate that reminded me of our mother. Particularly her hands, which were long-fingered, elegant, and so unlike mine. When Kate untied a lace, spooned flour into a bowl, or even turned a page, her fingers worked like a surgeon's in crisp, precise movements. Kate was feminine, something my mother valued in her oldest daughter. She was never loud, or brash. No one ever had to tell her to settle down, or to show some self-control. Kate was naturally careful. She'd never been clumsy, overbearing, or excessive in any way. Until last night. The fear and energy I'd seen in my sister when she'd woken up bleeding had been like a possession.

Rosie returned with a bowl of soapy water and a hard brush, and I left the room to select a fresh set of sheets and matching pillowcases from the linen cupboard in the passage – white cotton embroidered with pink roses, almost girlish. It seemed like a good choice.

Jack arrived quietly in his socks. He'd left his boots on the mat at the kitchen door, like my father used to do. He'd taken Kate to the hospital before it was light.

"What are you doing?"

"Making the bed."

"Let the maid do it."

He reached for the sheets in my arms. I twisted away from him.

"Your hands are dirty."

"Leave it, Eve." He peered through the bedroom door and took a sharp breath. Rosie was bent over the bare mattress with the coarse brush in her hand. The stain was dark with soap and water.

I pushed past Jack, putting myself between him and the stain, and laid the pile of clean laundry on the seat of Kate's vanity table. "I'm coming back," I said to Rosie, then took Jack's arm and steered him down the passage and through the kitchen. "Let's go for a walk."

In the yard, the pomegranate bush had grown taller, and was burdened with fruit, some of which had ripened and split on the branch. A crested barbet fed on the revealed seeds like carrion, and flew up to the roof as we came out onto the top step. I waited for Jack to pull on his boots. He was stunned and compliant, like a lost child being led somewhere safe.

I ducked under the washing line and Jack followed me through the gate. The road was dry, but still cool at the early hour, and without agreeing, we both turned towards the river. I walked a few steps ahead.

"How's Katie?"

"She was asleep when I left. They had to sedate her. The doctor says he thinks she'll be fine, but it'll take some time."

"And the baby?"

He shook his head and turned his back to me, patting his pockets until he found his cigarettes. He shook one out of the soft pack he always carried and held the filter in his teeth, then repeated the same pat down of all his pockets looking for a light. He struck a match, and I breathed in the pleasant smell of the first spark. Jack drew heavily on the lit cigarette and then offered it to me. I lifted it to my lips, aware of the slight dampness around the filter from his mouth. We stood in silence, passing the cigarette between us as the horizon slowly brightened. The early red glow turned to orange, then yellow, then faded to a pale blue. Every bird for miles was there to greet it.

"My dad always used to say, no matter what happened the day before, every morning the birds welcome the new day," I said, to fill the silence between us.

Jack dropped his cigarette stompie into the dust and ground it out under his boot. He immediately lit another.

"When will she be able to come home?" I asked.

"Doctor says we can pick her up in the morning." He dragged deeply on the cigarette and exhaled. "Ma will go."

"Not you?"

"There's too much to do here."

He nodded his head towards the bright green lucerne field where a team of labourers slowly gathered, preparing the first cut of the season. We both turned down the road towards the noise of the herd boy's whistles. The front row of the herd rounded the bend on their way to the river for their morning drink.

"I'm not sure I even want a baby," Jack said. He glanced at me, then quickly away. He put his hand over his eyes.

I waited for him to compose himself. Jack and Kate had slotted into this life, the life our parents had built, so quickly that it was easy to forget they weren't much older than I was. I appreciated for the first time the enormous gift my mother had offered me when she'd insisted I go back to school, and what Kate and Jack had been trying to tell me about the burden of their responsibility. Rosie's words beneath the oak tree the night of their wedding came back to me, "They are too young." I couldn't imagine being responsible for a family, a farm, all the people that worked there.

Jack swiped a sleeve across his face. "Sorry."

"It's not your fault," I said and took the burning cigarette from his hand. Our fingers touched and I lifted my face and blew the smoke with a deliberate expulsion of breath into the air. We moved to the side of the road to make way for the passing cattle.

The cows ambled past, their damp, grassy milkiness mixing with the dry smell of dust and their low bovine conversation. I nudged Jack's hand. "Remember when we used to race the herd down to the river." I smiled as I recalled the freedom of running. How the motion would transport me from the physical awareness of taking each step – landing heavily and pushing up – to a place beyond my body. "We'd set ourselves a challenge. Sometimes we'd have to make it to the end of the field, sometimes all the way to the willow." I lifted my skirt to reveal the pale stitch of a scar on my knee. "One of many bad landings."

Jack sighed out his cigarette smoke. "God, we had so much freedom."

"When do you stop running? I spent so much of my childhood running places. Then from one day to the next, I just stopped."

"It seems like a lifetime ago," he said.

"It was." I took the cigarette from him, dragged on the filter, and returned it, much reduced. The herd had passed.

He took a final pull, creasing his eyes against the smoke, dropped the filter onto the road and crushed the stompie beneath his boot. He looked up at the rising sun, then out to the men gathered around the harvester at the end of the lucerne field. "They're waiting for me."

"You should go to the hospital tomorrow, Jack," I said.

He looked at me. "I'll come with you, if you like. Kate is going to be heartbroken, she needs us."

"This is not the first time," Jack said.

"The first time?"

"With Kate, the bleeding." He could hardly say the words. "She had some before. Not nearly as bad."

The thought of the bloody bedclothes quietened us both for a minute.

"Why didn't she say?"

"She didn't tell anyone. It stopped and I think she thought it was over. Maybe she just wanted it to be over. I told her to rest, but she's… she's not herself."

"Did she go to her doctor?"

He shook his head. "I think she feels like it's some kind of punishment."

"Why would she think that?"

"I don't know, because it wasn't planned. Because we were together before we got married." He met my eye before looking away.

I blinked away the thought of Jack and my sister together.

"Then she started seeing this sangoma down at the compound. Rosie's daughter, Ruth, I think. Anyway, she's been giving Kate herbs to drink and this disgusting stuff to rub on her belly. It's like the fucking dark ages. She's been burning wild sage in the house. She says it's haunted."

"The farmhouse?"

"The whole farm."

"That doesn't sound like Kate."

"She's changed. It's like the pregnancy made her crazy. She reminds me of your mother."

"She's always been like Ma."

"I don't only mean the way she looks."

I looked away. I couldn't bear the thought of Kate vanishing into the hole our mother had lived in. Losing children, being afraid all the time. I couldn't stand to see that happen to her.

"Go tomorrow. She'll want you there."

"I don't know, Evie." Jack dragged the crushed stompie through the dust under the toe of his boot. "I don't know what Kate wants." He crossed the road and jumped over the fence, wading through the lucerne towards his men.

I waited to see if he'd look back. When he didn't, I went back to the house to retrieve the small tartan gift bag from under the Christmas tree.

Chapter Twenty-Four

Stitching Sunflowers | *April 1962* | Lasswade

It was important to remember the blessings, I told my sister. To feel gratitude for all the bad things that *hadn't* happened. It was hard to know how to reassure her after her third miscarriage in two years. Kate rubbed the soft baby blue yarn between her fingers before setting the ball back in the display basket.

"Madam?" The shop assistant returned from the storeroom and emptied a bag of sturdy yarns in shades of greens and greys out onto the counter. "These will be perfect for that pattern."

In the black and white picture on the paper envelope in my sister's hand, a man posed outdoors with a small boy standing at his side. A father and son, in their matching sweaters. Both smiled confidently into the distance, every hair in place. Kate put the envelope face down on the counter and picked out a ball of wool in a dark grey, which she squeezed, then handed to me. It was rough to the touch. My neck itched at the thought of it worn close to Jack's skin. I shook my head and selected a ball in a deep blue-green. The wool was softer and the shade would suit his colouring.

"This one," I handed it to Kate.

Kate passed the wool to the woman behind the counter.

"Will you be needing enough for both sizes?" she asked, flipping the pattern over and tapping her finger on the image of the little boy.

Kate shook her head and smoothed her skirt over her flat stomach.

"Just the man's, thanks," I said.

Despite being inside, I shivered in my short-sleeved blouse with my bare legs beneath my cotton skirt. On clear blue days like this one, it was easy to underestimate how cold April could be, and I'd forgotten to grab my cardigan when I'd rushed out of the apartment Libby and I shared in Johannesburg that morning. Libby's parents owned the flat, and I paid them rent way below what I knew was market value to live in the small second bedroom. Their accommodation was an act of kindness, which Mrs Peele explained away (to save my pride, I believed) as an act of convenience. "We'd far rather have you living with Libs than some stranger from God-knows where." It was a short bus ride to WITS, where Libby and I were both first year students.

Autumn had become, and still was, my least favourite season. Each year, as the air cooled and the leaves fell, my mood dropped with them. It was not the ideal time for me to be visiting the farm, and being here only made me long even more for hibernation. But my mother had taken the trouble to call all the way from London, to insist I spend the second anniversary of my father's death with Kate, telling me, "Your sister needs you, Eve."

"Righty-oh." The shop assistant lifted the glasses that dangled from a chain around her neck and held them on the end of her nose, peering down at the pattern. "You'll need about four of these then. Four shillings each. I'll get them wrapped up."

It would be a month at least before Jack needed a woollen jersey, but Kate needed something to do.

The bell on the shop door tinkled prettily, and a gust of outside air cooled the shop briefly, bringing with it the smoky hum of the main road.

"Quickly. Mommy must close the door. We don't want to let the cold in." A dark-haired, very pregnant woman bustled into the shop under the weight of a bag of groceries and a small boy on her hip. "Oh my word, you're getting so heavy." She slid the boy down her side to the floor, where she held onto his hand and positioned him a safe distance from the shelves of thread and bolts of fabric and boxes of buttons, all arranged according to shape and colour. "No touching, hey?" The movement had left the floral skirt of her dress hitched up slightly, to reveal the pale pink of her slip.

Kate caught the boy's eye and smiled. He stood up straight, shuffling the heels of his shoes together. They were dusty, and his knees sported dirty smears under his khaki shorts.

"Kate. Oh my goodness, both the Hunter girls. What a surprise. A *nice* surprise, of course," the woman said.

Kate straightened her spine and seemed to consciously blossom in the face of this social obligation as if she had flicked on some internal switch. I had not seen Zita Abelheira since Kate's wedding. She'd married a local boy, and lived next door to her parents who still ran the algemene handelaar. Kate seldom came to town, seldom socialised, and never invited anyone to the farm, but whenever I expressed any concern that she would isolate herself, thinking of our mother's lonely life, Kate would explain that there were simply too many reminders among the other mothers in her circle of friends of what her life might have been like. "And everyone looks at me with this pained expression on their faces. Like I'm terminally ill or something. I can't stand it." Seeing Zita here with her little boy and another on the way, I understood what Kate meant.

"We're shopping for wool," Kate gestured towards the pattern and the wool on the counter. She was speaking too loud, with forced cheer. "For Jack."

"That's nice," Zita said, a brief crease furrowed her brow, but she replaced it with a smile. "How is he?"

"He's well, thank you for asking."

"We never see you at church anymore." Zita's eyes drifted down Kate's body and Kate tightened her cardigan across her front.

"I can't believe Peter is already walking," Kate said, directing her friend's attention to her little boy. "The last time I saw him he was in your arms at his baptism."

The boy looked up at the sound of his name and took a few steps towards them. Zita tightened her grip on his hand and he stopped and edged back into the space next to his mom.

"Gosh, that was almost two years ago, Kate. Just before your wedding."

There was an uncomfortable shift in the air between us. Images from that day ran through my mind in a rapid, unwelcome burst, like a sepia slide show of someone else's life: the heat, the buzz, Kate in the silk wedding dress, which shifted across her body like a skin over the noticeable rise of her belly; Jack, as restless and vigilant as a meerkat; the endless stream of faces arranged in expressions of joy, mouths moving noiselessly. Everything was blunted by grief.

Zita smiled, a bit too wide. "They grow too fast," she said.

"He looks just like his father," Kate said.

"Well, boys should follow their fathers, I suppose." Zita rested a hand on Kate's arm, giving it a quick squeeze and rearranging her face into the expression of pity that I recognised as the pained sympathy Kate had tried to describe to me. Before Zita could offer any words of condolence, I grabbed Kate's hand.

"Sorry, Zita, I need Katie's help to pick out some buttons." I turned my sister to the button display.

The small shelf was slightly tilted to better present the six-by-six inch cardboard trays filled with buttons, which had been colour coordinated and ordered like a rainbow. In the same moment, Kate and I recounted the childhood rhyme, "Roy-G-Biv", out loud to one another. "Red, orange, yellow, GREEN, blue, indigo, violet." As girls we would shout the G. It was the odd-man-out and seemed to assert itself, the forceful GEE in the middle of the phrase. The shop assistant and Zita looked over at us giggling like children in church.

I sifted through the blue buttons, looking for a large round one for a turquoise coat I never wore due to the missing button. There were buttons with two holes lined up through the centre, others with four holes arranged in a square. Some were plastic, some metal, some covered in cotton or leather, and others wrapped in rough tweed. There were buttons the size of headache tablets, and others as broad and as flat as a jam jar lid. My heart broke for my sister. She couldn't help being aware of the whispered conversation and glances from the two women at the counter. Kate kept her back to them and sifted her fingers through the flat, round shapes. The buttons clicked pleasantly against each other.

With his mother distracted, Peter wandered close to us and watched us quietly. Kate pretended to pop a button into her mouth and the boy's eyes widened with excitement.

"They almost look like sweeties, don't they?"

The little boy shook his head. His two-year-old face was earnest.

"You are quite right," said Kate. "Never put anything that's not food into your mouth."

Peter joined us at the display. He reached into a low box and selected a large daisy-shaped button with white petals arranged around a cheerful yellow centre. He held the button out to Kate in his open palm. She crouched and took his offered hand.

If Kate had carried that first baby to term, he, or she, would have been eighteen months old by now. Probably walking, possibly talking. My chest constricted as I imagined a boy standing in front of Kate like Peter was, formed of flesh and bone, helping her pick out buttons. When Kate looked at me, I pretended my nose was itchy and managed a smile, feeling every muscle in my face strain with the effort.

"That's very pretty," Kate said, folding his fingers closed over the daisy button. "Except, my sister is buying a button for a blue coat and we need it to match this one." She showed him a turquoise button and Peter stepped forward, feet together, and bent his head over her hand, like a soldier taking a briefing. "Can you help us find one?" Kate said.

The little boy immediately began to scan the shelves and to offer us any button he could find that was in any way at all, round or blue.

"I hope he's not bothering you." Zita, finished at the counter, held a paper parcel in the crook of her elbow and her shopping bag in the other hand.

"Not at all. He's been very helpful," I said.

"Well, you've helped me too. You know how it is, shopping with children, it's impossible to get anything done." Zita stopped abruptly and her skin flushed a deep rose from her neck to her cheeks. She rearranged her shopping in her arms. "We'd better get on. He'll be calling for his lunch soon." She bent into Kate for an awkward kiss. "Let's not leave it so long between visits now. We'd like to see more of you and Jack."

"Yes, of course," Kate said, with a set smile on her face. I knew my sister well enough to discern that she had no intention of following up on the invitation. I was transported back to a dozen similar conversations between my mother and other women throughout my childhood. I was as amazed now as I had been then at the easy reliability of good manners to deliver the impression of sociability.

Zita pushed her ample bottom against the door and propped it open with her hip as she held a hand out to her son. "Come on, Peter. Say goodbye to Eve and Mrs Turner."

Peter lifted his open palm with the daisy-shaped button still pressed beneath his thumb.

"Thank you," Kate said, accepting the button from the little boy. She slipped it into her jacket pocket before returning to the counter to collect her parcel and pay for the yarn.

"No luck with the buttons?" the shop assistant asked.

"Nothing that matched," Kate replied.

I followed her out into the sunshine where Kate's car was parked on the street outside the store. I climbed in behind the steering wheel while Kate sat in the passenger seat with the parcel of yarn in her lap. I put my hand into my sister's pocket and pulled out the bright flower button. I rubbed my thumb over the yellow face, which was slightly raised in the middle of eight white, pointed petals. A small metal eye glued on the back would hold the button to the fabric.

"Have you resorted to robbing the haberdashery now?"

"Peter gave it to me." Kate snatched the button from me and closed her fist over it. A laugh burst out of her and she covered her mouth with her other hand and glanced back at the shop. The door remained closed.

"Jesus, Kate." This feeling of dread and responsibility was all too familiar. I could be eleven again, navigating my mother's unpredictable behaviour and moods. "You should take it back."

"It's only a button."

"That's not the point."

"It was a gift. You saw him give it to me." She gripped the button even tighter when I tried to take it out of her grasp.

"I'm not going to fight you for it."

Kate grabbed my wrist with an urgency I hadn't seen in her before. "You have to do it for me, Eve."

"No, just explain to the woman who helped us that it was a mistake."

"I'm not talking about the button," Kate opened her hand. Her palm was pricked with eight even punctures from the sharp petals.

I dug a tissue out of my bag, spat on it, and wiped at my sister's palm. "We can't return it now."

"I'm not talking about the button, Eve." Kate said again. The care she took in her pronunciation caught my attention.

"What are you talking about?"

My sister's eyes glittered and her cheeks were flushed. "Eve, you need to have a baby for me."

I sat back in the seat and stared at my sister, trying to arrange my features into an expression that adequately conveyed my horror. Or was it fear? I felt for an appropriate response and decided to go with concern. "Kate, I'm worried about you. Jack is worried about you. Even Ma, all the way from Surrey, England, is worried about you." I turned the key and shifted the car into gear. Before I could release the brake, Kate grabbed my arm.

"It's my fault, you know."

"It's just a button." I knew that we'd moved on from any discussion of buttons, but I did not want to follow Kate down the path she was trying to lead me.

"Not the button. Losing the babies."

"It's no one's fault, Katie." I kept my foot on the brake.

"How come women like Zita can make babies so easily, one after the other. She's pregnant again, did you notice that? I mean, Peter isn't even two yet and she's going to have another." Kate wasn't crying, but her voice pitched with emotion. "It's so easy for her. It's not fair."

"You're right, Katie. It's not fair, but it's also not your fault."

"Even Ma could have children and she was a terrible mother."

"She had her own problems."

"I never asked myself if I wanted children, Eve. Really, really wanted a child of my own. I only thought of them in relation to me being a mother." She jabbed a finger at her chest.

"That's alright, Katie."

"No, it's not. Because I only thought of myself as a mother compared to Ma. How one day, I could show her how to do it right. How to be a proper mother. To prove to her that despite everything – despite her distance and her sadness and her loving her dead son more than she loved us – that I could still be a good mother. Even with her broken example, I could do a good job. But I never thought of the reality of having a child in all this. I only thought about myself. Me being a better mother than she ever was."

I took both my sister's hands in mine. "It is not your fault, Kate. It's medical or physical, some cruel trick of nature. You aren't doing anything wrong."

"But then why can't I hold onto my babies?" She dug her fists into her belly. "Now that I really want a baby for all the right reasons, I can't have one, because I'm not worthy. I'm being punished for wanting to punish Ma."

"She's not even here. She has no power over your pregnancies."

"Please help me. There's no point otherwise." Kate's eyes were wide and liquid with a deep fear of her own.

"No point in what? You're so young. You've got time, and you've got Jack."

"If we are not a family, there's no point in us. In Jack and me. I know he doesn't want to be here, that he stayed because of his father." She covered her face and began to sob, bone-wracking, jarring sobs that seemed to come from somewhere so deep and so bleak that I felt my own heart break.

I pulled Kate into my chest and held her until she regained her breath. "It'll be alright, Katie."

She pushed herself out of my arms. "No, it won't be alright." She slumped back into the passenger seat. "If you loved me…"

"That's not fair. I do love you."

"Jack would agree to it."

"This is beyond belief. I'm not having a baby with Jack. You can't ask this of me."

"You can wear this." She untucked her blouse, and from beneath the waistband of her skirt, Kate pulled out a thin length of braided leather that was tied in a loop around her waist. Beads and shells and bits of bone were knotted along it at regular intervals. "Ruth gave it to me. It's a fertility belt." Kate picked at the knot with frantic movements.

I grabbed her hands. "Stop, please. This is crazy."

"I'm not crazy!"

"Imagine Ma's face if she heard what you were saying, Katie."

"It'll work. Ruth threw the bones and she knows things, Eve. She saw you with my daughter."

I couldn't reply. Could barely catch my breath. I engaged first gear and released the brake. I rolled down my window and waved my hand to indicate to the passing traffic that I was about to pull out. "Jack would never, *ever* agree to this. It's madness."

"I'm not mad!" I couldn't tell if Kate was crying tears of pain or shame or desperation. She shrunk into her seat and glared out of the car window as we drove through town.

It was heartbreaking. The whole idea was unthinkable, and yet I still found myself wondering if I was cruel to deny my sister the one thing she'd always wanted. The thing she believed would make her whole. Could I really do this for her? I thought again of my mother, a look of horror on her face. I thought of Jack, his pale dull eyes, his back moving beneath his cotton shirt, the way he shaped his lips and blew perfect smoke rings into the air. I pictured his face above mine, his mouth relaxed in pleasure, and shook the image out of my head. No. It was unconscionable. I couldn't trust myself with this. I couldn't trust myself not to be selfish, not to put my own motives above my sister's, to offer her the hope of a child just so I could be with him again.

"What if I can't have children either?"

"I told you, Ruth has seen you with a girl. With my child." She took one of my hands off the wheel, pressed the bundled-up fertility belt she'd unknotted from her waist into my palm, and closed my fingers around it. She squeezed my fist closed. "Please, Evie. I have no one else."

I drove past the bank and braked at the stop sign at the corner. The Presbyterian Church cast a thin shadow across the road on the opposite side. I checked my rearview mirror. I could still see the sign that marked the entrance to the haberdashery halfway down the block, and I watched the door for any movement until the car behind me hooted its horn. Instead of heading straight past the church, I turned right, deciding to take the long way home.

Chapter Twenty-Five

The Red-Chested Cuckoo | *December 1962* | Lasswade

I planned my arrival at the farm for a day when I knew nobody would be there. The last time I'd visited had been in April and I noted with pleasure the way summer had brought the farm to bright green life. Rosie was on her annual leave. Kate had gone to Johannesburg to visit Margaret and finish her Christmas shopping. Libby had been kind enough to lend me her car for a few days, which allowed me to park under the oak tree and let myself in without having to announce myself.

The house was quiet. I wandered through each room like a thief, stroking my fingers over all the things I knew, and the new things that had been added since I'd moved away. In the sunroom, I sat with a slip of the chair's legs on the wooden floor in front of my mother's desk, and rested my palms on the cool, smooth wood. The frangipani flowers outside the window displayed their bright-cerise, open-mouthed invitation to the bees who visited one by one, each leaving with a sip of nectar and fat yellow knees. I slipped open the drawer and pushed my hand right to the back where my fingers bumped up against my mother's silver cigarette box. One of the corners was dented. I traced the initials etched on the front and pressed down on the latch. The lid sprung open. The elastic that clipped over the cigarettes had stretched and frayed, but the box was empty anyway. I lifted it to my nose and sniffed.

A red-chested cuckoo, known for nesting in another bird's nest, called *piet-my-vrou, piet-my-vrou*, in the yard. I closed my eyes, taking in all the sounds and smells, and the way the light moved around the room behind my eyelids. It was all so familiar that I almost expected to open my eyes and find myself on a day in my childhood: my mother in her bedroom across the hall, my father at the dairy with his dogs, Rosie ironing with the regular click and hiss of the old metal iron, Kate lying on her belly on the carpet, playing with George or reading a book. I crossed the room to the piano and pressed down on the keys, shocking the afternoon awake and sending dust up to dance in the light.

In the second bedroom, I changed out of my cotton trousers and the light blouse I'd worn for the drive and shook out a summer frock I'd packed when I left Johannesburg – a dress that I loved, but did not often find the occasion to wear. It was a halter neck, cinched at the waist with a full skirt that brushed my knees, in a pale blue that favoured my colouring. I wanted to look my best. My mother would love this dress. She'd love to see me in it, but she wouldn't love the reason I wore it today.

In the bathroom, I powdered under my armpits, wet a hand towel, and wiped between my legs. I brushed my hair and applied a single swipe of lipstick from Kate's vanity case.

Barefoot, I left the house via the kitchen door.

Rain the night before had washed the world clean, and a pair of russet-headed hoopoes hopped in the furrows ahead of me, pulling earthworms out of the soft sand. I crossed the top pasture, where damp soil pushed pleasantly between my toes as I waded through the thigh-high grass. I climbed the stile into what had once been the Turners' property, but was now part of Lasswade, since Jack had inherited his father's farm after his parents had been killed in a car accident the previous year. I lifted my skirt to prevent it from catching on any loose nails or splinters. The barn's wooden structure grew taller as I approached – the place where I'd helped my father birth a calf, and where he'd died just a few months later; where I'd seen Tommy Turner raise a gun to his head and that had burned to the ground; where Jack and I once lay in the hay and read *Lady Chatterley's Lover*. Now rebuilt, the barn stood as a memory and a memorial. The smell of smoke had been replaced with the smell of fresh wood and paint. Weavers dipped with bright yellow flashes in and out of new nests hanging in the recovered blue gum trees.

I smelled his cigarette smoke before I saw him. Jack sat on the bonnet of his truck, looking across the patchwork of fields towards the poplars that curved with the shape of the river. He turned with some sixth sense. I knew Kate had spoken to him about what she'd asked of me, but he and I had never acknowledged the request to one another, and I had not given him any warning that I'd be here today. I did not know if he was in agreement with Kate's plan, or if he'd dismissed it as an impossible madness, like I once had. He sat very still and watched me approach. I was transported back to the day at the river, when I'd gone to find him, certain he'd choose me. I'd been braver then, but I'd still needed his participation, and I needed it even more today. My heartbeat pounded into every extremity, but I was not afraid. Instead, a calmness flowed through me. A certainty that this was the right place for me to be. I felt for the twist of beaded leather that Kate had pressed into my fist with such urgency eight months before, and that I had finally, after many sleepless nights, knotted around my own waist.

When I was close to the barn, Jack took a final deep drag on his cigarette before rubbing it out against the sole of his boot. He flicked the dead stompie away, pushed himself off the truck, and came to meet me.

We lay on the hay with our bodies mirroring one another's, like we'd stepped back through time to what might have been. Legs and arms starred. My right hand touched Jack's left, and his left foot rested against my right ankle. I thought again of paper cutouts, of endless families in a chain of connected bodies. Foot-to-foot, finger-to-finger. The negative space between us was as essential to the pattern as it had been before, but filled today with understanding and choices, and mostly, with Kate. I allowed myself to feel my sister's presence and to respond to the close proximity of Jack's body. Our breathing started to match one another. In, and out. In, and out. I closed my eyes and tried to empty my head. I knew that this was the final moment we could stop this from happening, and that it would probably be up to me. I also understood that a part of me wanted to be here, wanted it so much that if I could just quiet the voice in my head, I could do this until it was done, and be glad.

We didn't speak. After a few minutes Jack rolled towards me.

I was ashamed at how much pleasure I took from him, ashamed at how hungry I was for him, and ashamed that this act of love for my sister was as much for me as it was for her. I arched against him. Jack stopped and lifted himself up onto his hands. I opened my eyes. His eyes were wary and questioning.

Excitement, fear, and pleasure at the culmination of a lifetime of love and friendship mixed up inside me with sorrow for what I knew we all stood to lose if I said yes to him now.

I nodded.

March 1975 | Lasswade

The road to Lasswade is straight and long and lined to the horizon on both sides with yellow veld. The turn to the farm is unmarked and comes up after a small rise, where the dirt track meets the tarmac in a loose drift of sand and stone. The ground that was pushed aside when the track was first made has healed over with wild grasses, whose seeded heads tremble with our return.

Acknowledgements

Thank you Colleen Higgs at Modjaji and Jessica Powers at Catalyst for guiding *The Light Remains* into being. I'm enormously grateful to my mentors at the Fairfield University MFA program, where this story first came to light, for everything you taught me about writing craft—Rachel Basch, Eugenia Kim, Karen Osborn, and the late Baron Wormser. Thanks to my sister-writers for your notes and friendship, and occasionally guiding me back from the I-can't-do-this-anymore brink, especially Ellyn Gelman and my lovely mermaids, Elise Chidley and Sam Grieve. Thanks to Tanya Farber, Mark Winkler, and Chris Belden.

Thank you Mom and Dad, for encouraging the artistic life.

Thank you Grant, for all your support in every way. I love you.

Thank you Thomas and Chloe, the constant lights in my life.

www.ingramcontent.com/pod-product-compliance
Lightning Source LLC
LaVergne TN
LVHW091051080826
845145LV00002B/700

* 9 7 8 1 9 6 0 8 0 3 4 7 4 *